THE SECRET INGREDIENT TO MURDER

Terry Ambrose

THE SECRET INGREDIENT TO MURDER

Seaside Cove Bed & Breakfast Mystery #8

Terry Ambrose

BOOKS BY TERRY AMBROSE

Seaside Cove Bed & Breakfast Mysteries

A Treasure to Die For
Clues in the Sand
The Killer Christmas Sweater Club
Secrets of the Treasure King
Treasure Most Deadly
Lies, Spies, and the Baker's Surprise
Dead Men Need No Reservations

McKenna Mysteries

Photo Finish
Kauai Temptations
Big Island Blues
Mystery of the Lei Palaoa
Honolulu Hottie
North Shore Nanny
A Damsel for Santa
Maui Magic
The Scent of Waikiki
Mystery of the Eight Islands

License to Lie Series

License to Lie
Con Game
Shadows from the Past

Anthologies with Stories

Paradise, Passion, Murder: 10 Tales of Mystery from Hawai‘i
Happy Homicides 3: Summertime Crimes
Happy Homicides 4: Fall into Crime
Happy Homicides 5: The Purr-fect Crime

COPYRIGHT

THE SECRET INGREDIENT TO MURDER

ISBN: 979-8-9900457-0-5

Cover design by Dar Albert

ABOUT THE AUTHOR

Once upon a time, in a life he'd rather forget, Terry Ambrose tracked down deadbeats for a living. He also hired big guys with tow trucks to steal cars—but only when negotiations failed. Those years of chasing deadbeats taught him many valuable life lessons such as—always keep your car in the garage.

Terry has written more than a dozen books, several of which have been award finalists. In 2014, his thriller, "Con Game," won the San Diego Book Awards for Best Action-Thriller. His series include the Trouble in Paradise McKenna Mysteries, the Seaside Cove Bed & Breakfast Mysteries, and the License to Lie thriller series.

You can learn more about Terry and his writing at terryambrose.com.

1

ALEX

SEPTEMBER 10

Hey, Journal,

The house is a lot noisier than it used to be. Our new guest, my baby brother, is a super-big attention seeker. He's cute, sure, but he's an awful lot of work. I never thought about that part when I said I wanted a little brother.

Diapers, feedings, crying super early in the morning... I didn't sign up for this! Mom says it's like living with a tiny, very demanding, opera singer. Once Mom called him that, Dad started in, too. Now he's calling him our mini Pavarotti.

At least it's not all chaos. I visited Grandma Madeline at Howie's Collectibles this afternoon on my way home from school. Ever since I started making deliveries around town for a couple of the shopowners, I've seen her at least twice a week. She's gonna have another delivery for me tomorrow. That'll put me halfway to my goal! In a few weeks, I'll have enough money for the antique clock me and Grandma Madeline are gonna give Mom and Dad for their first anniversary!

While I was at the store, I asked Grandma Madeline a bunch of questions. She finally spilled the beans. She told me Mom was just as cranky as my brother. When she told me that, I said I guess the apple doesn't fall far from the tree. She said, 'Oh, no, dear. Having a baby is like seeing your own quirks come to life but in a much smaller, diapered version. It's like watching a rerun of your own show but with more spit-up!"

Guess what? I made a new friend today, too. Her name's Veronica. She's a few years older and super cool. We walked to Marina Park and sat on one of the benches. Her hair is even redder than mine. She's also got wild curls and a fun laugh. We've totally got a bond between us even though she's older than me. Her mom died two years ago. That's just about the same time me and my dad moved to Seaside Cove. Veronica says she was always super close to her mom, and she grew up baking with her in the family home. She got all teary when she talked about it. I totally get it that she wishes she could have those days back, but wow, she can't. I can't even imagine what it would be like if I lost Mom or Dad.

Veronica says her Uncle Tyler is the only family she has left. I guess they moved to Seaside Cove a few months after he sold the family's bakery. It was a super-big deal because her mom made these famous flourless chocolate brownies. The new owners are threatening to sue her uncle because he didn't turn over the secret ingredient for the recipe. Veronica's mad because her mom promised the business to her before she died. And there's some guy Veronica says is trying to buy the secret ingredient for a lot of money.

I can't get the picture of how sad she looked out of my head. She was sitting on the bench with her curls blowing in the wind and telling me this whole story. She said she's totally over her uncle and just wants to get away. She's even been looking for a job so she can make enough to escape from her uncle. I hope she doesn't because it's kinda cool having an older friend.

All her problems remind me of something my dad said. He told me that life can throw curveballs at you. He's right. And talking to Veronica made me realize my baby brother troubles are kinda small. LOL. No pun intended, Journal! Oh well, I guess we've all got our stuff, huh?

Gotta go. Mom says she needs help with dinner in the kitchen.

xoxo,

Alex

2

RICK

THE FOYER OF THE SEASIDE Cove Bed & Breakfast was drenched in an inviting warmth, a stark contrast to the chill outside. Though it was the middle of the afternoon, the golden light from ornate lamps left on for ambiance cast long, dancing shadows on the dark wood of the banister leading to the second floor. A fire crackled in the hearth, further adding to the atmosphere. The decor was tastefully romantic, with twin couches facing each other in front of the fireplace and an assortment of vintage trinkets Marquetta's mother had given them scattered around, creating an atmosphere of timeless elegance.

Rick Atwood rested his fingers on the polished surface of the front desk, admiring the subtle beauty of the house he'd inherited from his grandfather. Captain Jack might not have had much business sense and might have nearly bankrupted the B&B, but he had done an amazing job of renovating the old Victorian.

This was the time of the afternoon when things felt slow. Alex was still at school, and they were still waiting for the arrival of new guests. In between arrivals, he occupied himself with a crossword puzzle. So, when the front door opened, he was surprised to see Alex and a friend framed against the bright daylight streaming through the door. Behind Alex stood an older girl with wild red curls and ashen skin.

"Daddy," Alex began, her voice laced with concern. "This is Veronica Campbell. She fell into the planter outside the Rusty Nail. She's a friend of mine."

Veronica gave Rick a small wave, then clutched her arms to her chest. She seemed out of place amidst the quaint charm of the B&B, like a bird thrown off course in a storm. A friend? Rick didn't like that thought. This girl was obviously several years older than Alex. She was maybe what? Seventeen? Something in her appearance, perhaps the boldness of how she dressed, told him she was a firecracker just waiting to explode. Since when did Alex hang out with kids who were so much older?

Rick rose from his perch behind the desk, his gaze shifting between Alex and Veronica. The girl was visibly shaken. He resolved to talk to Alex about her new friend later. For now, he felt compelled to help. "Are you alright, Veronica?"

The girl gave him a tentative nod. "I'm just a bit shaken, that's all." Her voice was frail, like thin ice on a winter pond.

Alex moved closer to Veronica, but Veronica stepped away and paced the room. Her translucent skin practically glowed in the firelight. The young girl was a storm of emotions, her haunting brown eyes flashing a mix of anger and fear. The emotions seemed to subside when she stopped and gazed at a towel animal sitting on one of the end tables.

"My mom and I used to make those…" she whispered. As quickly as they'd dissipated, the anger and fear returned.

"What happened?" Rick asked.

"I've been trying to get a job, but nobody wants to hire me." She went to the stairs, rested her hand on the dark wood of the banister, and let her fingers stroke the smooth surface. "Retail stores, boutiques, I've tried them all. No one's hiring." Veronica continued as she twirled a lock of hair around her finger. "So I thought, why not try the restaurants?"

Rick couldn't help but admire her tenacity. As young as she was, she was already shouldering responsibility. More than some adults he knew. He encouraged her to continue, pretty sure he knew where this was going. No work in town.

"That's when I saw him," she sneered.

The sudden turn caught Rick off guard. "Who?" And what did this have to do with a job search or her current condition?

"My Uncle Tyler. He was at the Rusty Nail. And he wasn't alone. He was with Gideon Styles. The man is scum."

Harsh words, thought Rick. Once again, this girl had caught him off-guard. He raised an eyebrow, curious as to why she hated this man so much.

"Veronica's uncle is going to sell the family's secret recipe, Daddy." Alex blurted.

"The Secret Ingredient was my mom's legacy. It was supposed to be mine! But my Uncle Tyler's going to sell the most valuable part before I even have a chance to inherit it!" Veronica's words tumbled over each other in a mad rush.

The situation was starting to come into focus. Rick felt a pang of sympathy for Veronica. He could see the desperation in her eyes. And, having struggled to make things work the year after he inherited the B&B, he certainly understood the fear of losing a family's legacy. He reached out to place a comforting hand on her shoulder.

"Veronica," he said gently, "Sometimes, things aren't what they seem. You should talk to your uncle. Hear his side of the story. And remember, no matter what happens, your mother's legacy lives on in you."

Tears glistened in Veronica's eyes, and though she tried to force a smile, her pain was evident. Rick couldn't help but admire her strength. In the face of adversity, she was standing tall, ready to fight for what she believed in. Or, at least, that's how it appeared. He could see why Alex had taken a liking to her. They had the same spirit. The same fire. Unfortunately, he knew Alex would do anything she could to help her friend. He just hoped this new friend wasn't taking advantage of his daughter.

"Alright, kiddo," Rick said to Alex, "Let's take Veronica to the kitchen. I think we should move this conversation to someplace a bit more private. And your mom's there. Maybe she can help."

"Awesome," Alex said. "Mom will know what to do."

Rick agreed. If there was one thing he'd learned over the past couple of years, it was that Marquetta always seemed to know what to do. After relocating to Seaside Cove and divorcing Alex's birth mother, the B&B had become Rick's sanctuary, a refuge from the storm of life. Here, he'd learned to trust—and love—again. He hoped it could offer some comfort to Veronica as she allowed herself to be led toward the back of the house.

They entered the kitchen, the room Rick considered the heart of the B&B. It was like stepping into a warm hug. The white marbled granite countertops gleamed under the overhead lighting, giving the room a welcoming glow. Five mullioned windows overlooked the back patio and the ocean beyond, offering a view that could soothe even the most troubled soul. The room smelled of fresh bread and cinnamon—the scent of home.

"Hey," Marquetta said as she looked up from her seat at the center island. Rick recognized the paper in front of her as the next day's menu. Marquetta had tied her brown hair back with a red scrunchie, and her gray eyes sparkled with an inner light. She was a woman of strength and warmth. A comforting spirit. Kind of like a bowl of hot soup on a cold day.

Alex ran to Marquetta, gave her a hug, then introduced Veronica and told her what had happened. "We need some help."

Marquetta turned her gaze to Veronica. Her eyes softened, and she wiped her hands on her apron before she stood and gave the girl a smile that was as warm as a summer's day.

"Oh, Sweetie," Marquetta said, her tone gentle and soothing. "I'm so sorry for your loss." Without hesitation, Marquetta pulled the girl into a hug. There was no awkwardness, no hesitation, just pure, heartfelt compassion.

Veronica seemed to melt into Marquetta's embrace and murmured, "Thanks."

"You're safe here," Marquetta said. "Nothing bad will happen to you here. We won't let it."

Marquetta pulled out a first-aid kit from the cabinet and stood beside Veronica. She examined the girl's scrapes carefully, cleaning and dressing them with gentle care. All the while, she spoke to Veronica in a soothing voice, coaxing her to open up about what had happened.

After a few minutes, Veronica finally began to speak, her words again tumbling out in a rush. She explained how she had fallen while running away from her uncle, who she believed was trying to take away her inheritance. Rick listened to her story with a sympathetic ear, nodding in understanding.

"That sounds really tough," Rick said. "Would it help if I took you home and helped you talk to your Uncle Tyler?"

Veronica's face lit up with gratitude, and she nodded eagerly. "Yes. Thank you."

The drive took only a few minutes, but as they turned onto the quiet side street a few blocks from downtown Rick felt his gut clench. Police Chief Adam Cunningham's 4x4 was parked in front of the Craftsman-style home. The sight of the police vehicle sent a surge of apprehension through him. Had Veronica's uncle reported her missing? Or had something else happened?

The house itself looked like something from a Norman Rockwell painting. Its low-pitched, gabled roof had wide, unenclosed eaves overhanging the weathered gray shingle siding. Exposed rafters and decorative beams under the gables added a touch of rustic charm. The house's front porch spanned the entire width and featured square columns that extended to the ground, creating a sturdy and well-built appearance.

As Rick approached Adam's 4x4, he noticed that Veronica had gone pale and asked, "Are you okay?" He kept his voice steady despite the unease twisting his insides.

Veronica's eyes were wide, her gaze fixed on the Chief's vehicle as she spoke in a voice barely above a whisper. "Why are the police here?"

Rick shook his head. "I don't know. Why don't we find out? Together."

He cut the engine and climbed out of the car. Veronica clung to his side as they approached the front door. The porch creaked under their weight, adding to the tension. As he raised his hand to knock, Rick took one last look at Adam's 4x4, a sense of foreboding settling over him.

Whatever was waiting for them inside the house, he felt sure it was more than Veronica being late.

Rick pushed open the front door of the 1920s home, a sense of dread rising into his throat as he looked around. The thick, heavy trim around the doors and windows was marred by scratches, the built-in cabinetry and shelves had been thrown open and their contents scattered across the hardwood floors that once shone with a rich, warm glow. Despite the mess, Rick couldn't help but notice the lack of severe damage. Whatever happened here, the physical damage was repairable. He wasn't so sure about the emotional damage.

"Uncle Tyler?" Veronica called out. Her voice echoed through the house, her tone filled with worry.

Rick shook his head, trying to offer her some comfort. He gripped Veronica's arm when she took a step in front of him. "Let me go first. We'll find him." His voice remained steady despite the chaos around them.

"Hey, Rick," Police Chief Adam Cunningham said as he entered the living room, his face a mask of concern. "What are you doing here?"

"Adam, this is Veronica Campbell. She's the niece of Tyler Winkle. She spent a little time with us at the B&B, and I was just bringing her home. Why are you here in the house alone?"

"We got an anonymous call about a break-in, and when I got here, the front door was ajar." Adam cocked his head to one side and eyed Veronica. "Ms. Campbell, I'm sorry to be meeting you under these circumstances. Why were you at the B&B?"

"Veronica fell into the planter in front of the Rusty Nail, and Alex brought her home. I volunteered to drive her here, but then we saw your vehicle. Is this just a case of vandalism?"

"Burglary," Adam said, his words punctuated by a heavy sigh. "But not your usual type. No smashed windows, no broken doors. If you look closely at the damage, it all looks very calculated. They didn't take the expensive stuff either. My guess is that whoever did this was looking for something specific."

Rick frowned, taking another look around. Adam was right. The disarray, the damage, it all suggested a burglar who knew what they were after. Someone who wasn't interested in the valuables scattered around the room.

Veronica's voice cracked, and tears welled in her eyes. "They wanted the chocolate recipe. It's been in our family for generations. My uncle kept it in a safe in his bedroom."

She rushed through the door Adam had used seconds before. Rick and Adam followed her past a bathroom with a clawfoot tub, a pedestal sink, and hexagonal floor tiles that added a classic touch. After turning into the last room on the right, a spacious bedroom with a built-in desk, she went straight to a small, open safe tucked away in the corner.

Veronica stood before the safe and jabbed a finger at the open door. "It's gone," she croaked. "Somebody stole the recipe."

Rick noticed Adam was looking exactly the way he felt—suspicious. This was no ordinary break-in. If Veronica was right, whoever had done this had been after one thing. What was so important about that recipe, and why had they done all the damage to the rest of the house? None of this made sense…unless someone wanted it to look like a break-in when it wasn't. Rick caught a glimpse of Veronica's face. Her devastation seemed real. Then why, for about the third time since he'd met her, was his gut twisting with uncertainty? He had a feeling Alex's new friend knew far more than she was revealing.

3

RICK

STANDING IN THE CENTER OF Tyler Winkle's bedroom, Rick allowed himself a few seconds to take in the scene. An open safe. Papers strewn around in disarray. And a distraught teen standing defiantly amidst it all.

"Chief Cunningham," Veronica said, her voice trembling with a mix of anger and fear. "I'm telling you, someone stole our family's secret recipe."

Adam, a broad-shouldered man with an easy grin, narrowed his gaze at the young girl. "You're positive it was in here?"

Veronica's face reddened with what Rick now recognized as a rebellious streak. Not only did this girl have a spirited personality, but she was stubborn, too.

"No, I'm not positive! My uncle had it and wouldn't share it with me. For all I know, he staged this!"

Rick winced at the accusation. Lashing out at her uncle wasn't going to help anything, and he still had a nagging doubt about Veronica's role in all of this. They needed to talk to her uncle. They also needed to get out of this room before they contaminated it any further. "Adam…"

"I know. Let's move this into the kitchen. Please, Ms. Campbell, don't touch anything. We need to preserve the scene."

Like the B&B, the kitchen was the heart of the old Craftsman home. Another rush of sympathy flooded Rick's veins as he looked around the once-charming room. The shaker-style cabinets were now flung open like the pages of a tragic novel. The butcher block countertop, which had probably been clean and gleaming before the break-in, was littered with papers and debris. It was as if a tornado had swept through, leaving chaos in its wake.

Rick caught the look of shock on Veronica's face as she absently ran her fingers over the edge of the countertop. She looked at Rick with tears in her eyes and croaked, "Why would anyone do this?"

"I don't know," Rick whispered, suddenly feeling ashamed for thinking she'd somehow been involved. Only a professional actor could fake that kind of shock. "Adam, we have to find out who did this."

He was also sure there was more to this break-in than just a stolen recipe. His gaze swept over the chaos, and Rick allowed his reporter's instincts to kick in. He found himself mentally crafting a headline—*Famous Bakery's Secret Recipe Stolen: Hurricane Hits Seaside Cove Kitchen.*

Rick shook his head and studied Veronica's face. Her eyes were filled with anger as she returned his gaze.

Suddenly, she exploded, "This is all because of that scum Gideon Styles!" She craned her neck forward, her fiery locks giving her the appearance of Medusa about to explode. "You have to arrest him, Chief! He stole our family's secret recipe."

The girl was obviously in what Rick called blame mode. How long she'd lash out like this, he didn't know. But she'd already accused her uncle—and now Styles. Who else she might want to blame was anybody's guess. What he did know was that they needed evidence to do anything. "Veronica, I'm sure the chief has a plan to gather evidence so we can bring the perpetrator to justice. Right, Adam?"

"Right. Ms. Campbell, I need proof of their involvement before I can arrest anyone. We will figure out who did this. And I can assure you, once we do, they'll face justice. Rick? Are you in?"

"Of course, I'll help," Rick said reluctantly. Less than an hour ago, he'd been working a crossword puzzle and waiting for guests. Now, he was being pulled into the role of police consultant once again.

The corners of Adam's green eyes crinkled with appreciation. "Thanks, buddy. Ms. Campbell, I'll have my deputy dust the safe and the other hard surfaces for fingerprints. Maybe we'll get lucky. We can also talk to the neighbors."

Veronica rolled her eyes. "What good will that do? Everybody ignores their neighbors."

"Maybe where you come from, Ms. Campbell. But in Seaside Cove, we're quite likely to find a witness."

"What about the sheriff, Adam? Won't they send out a forensics team?"

"For a home invasion? No. You know what it would take to get them here. Unfortunately, we're on our own."

Veronica whirled her arms around at the room's disarray. "You're kidding, right? This is a crime scene!"

Adam gave her a sympathetic smile. "Welcome to small-town law enforcement, Ms. Campbell. Actually, for something this small, you'd probably have the same problem in the big city."

"This isn't small. That recipe's priceless!"

Unfazed by Veronica's drama, Adam pulled out his radio. "Sorry, Ms. Campbell. That's the reality of it." He pressed the button and told Deputy Amy Kama where to meet them. When he finished, he looked at Veronica with sympathetic eyes. "Just because we're dusting for prints doesn't mean we'll find anything. Don't get your hopes up."

Having already heard one story about Gideon Styles at the B&B, Rick felt compelled to guide the conversation. "Veronica? Why don't you tell us about this Gideon Styles? What makes you think he's behind this?"

"Because he's a crook!"

There it was again, that fiery teenage spirit. It was the same problem he sometimes had with Alex. "Can you be more specific? What exactly has he done to make you think he'd steal the recipe?"

Veronica crossed her arms over her chest. She glared at Rick, and then her tough exterior cracked. Her eyes again welled with tears as she spoke. "Right after my mom died, my Uncle Tyler met with him. My uncle wanted to sell the business and move away. I told him my mom had promised it to me and that I wanted to stay and run it."

Rick avoided looking at Veronica and instead focused on the mess around them. He felt a twinge of sympathy for the girl even as his suspicions about Veronica's family drama resurfaced. He focused on the details around him to keep himself from spinning theories and instead resorted to the process he'd used when working on a big story back in his reporting days. Ask questions. "When did your mom die?"

"Two years ago."

"So you were fifteen. How did you expect to run the business?"

"I didn't mean, like, right then," Veronica huffed. "You know, I thought my uncle could run it for me until I turned eighteen."

And then what? She'd dismiss him like an unwanted employee? "Had you ever worked in the bakery?"

"Of course! I made chocolate and baked with my mom since I was little."

"How did your mother die?" Adam asked.

"She was murdered."

Rick's breath caught. The poor girl. No wonder she was so angry. "And did they ever find the killer?"

The girl shook her head, the sadness in her eyes the only answer Rick needed. So much tragedy for someone so young. Nothing about this situation made sense. How had Alex met Veronica in front of the Rusty Nail right as the girl had fallen? How had she known her uncle was there with Gideon Styles? How had Styles done all of this?

Rick shook his head to fight back the barrage. Fortunately, he knew the owner of the Rusty Nail and could easily verify what had happened there. At least that way, he could keep up the appearance that he believed what Veronica was telling them. There was one thing he could do to test the truthfulness of her story—have her tell it again.

"Veronica, you and Alex explained what happened at the Rusty Nail to Marquetta and me, but the chief doesn't know about it. It could be relevant, so could you go through that for him?"

She rubbed her arms with her hands as she began, "I told Rick before that I've been looking for a job in town. I went to all the shops downtown, but nobody was hiring, so I finally decided to try the restaurants. That's why I went to the Rusty Nail. But when I got there, I saw my Uncle Tyler meeting with Gideon Styles."

Adam's green eyes darted toward Rick, conveying what was hopefully the same question Rick had. How did Styles come to be in two places at once?

"Do you know what they were talking about?" Adam asked.

"I'm sure they were talking about how to make this happen. I think my uncle decided he couldn't sell off the secret recipe because of me, so he must have decided to have Styles steal it. They'll split the money when Styles sells it."

The crease that had been in Adam's brow since Veronica began deepened. "You're alleging that your uncle intentionally had someone break in, vandalize your home, and steal a valuable asset?"

Without hesitation, Veronica gave them a definitive answer of yes. She also said she wanted to file charges. Between her defiant stance and her fiery hair, it was like looking at a young phoenix rising from the ashes. The sight of her confidence again stirred something deep inside of Rick. Pity? Sympathy? Fear? His throat tightened, a lump forming that he quickly swallowed down. His palms felt strangely clammy, and he had to fight the urge to reach out and comfort her—or question her motives.

"Are you saying you'd like to file a police report, Ms. Campbell?"

Adam's gaze bore into Veronica's, but she didn't back down. Instead, she stared at him and spoke in a confident voice. "Yes."

"I think we're getting ahead of ourselves," Rick said. "Veronica, think about what you're saying."

She squared her shoulders and took a deep breath. "I'm tired of secrets. I'm ready to bring the truth out into the light." She seemed to be steeling herself against some invisible force—perhaps the ghosts of the past?

Adam, grim-faced, pulled in a deep sigh, then turned toward the kitchen door. He raised one hand but was interrupted by a booming voice.

"What the devil happened to my house? And who are you?"

A sturdy man with broad shoulders and hands that betrayed many years spent kneading dough and moving bags of flour stood in the kitchen doorway. His hands trembled slightly. Was that a sign of the guilt and regret he carried? Or anger over finding strangers in his home and his house vandalized? Either way, Rick knew as sure as the sun would set over the ocean tonight that this was Veronica's uncle, Tyler Winkle. And he hoped the man was less volatile than his niece.

4

Rick

Tyler Winkle seemed unconcerned with introductions. He simply brushed off the fact that the Chief of Police was in his kitchen and demanded that Veronica explain why she'd brought strangers into his home. And why had it been ransacked? What had she done? After the third question, Adam cut Tyler off by moving in front of him and staring him down. Once cowed, Veronica's uncle put his hand to his heart as he looked around.

During his days as a reporter, Rick had learned that having empathy for the victim of a crime was one thing, putting yourself in their shoes and feeling what they felt was entirely different. He tried to imagine how it would feel to walk into this kind of chaos in his own kitchen and failed. It was just too big of a leap.

Tyler's eyes narrowed as he took in the disarray, a mix of frustration and determination evident on his face. He focused on the small breakfast nook, which had been turned into an impromptu workstation. The built-in bench was littered with scattered papers, further evidence of the break-in's aftermath. Finally, Tyler seemed to realize he couldn't bulldoze his way through this mess.

"What happened here? Who called you? Why are you in my house?" Tyler trembled as he looked around again and turned his irritation on his niece. "Veronica?"

Adam moved so that he stood between the two. "Mr. Winkle, I understand why you're upset." He went on to explain how a neighbor had called in what they thought was suspicious activity and how he'd found the front door ajar when he arrived.

"I have a suggestion, Adam," Rick said. "Why don't I talk to Tyler while you continue our discussion with Veronica?"

Veronica watched her uncle with wary eyes. "Uncle Tyler, I understand why you're so angry." She gently reached out and grabbed his arm. "But let's just try and talk this through."

Who was this girl? This was a completely different version of Veronica than the one Rick had met earlier. Compassion? Sympathy? He hadn't seen those traits before. The sudden change gave Rick pause. Here she was, standing amidst the chaos of an obvious ransacking of her home, and she'd somehow turned off her anger and grief. How had she made the switch so suddenly? The change felt way too smooth and polished. It was so smooth that his initial questions about her relationship with Alex came flooding back. He had to solve the case—if only to end the relationship.

Without waiting for Adam to agree, Rick took Tyler by the arm and started to lead him away. "I have something to show you in the master bedroom. Why don't we go back there so we can talk? Don't worry, Adam, we won't touch anything." As Rick led the way, he added, "It's about your safe."

A look of shock crossed Tyler's face. "How did you know I had a safe in my bedroom?"

"Your niece told me when I brought her home."

Tyler started to say something, then his jaw dropped, and he sucked in a breath. "Oh, God. No. Don't tell me they got the recipe."

"It would appear so," Rick said.

As they left the kitchen, Rick heard Adam say, "Now, Ms. Campbell, let's begin at the beginning."

Tyler seemed in a daze as they walked to the master. On the way, Rick noted the attention to detail throughout the house. Even the light fixtures had been crafted from hammered copper and brass, complementing the natural materials used throughout the rest of the home.

When they reached the bedroom, Rick put a comforting hand on Tyler's shoulder. "I'm sorry this has happened," he said quietly. "It's okay to feel overwhelmed right now, but we'll help you get through it."

Tyler stared across the room at the safe as he slumped against the wall. Slowly, the color drained from his face. He looked toward the kitchen, and the corners of his mouth twitched. "Does Veronica think I had something to do with this?"

Interesting question, thought Rick, given the conversation they'd had with her. Rather than answering, Rick sidestepped the question. "Let's focus on the safe and figure out what happened. We'll start with the basics. Was it locked?"

"Of course, it was." Tyler pushed off the wall and stumbled over to the safe.

"Don't touch anything," Rick cautioned. "The police still need to dust for prints. What else was in the safe besides this recipe?"

"I didn't keep a detailed inventory or anything like that." Tyler grumbled, then quickly added, "But I do remember there being some important documents in there. Some of them were financial records. Others were personal papers for family members."

Family members? From what Veronica had said, she and her uncle were the only family left. "Anything someone might want to steal?"

Tyler shook his head. "I can't think of anything valuable enough to risk breaking into a safe for." He turned away and put his hands on the wall as if searching for an answer.

Maybe the best thing was to do the same thing Adam was with Veronica and begin at the beginning. His instincts told him to keep the information he gave out to a minimum. Maybe that would net him more information than what Veronica had provided. "Tyler, why don't you explain to me why this recipe is so valuable?"

"That recipe's been in our family for almost a hundred-and-twenty years. Over the generations, we built a reputation and a business everyone thought would last forever. That is, until our brother took over. A first-class cheapskate is what he was. He tried to modernize the recipe by substituting cheaper ingredients. It was never as good as the original. We lost business until Maxine stepped in and salvaged what was left."

Rick noted an uptick in Tyler's irritation level when he mentioned his brother. He also chalked up Veronica's earlier statement about there being no other family members to her propensity for drama, which she seemed to have plenty of. Curious, he asked, "Do you and your brother get along?"

"Haven't seen him in years. Can't stand the guy. He ruined our family chocolate business."

"I don't understand. I thought you and your sister were bakers, not chocolatiers."

"The missing recipe is for the chocolate we used in our baked goods. It's the chocolate we used that made The Secret Ingredient Bakery famous. Maxine figured out how to incorporate the original chocolate recipe into our baked goods. My sister was a genius. She was always a better baker. I could never measure up to her standards."

Rick cast another glance at the door of the safe, which hung open to expose only an empty shell. "So, how valuable is this missing chocolate recipe?"

Tyler paused, then quietly said, "Some people think that if they can get their hands on the original recipe, they could make a fortune. I was hoping to capitalize on the interest and sell it so we'd have the money to send Veronica to a good college. I don't want her growing up to be a baker. She should be able to do something she enjoys, not be chained to a hot kitchen her entire life."

A pang of sorrow rippled through Rick as he listened to Tyler. He couldn't help but think about the picture of Alex he kept stored in his wallet. He had always hoped she would find her own way in life. Rick studied Tyler, wondering how he and his niece had grown so far apart. He made a silent promise to ensure that Alex would have the freedom to carve her own path and explore her passions without being chained to the legacy of a family business. But he'd also give her the chance to take over the business if she wanted.

Rick pulled in a slow breath. The chains of a family legacy. Was this the event that would break them? It was tempting to think Tyler—or even Veronica—had been willing to put an end to what they perceived as a burden.

"These people you're referring to. Would any of them go to such lengths to steal your chocolate recipe?" Rick asked, his gaze steady on Tyler's. Rick's tone had been calm, but the question hung heavy in the air between them, clouded with implications about trust, deceit, and the dire consequences of greed.

"I don't know why anyone would take such extreme measures."

Rick didn't know who was worse—Tyler or Veronica. They both were quick to make general accusations, but neither had anything concrete to back up their claims. Rick made a show of looking around the room. An overturned lamp lay on the floor, its shade now cockeyed and broken. "Chief Cunningham thinks this burglary was not just about the chocolate recipe."

Tyler's brow furrowed, and he pressed his lips together in a tight line. "What are you saying?"

"I'm saying that someone might have done this damage to hide an ulterior motive."

"What motive?" Tyler demanded.

"I don't know. You tell me. It's your home." Rick responded. His words were soft, but the implications, serious. He held Tyler's gaze, looking for any signs of evasion.

There was no question; Rick definitely wanted answers. Not just the surface issues that Tyler and his niece kept throwing out, but what was the root cause? Rick resolved not to stop until he got the answer. Tyler seemed to understand this, too, as a hint of worry crept into his eyes.

"Veronica told me earlier that she was upset after she saw you meeting with a man named Gideon Styles," Rick said matter-of-factly. "Do you know why she was so upset? What about your meeting? Could it have something to do with this burglary?"

Tyler blinked, his expression unreadable. He started to say something, stopped, then spoke quietly, "I don't know."

"No, Tyler. I think you do. Either that, or you don't know your niece well at all. Please, be honest with me."

"Veronica is troubled," Tyler said slowly. "She seems to be obsessed with Gideon Styles." He shook his head again, his expression grim. "You don't suppose she did all of this, do you? Maybe I should do something. You know, maybe get her some help."

Rick's eyes narrowed as he read Tyler's response. His mind was racing, trying to make sense of what was going on. A knot formed in his stomach, an unease he couldn't shake off. These two were both way too quick to point fingers at each other. It was all too easy, too convenient.

The girl had her issues, and apparently, so did her uncle. But to go to such lengths? Rick was having a hard time buying into their stories. There had to be more, something that he was missing.

"Tyler," Rick began, suspicion creeping into his voice, "That's a heavy accusation to make without concrete proof. What you've told me so far is that your niece has emotional problems stemming from the death of her mother. Okay, I get that. But the damage done here suggests an act of calculated destruction, not just an emotional outburst. And the timing with Gideon Styles—it's too neat. Are you sure there's nothing you're hiding?"

Tyler's eyes widened, and he threw up his hands in an exaggerated gesture. "Hiding? Me?" He laughed nervously. "Rick, I assure you, I'm as baffled about this as you are. And as for Veronica, I'm just worried about her, that's all. After her mother's death." His voice wavered a bit, betraying a feigned surprise.

Tension filled the air as Rick zeroed in on Tyler's efforts to sound shocked and appalled. "Sure. I get it. You want what's best for your niece. Tell me, how did she react when her mother died?"

"It was hard for her. She didn't take it well. She was really angry with me at first. She even blamed me for Maxine's death at one point. But Maxine was my sister, and I'm sure Veronica has finally realized I would never have done anything to hurt her."

Talk about someone sticking their head in the sand. Tyler sounded like a man who had no clue what his niece felt. In the short time the girl had spent at the B&B, she'd implied plenty about her uncle. They were completely out of sync. Rick took a final look around the room. He took a slow, measured breath. Even though these people were the victims, it seemed they had plenty to hide. Family secrets. He hated digging into them. But it looked like that's what it was going to take.

5

ALEX

September 11

Hey Journal,

I can't believe what just happened! I'm so bummed out. I brought my new friend Veronica home to get her some help after I saw her fall into the planter at the Rusty Nail. After I helped her get back on her feet, she was totally different from when we first met. Then, she was super cool and funny. Now, she's like all dark and moody. That's why I got Mom and Dad involved. I thought we were gonna figure out a plan to help her with her Uncle Tyler.

Mom was awesome and consoled Veronica, but then my dad started pushing her to talk with her uncle. When she agreed, I totally wanted to go with her so she'd have a friend there, too. Right?

Then, out of nowhere, Dad decided he'd take Veronica home himself! I mean, what? I was totally left out of the loop. I was supposed to be the one there for her, and now I'm just...here. I'm clueless about what's going on and it feels like a major letdown.

But, you know what, Journal? This hiccup isn't gonna stop me. I'm determined to help Veronica, no matter what. She's my friend, and she's going through such a tough time. I can't just sit around doing nothing. I'm going to figure out another way to help her. Tomorrow's another day, right?

xoxo,

Alex

6

RICK

TYLER WINKLE PACED NERVOUSLY, HIS eyes darting around the room as he moved. His shoulders were hunched forward with the look of a man whose guilt weighed heavily on his soul.

"So, Tyler," Rick began, his voice calm and tinged with curiosity, "I've been trying to piece everything together. Can you walk me through what happened to Veronica's mother?"

"What do you mean?"

"What happened the day Veronica's mother died? That loss seems to be tearing your niece apart."

"She was my sister! That loss weighs on me, too. I don't see why Maxine's murder is any business of yours."

"I think it is for two reasons. First, there's a lot going on between you and your niece. Second, as Chief Cunningham and I have both stated, we don't think this was any ordinary robbery. The only thing we know for sure is that your family recipe is gone. The vandalism…" Rick motioned with his arm at the mess around them. "We're not sure yet what the motive was for this. So, tell me about that day."

Tyler looked up, meeting Rick's gaze with a mix of sadness and regret. He took a deep breath, and his voice trembled as he spoke. "I was supposed to be the one working, but I had a terrible hangover. I asked Maxine to cover for me at the bakery."

Rick felt his gaze narrow. A hangover? Was Tyler an alcoholic? That could account for the angst in this home, especially if Veronica knew the truth. Then again, how could she not? "Does your niece know?"

"I…I'm not sure."

"Don't delude yourself, Tyler. Kids pick up a lot more than we give them credit for." Rick resisted the urge to pummel Tyler with questions and instead chose to observe. He watched Tyler's hands fidget, his fingers tapping anxiously against his thigh. It was clear he carried the weight of Maxine's death on his conscience.

With desperation creeping into his voice, Tyler continued, "I never imagined something like this would happen. I blame myself every single day."

A flicker of sadness shown briefly in Tyler's eyes. It was a look Rick knew all too well—the torment of regret and the gnawing feeling of responsibility. "I know this feels like I'm prying, but do you drink a lot?"

"Not anymore. I haven't had a drop since the day Maxine died."

"I see. Tyler, I understand that you're hurting, But in order to figure out who broke into your home, we may need to look at different aspects of your life."

"I'll do whatever it takes to find the truth." Tyler's voice cracked under the weight of the sorrowful load he'd been carrying.

Rick's heart went out to him, recognizing that he and his niece were both tangled in a web of grief and unanswered questions. "Alright, then. I need details, basically, a timeline of the day your sister was killed."

"Maxine got to the bakery around 7 a.m. There was nothing special about the day. It was ordinary, just like any other. She was supposed to be there until three." He paused, his voice threatening to break. "At the end of the day, she put together the bank deposit like normal, then locked up and started walking to the bank. She never made it. An addict who needed a fix stuck a gun in her face and demanded the cash."

Rick was silent, letting Tyler compose himself before he continued.

"Maxine resisted, so the guy shot her and ran. All he got was a few hundred bucks. The worst part is the cops never caught him."

"And Veronica blames you because you were the one who was supposed to be working that day."

"I suppose so." Tyler's body deflated as he said the words. "She's not the only one. I blame myself, too. I should have been there."

"I'm sorry for your loss. Have you and Veronica talked at all about it since?"

Tyler shook his head, and he looked away. "No. Not really. I think she's too upset to talk."

It seemed impossible that Tyler could be so clueless about what his niece knew. Unless he was just in denial. Even at that, if Tyler tried, he and Veronica probably could talk to each other and accept their shared grief. "Earlier, you said the stolen recipe had been in your family for over a hundred years. But Veronica led me to believe it was created by her mother. Can you clarify that?"

"In 1903, Veronica's fourth-great-grandmother, Sadie Smith, worked for Milton Hershey. They worked closely on a recipe for chocolate for his new company. Hershey thought what Sadie came up with was too dark and bitter for the general public, so they put it aside. Later, when Sadie married and left the company, she and her husband opened a chocolate shop using the recipe. It's been the family secret for generations, and now some thief has it. Veronica's going to be devastated now that it's gone."

Rick ran his fingers through his hair and thought about what to do next. He'd seen Veronica's rage firsthand and agreed. Veronica was filled with all kinds of negative emotions. Her mother's death had left an open wound. One neither she nor her uncle had dealt with. And now, somebody had stolen the only thing they had left. "Did anybody in Seaside Cove know about this chocolate recipe?"

"Not unless Veronica told them. I haven't told anyone around here."

"So we can be pretty sure that whoever committed this burglary was from out of town. Which means somebody found out you were here and came here to get the recipe. Could it have been the man you were meeting with at lunch? What was his name?"

"Gideon Styles. He's a broker. No, he wouldn't have done this," Tyler said firmly.

Rick paused to reconcile the timing of the break-in with a lunch in which Tyler had intended to sell the very item that had been stolen. Coincidence? Not likely. "Are you sure it wasn't Gideon Styles?"

Tyler covered his mouth with his hand and coughed several times. "Sorry, guess I caught a piece of dust or something," He patted his chest with his hand.

Rick eyed Tyler closely, certain that the man was making a bad attempt at covering up more than a cough. Maybe there was a different way to get the answer he was looking for. "If it wasn't Styles, then somebody else followed you here. Why did you move to Seaside Cove, Tyler? Was there someone you were trying to get away from?"

"No. It was to protect Veronica. She was always such a good kid until her mom was killed." Tyler paused. His eyes misted over, and he placed his fingers over his mouth. "The two of them loved to make towel animals. It was Maxine's last Christmas. She and Veronica spent hours making swans. They used them in the bakery window as part of our holiday decorations. The display was a massive hit with the customers."

Tyler stopped, bit his lower lip, and gazed across the room at nothing. When Rick asked if Tyler was okay, the man started.

"Sorry. It was the last time Veronica was truly happy. Ever since Maxine died, Veronica has had trouble with the law. About six months ago, the police raided a party where there was underage drinking going on. Veronica was there, and while she wasn't arrested, word got around that she had been involved."

"I see. Was there just the one incident?"

Tyler's face darkened. "Another time, she was in possession of drugs and faced charges of delinquency. That was enough to get her kicked off the track team." He shook his head sadly. "I wanted to get her away from that environment. She'd been through so much back home, so I thought Seaside Cove might be the perfect place for us to start over."

"Until today, has it been?"

"Yes," Tyler said with a genuine smile. "It's been amazing." As quickly as it had come, the smile fell away, and Tyler seemed to slip back into darkness. "But now I'm afraid Veronica will never be able to move past all the pain and anger she has inside. She won't let anyone close enough to help her heal."

"Speaking of that, she believes Gideon Styles is at the root of all this. You said he's a broker? Of what?"

"Veronica's got it all wrong. He's an honest man that she doesn't like. You know how kids are. Gideon and I were having lunch at the Rusty Nail when Veronica walked in. That's it. Just lunch. And she had a meltdown. Right there. She started making accusations about me trying to steal her inheritance and a bunch of other nonsense."

Rick noted the hard edge in Tyler's voice and how he'd clenched and unclenched his fists as he'd spoken. "Such as?"

"That I was just trying to get my hands on her money. That I wanted to use it to support myself. That I didn't love her." Tyler continued, his voice growing in intensity. "She accused me of conspiring with Gideon to sabotage her life. The whole place was watching. It was embarrassing, to say the least."

"Are you absolutely certain that Styles had nothing to do with the robbery?"

"Of course I am! Veronica's just imagining things."

Rick paused to consider Tyler's response. A little too fast. A little too forceful. It was too soon to be calling anyone a liar, but something was way off in this house. As Rick studied the man's face, he couldn't help but note a mix of characteristics. So far, he'd seen glimpses of the same anger in Tyler that Veronica bore, but unlike Veronica, Tyler had also come across as disciplined. A current of pessimism and an unforgiving nature ran beneath the veneer of control. It appeared that Tyler was a man who held onto grudges, carrying the weight of past wrongs—even when those might be his own. No wonder it was so difficult for Veronica to find the understanding she so desperately needed.

"Yes or no—were you and Gideon having lunch to discuss closing a deal on the recipe?"

Tyler uttered a begrudging, "Well, yes. He offered, but I never agreed. He didn't get upset about it or anything. If that's what you're implying. Like I said, he's an honest guy."

Rick was beginning to see the full picture of this tangled web. It was clear that Tyler wasn't being entirely truthful. Rick wondered why he should believe that Styles was honest. Circumstances said otherwise. The man had come here to get the recipe without warning. What honest businessman did that?

The other big doubt Rick had centered around Tyler's motives for moving to Seaside Cove. He now doubted those motives were as pure as Tyler claimed. It might be premature to lay blame for the robbery at Tyler's feet, but Rick was sure Adam would want to talk to Gideon

Styles. He certainly did. "Let me be direct, Tyler. Did you have any enemies? Someone who would want to do this to you?"

Tyler shook his head, refusing to look Rick in the eye. "No," he finally muttered.

"You're absolutely positive?"

Continuing to avoid Rick's gaze, Tyler let his silence stretch on. His anxiety practically filled the room. Finally, he nodded, his voice barely above a whisper. "Yes, I'm positive." His eyes flickered with a fiery emotion Rick couldn't pinpoint.

Rick made a mental note to follow up later. Family secrets. Buried deep. He suspected that if they were going to get to the bottom of who had broken in, ransacked the house, and stolen a recipe, he and Adam had to unearth those secrets. In that process, would he discover the real reason behind Veronica's anger? No doubt. This was going to be tricky and could open old wounds that had not yet healed.

The sudden sound of Adam's voice pulled Rick's attention away from Tyler. "Rick, we need to talk. It's urgent."

Adam stood in the doorway to the master, the look on his face telling Rick that, indeed, this conversation had to happen right now. Holding up one finger to indicate Tyler should wait for him to return, Rick crossed the room and lowered his voice. "What's up?"

"I received a call. We have a homicide on our hands. Deputy Kama's at the scene." Adam looked back at Tyler, grimaced, and lowered his voice so only Rick could hear. "I need you to stay here and keep an eye on these two."

Rick glanced over at Tyler, who was watching them intently. His brow furrowed, and his confidence was visibly shaken by the interruption. Adam held out a piece of paper. Rick looked down and read what Adam had written. He lowered his voice so Tyler couldn't hear him, "And Veronica?"

"She's in the kitchen. That's the best place for both of them for now. I know this is asking a lot."

"No worries, Adam. You go deal with this. Do you want me to say anything about it?"

"I'll let you make that call." With a single, grim nod, Adam turned away and headed out the door.

After Adam was gone, Rick walked slowly over to where Tyler stood. "Veronica's in the kitchen. Let's join her."

"What's going on? Why's he leaving?" Tyler demanded.

"I'll tell you both at the same time. Let's go." Rick cocked his head toward the bedroom door, then followed Tyler into the kitchen.

Veronica watched them both suspiciously as they entered the room, her face a mask of worry. "Why did Chief Cunningham leave?"

Rick held up his hand. "I'll tell you both, but first, I have a few questions."

"I demand to know what's going on here!" Tyler shot back.

He could demand anything he wanted, thought Rick. But the interruption was a game-changer. They were now dealing with murder. Gideon Styles was dead. And the two people who lived in this house both had reasons to kill him.

7

RICK

A PALPABLE TENSION PERMEATED THE air in the kitchen as Tyler and Veronica glared at each other, then Rick. The silence, stifling as it felt, was exactly what Rick wanted. The refrigerator kicked on, its hum filling the air like distant echoes.

"I won't sugarcoat this," Rick began, his every syllable resonating with a seriousness that immediately caught their attention. "You could both be in trouble." The statement hung in the air, a tangible threat that cast a chill over the room.

"What…what are you saying?" Veronica's pale skin turned almost translucent as the fear of the unknown threatened to overwhelm her.

"I don't think you've been entirely truthful with me," Rick said, his eyes fixed on Veronica. "Neither have you," he turned to Tyler. "That call Adam received?" It was to report that Gideon Styles is dead. I suggest you both take a step back and think about what you've told me. Your stories contradict each other, and you're both blaming each other." Rick paused and surveyed the room. "For all of this."

Veronica's jaw went slack, and she slumped against the counter. She ran her hand down her throat as her eyes darted between Rick and her uncle.

Tyler, to Rick's surprise, stepped forward. He squared his shoulders and lifted his chin in a defiant posture. "You're right. I wasn't entirely forthcoming with you." He turned to Veronica, then back to Rick, a stern expression on his face. "Are we suspects?"

"As of this moment, no, but if I were you, I'd start telling the truth. Now."

Veronica's rebellious attitude evaporated like mist caught in the morning sun. She went silent, and the vulnerability Rick had seen when they first met returned. Her pale skin made her green eyes stand out even more, but as she took a deep breath, she looked at Rick with determination. "I'll tell you everything," she said, her voice a hoarse whisper. "I just…I'm just feeling so overwhelmed." Rick nodded, seeing a remnant of what he hoped was a need to set things right.

Though he was a sturdy build, Tyler was shorter than Rick, a fact Rick planned to capitalize on as he fixed Tyler with a look of irritation. The room's power dynamic seemed to shift visibly as Rick's gaze bore into Tyler's. The silence was a strong reminder of the tension and uncertainty surrounding this entire situation.

"Yes," Tyler said calmly. "The truth."

"Good. Now we understand each other. Veronica, at the B&B, you told me you ran out of the Rusty Nail when you saw your uncle with Styles. Is that really what happened?" Rick pressed, his voice expectant yet firm. "Start from the beginning."

After going through the entire sequence of events again, Rick was convinced she was telling the truth. At least, in part. "And where did you go after the Rusty Nail?"

"I was with Alex. That's when she brought me back to your place."

"That's where you went? With that girl?" Tyler turned his gaze from Veronica to Rick. "And she's your daughter?"

"Yes, she is." Rick let the expression on his face say what he wouldn't say out loud—I'm not taking any crap from you. "Tyler, it seems obvious that you were not just meeting to have lunch with Styles. What was the nature of your meeting with him?"

Tyler blew out a long breath and shifted to one side, then looked at Veronica. "If Gideon's dead, I guess he can't hurt you now."

"What's that mean?" Rick demanded.

"He showed up and told me he had another offer for the recipe. We agreed to go to lunch. That's when he said he needed to reduce the amount he could pay." Tyler paused and looked away as if he was afraid to meet Rick's gaze. "He said he could only give me half of what we agreed on."

"I knew you were trying to sell it!" Veronica rushed to her uncle and beat him on the chest with her fists. "I hate you! I hate you!"

When Tyler made no move to stop her, Rick quickly intervened, gently pulling Veronica aside and looking once more at Tyler. "What did you say to him?"

"I told him there was no way I'd sell for half. That we'd already agreed to a deal." A tear formed in the corner of Tyler's eye, and his expression turned to one of shame. "Veronica, sweetheart, I turned him down the last two times because of you. I knew you'd never forgive me if I sold. But lately, I've been thinking. I know your mother wanted you to go to college, and the only way I could afford it was to sell. It's what your mother would have wanted."

"Liar!" Veronica spat. "Mom wanted me to have the business. She always said it was my inheritance."

"Veronica," Rick said quietly. "Let's listen to what your uncle has to say. Alright, Tyler, after you turned him down, what happened?"

Tyler swallowed hard, ran his hands through his hair, and then looked at Veronica. "That was about the time you walked in. When you started yelling, I was surprised that Gideon wasn't bothered at all. Then you ran out, and I panicked."

"So what did you do?" Rick asked.

"I left Gideon and went after her, of course."

"Did you see her fall?"

"Yes." Tyler grimaced and avoided Rick's gaze.

"But you didn't try to help her when she fell in the planter?"

"She didn't want my help. She made that clear." Tyler paused, then folded his hands in front of him. "When I went back inside, Gideon said it was time to make a deal. Basically, he told me I was out of time. He said if I didn't agree to sell him the recipe, he'd use his influence to make sure Veronica never got into college."

"That's what you meant when you said he couldn't hurt Veronica now?"

"Yes."

Rick studied Tyler for a few seconds. With a high forehead beneath wavy, dark hair, Tyler appeared to be a hard man. Could he be the kind of man who would commit murder? After a long pause, Rick said, "You realize everything you're telling me is making it sound like you had a very good motive for wanting to see Gideon Styles dead."

"I do." Tyler's voice was again determined. "But I didn't have anything to do with it. I swear."

Rick muttered a soft "Mm-hmm" before turning his attention back to Veronica. "My gut says your uncle is telling the truth. But there's still something off about this whole situation." He looked at Tyler and raised an eyebrow. "How well did you know Styles?"

"The first time we met was right after my sister died. At the time, Veronica and I were both still grieving so much that I couldn't bring myself to sell. The second time I met him was when I decided to move us to Seaside Cove. He wanted to buy the recipe from me then. But I still couldn't bring myself to sell it because I knew what it would do to Veronica."

"So, how did you leave things with him?"

"I never thought I'd see him again, but then he showed up in Seaside Cove. We'd settled in, and Veronica was going to be going off to school in about a year. I figured there wouldn't be any other chance for me to sell it if I didn't agree this time."

"What's it worth?" Rick asked.

"Millions!" Veronica blurted.

Rick gazed at her, hoping his skepticism didn't come through too strongly. "Millions?"

Tyler winced, shook his head, and reached out to his niece. "Veronica, you know it's not worth that."

Veronica stepped back and glared at him, her jaw set. "Well, it could be. Me and Mom always talked about how we could make it something big again."

"Gideon wasn't offering millions. He originally offered fifty thousand dollars." Tyler paused and looked down. "But I still said no. I couldn't do it—not when I knew how badly Veronica wanted it."

Rick felt a soft ache in his chest for both of them. The adult, fully aware of the realities of the business world, trying to insulate his young niece from that reality. And Veronica, really, not much more than a child with unrealistic expectations. He looked down, then back up, meeting Tyler's eyes with an empathetic gaze. His voice softened, "That's quite the dilemma."

Veronica's lower lip trembled, and she looked at Tyler pleadingly. "I'm the reason you didn't sell?"

Tyler's mouth opened slightly. He sounded exasperated when he said, "Of course. Everything I've done over the past couple of years has been for your benefit. Even the move to Seaside Cove. I had to get you away from the bad influences in the city. The only reason I wanted to sell was to get you a decent college education. I don't care where you want to go. That should be up to you. If you wanted, you could have used the money to go to culinary school. I just wanted you to have a good chance at making it in this world. For me, this recipe was never about improving my lot, and it was all for your benefit."

Suddenly, Veronica stepped forward and let Tyler embrace her. The muscles in his arms tensed with emotion as he tightened his grip. He looked up at the ceiling, then bit his lower lip and closed his eyes. When he opened them, they were moist, and he blinked several times as if trying to hold back tears.

"Tyler, you described Styles as an honest man, yet he showed up without advance notice and lowered his offer, then tried to apply pressure on you by making threats against your niece. That doesn't seem like a very honest businessman to me. He wasn't. Was he?"

The muscles in Tyler's jaw tightened, and the blue in his eyes now looked like steel. "No."

"Why'd you lie?"

"Because at first, I thought I had to protect Veronica from Gideon's threats. Then, once you told me he was dead, I knew that telling you the truth would make me look guiltier than I already do."

"Lying makes it even worse, Tyler. So, what is the truth?"

"I couldn't stand Gideon. I always had a feeling the man was trying to swindle me. Now that this has happened…" He paused and gestured around the room. "I'm pretty sure Gideon must have been behind this. As for how he did it, I don't know. But he's been trying to get the recipe for two years now, and I'm sure he'd stop at nothing to get what he wants."

"Why'd you deal with him if you didn't trust him?"

"I was desperate to help Veronica."

Was that another half-truth? "Did he know you had a safe?"

"Yes. I stupidly told him about it at lunch. I never thought he'd resort to theft to get his hands on it, though." Tyler shook his head and tightened his grip around Veronica as if trying to protect her from danger. "I can't believe I let him into our lives like this. It's all my fault."

"When exactly did you tell him about the safe?" Rick pressed.

"Right after he threatened to keep Veronica out of college. That was just before she showed up."

"And after that was when you went outside to check on your niece?" Rick craned his neck forward.

"I suppose so."

"Which would have given him time to call an accomplice."

Tyler's shoulders slumped again. "What have I done?"

Yes, thought Rick. Wasn't that exactly the right question? "Where did you go after lunch, Tyler?"

"For a walk. I had so many things to sort out. I was trying to figure out how to protect Veronica and the recipe, without putting her in danger. But it seems like Gideon was a step ahead the entire time."

Rick shook his head. "That's not entirely true. He might have been one step ahead of you, but the man's dead. Someone killed him. Unfortunately for you, given your relationship with Styles and lack of an alibi, Chief Cunningham will probably consider you his number one suspect."

8

ALEX

I KNOCK ON THE DOOR of the Jib Room, not even knowing who I'm looking for. My mom asked me to bring our newest guest some extra towels. When the door opens, a tall man with broad shoulders stands in front of me. He's handsome. Has a smile that makes me want to stop and gawk. Heck, his smile's so warm that it could melt butter. He introduces himself as Barrington Rhymes.

Oh, right. Duh. That means I'm supposed to say something. I shove the two towels at him. "My mom asked me to bring you these." Oh, man. I sound so lame.

"You must be Alex." He takes the towels from my hands and smiles again. "Thanks. I need to make a towel roll so I can stretch out my back."

Wow. He's totally smooth. And handsome. His voice is inviting and friendly, with a hint of professionalism. "Sure. No problem. Are you staying here long? We can get you more anytime you want. We don't want you to be uncomfortable." Ugh. That didn't come out right, either.

Mr. Rhymes smiles again. "I'll be here for two weeks on business. It's nice to know that you're all so accommodating."

Two weeks? Whoa. "That's a long stay for us. We get mostly tourists, and they're only here for a few days. What kind of business are you in?" I'm totally trying to sound cool and casual, not lame like a little kid, and it's so not working.

"I'm a consultant," he says with a slight grin. "I have meetings lined up while I'm here."

"Do you travel a lot, Mr. Rhymes?"

"Please, my father is Mr. Rhymes. Call me Barrington."

Now he's laughing, and I'm embarrassed. Talk about feeling like a little kid. Suddenly, my jaw drops open just a little. I know somebody who would be perfect for him. If he's single. And he doesn't travel too much.

"I'll bet you have like millions of frequent flyer miles!"

He laughs again. He's easy. Relaxed. Oh, wow. I'm loving this guy for Miss Redmond. She's not just any ordinary teacher; she's got this air of mystery surrounding her. Her blonde hair falls gracefully over her shoulders, and her eyes are like deep pools of wisdom and knowledge. I can't help but imagine her as the leading lady in some romantic movie—opposite Mr. Barrington Rhymes.

"I do have a lot of miles, but I really don't like traveling that much. I'd rather settle down in a place like this little town. It's quaint. I love the way the sea breeze brings in the salty air. This is my idea of heaven. You're lucky to live here."

This is totally game on. Maybe I should call it Operation Blind Date? My face gets warm because I realize I can't just ask him if he's single—or can I? "I love it here, too. We moved here from New York, and I hated it at first. But it's so peaceful here compared to the hustle and bustle of the Big Apple."

He gives me a lopsided grin. "Hustle and bustle? Aren't you a little young to be knowing about that?"

I can't help but giggle. "It's something my dad says sometimes. The adults were the hustlers and bustlers—not me!"

He smiles so wide that it almost seems impossible to contain his enthusiasm. He leans closer to me, and I swear there's a sparkle in his eyes. There is gonna be so much chemistry between him and Miss Redmond that the test tube's gonna blow up!

"So, do you have kids?"

"No. Sadly, I'm still single. But I'll tell you this. I think if I had a daughter, I'd like her to be like you."

I can hardly stop smiling. This guy is amazing. Miss Redmond is going to love him. My phone pings, and I pull it out of my back pocket. It's a text from Veronica.

"I guess you'd better get that, Alex. Thanks for the towels."

"Have a great day!"

He slips the door closed, and as I turn away, I can still feel the big, stupid grin on my face. When I get to the second-floor landing, I take one last glimpse at the Jib Room door. Talk about a potential happily ever after in the making. It isn't until I read what Veronica wrote in her message that I stop smiling.

—Gideon Styles is dead. The cops found his body at the Seaside Cove Inn. Meet me there. Now!

9

RICK

RICK STUDIED THE BODY OF Gideon Styles. Blood had pooled onto the asphalt where the body lay close to the dumpster. He looked again at the plastic baggie in his gloved hand. The baggie contained a single piece of paper with only a few words written on it. Seventeen words, to be exact. And, to be truthful, the words didn't even make much sense.

"This is the only clue you have? Don't you have anything else?" Rick asked.

"Nope. Not even a wallet. I've got Deputy Kama checking the dumpster."

At the mention of her name, Deputy Kama popped up, her brown eyes smiling playfully over the rim of the dumpster. "Hey, Rick. Care to trade places?"

"No thanks, Amy," Rick snickered. "I think you're doing a fine job in there."

After the deputy ducked back down and the sounds of her rummaging around returned, Rick nudged Adam with his elbow. "Boy, has she changed."

"Love will do that to you," Adam whispered, then raised his voice to a normal level. "We're hoping our killer tossed the wallet in there. I went to the office, dragged Ray Villari out here, and he identified

Styles. He remembered him from when he checked in. Styles claimed he was in town for business."

Surveying the scene, Rick thought it looked like someone had walked up to Styles, put a few slugs in him, and walked away. "Business, alright. And not the kind that's honest. Tyler finally leveled with me. It sounds like Styles came here intending to walk away with the family's recipe no matter what. Did Ray tell you anything else? Anything at all?"

"Nope. You know Ray. Mr. Chatty."

"Takes the expression, 'a man of few words' to a whole new level," Rick muttered. He stretched his back and shoulders, then held up the baggie. "And this is all there was on the body? No keys? What about a room key?"

"Nope. Which means maybe our killer went up to Styles's room."

"Precisely."

"And since Ray gave me a key and told me to free up his room ASAP, I thought we might want to check it out."

"I can't believe it. He cooperated without an argument?"

"He wants his room back so he can rent it out again."

"Seriously? That's all it took?"

"Didn't say that. I did have to threaten him with obstruction, but only once."

"He's getting better. Okay, mind if I go up there now?"

"I'll go with you." Adam's expression was grim, the little lines around the corners of his green eyes crinkling with concern. "You got this under control, Deputy?"

"Got it, Chief!" Deputy Kama's voice sounded hollow as it came from within the dumpster.

"Okay. Let's go," Adam said.

A squeal from the dumpster caused Adam to do an about-face. "Are you okay, Deputy?"

"I'm good, Chief. I found it!" Deputy Kama popped up. This time, she was waving a wallet in the air and had a satisfied smile on her face.

"Along with plenty of filth and gunk," Rick said.

"Nice job, Deputy," Adam said as he took the slimy mess from her. "When this is all over, go home and get cleaned up."

"Thanks, Chief. I smell like…" She raised her arm, smelled the sleeve of her uniform, and made a face. "Ewww. Never mind."

Adam placed the wallet on the hood of his vehicle, which he'd strategically parked to block access to this part of the parking lot. Rick and Deputy Kama watched as he pulled out a driver's license, a credit card, and the photo of a petite woman with dark hair and warm brown eyes. He turned the photo over, but there was no inscription on the back.

Turning back to the body, Rick noticed a wedding ring on Styles's finger. "Hey, Adam, Styles was married."

"It would appear so. Let's see if there's an inscription inside. Maybe it will help us figure out who this woman is." Adam turned and looked at Deputy Kama. "Do you want to do the honors, or do you want me to?"

Deputy Kama looked shocked as she gaped at Adam. "You're giving me a choice?"

"You did volunteer for dumpster duty. Why not?"

"Ah, what the heck?" Deputy Kama stepped over to the body and made quick work of the task. She slid the ring off Styles's finger and turned it over in her hands. "Look at that. It says, Leslie and Gideon Forever."

She held out the ring, but Adam shook his head. "Just bag it. All we have to do now is find a woman with dark hair and brown eyes named Leslie." He turned to Rick. "Piece of cake, right?"

Rick barked out a quick laugh. “Sure, buddy. Let’s take a look at the room. Maybe we’ll get lucky and find a last name.”

“I’ve got this under control, Chief. The ME and the forensics team should be here in a few minutes.”

“Okay. Rick and I will take a look at our victim’s room before we lose it to the Sheriff.” Adam motioned with his head for Rick to follow, then walked toward the stairs.

By the time they reached the second-floor landing, Rick’s mind was reeling with questions about who killed Styles and why. He shook off the thoughts, determined to focus on the search of Styles’s room.

Adam knocked three times on the door, but there was no answer. He pulled the key from his pocket and smiled. “Only once.”

“Next thing you know, Ray will actually be cooperative,” Rick snickered.

“That’ll be the day,” Adam said as he pushed open the door.

The musty interior of the room smelled of room deodorizer and stale air. The furnishings were modern cheap with just a touch of dingy.

“Why doesn’t Ray paint these rooms a brighter color?” Rick asked. “Paint’s cheap.”

Adam rubbed his fingers and thumb together. “You know why. Closet or dresser?”

“I’ll take the closet.”

Rick quickly found the usual items: a few shirts, trousers, and shoes. He almost missed the tattered notebook tucked into the back pocket of a pair of pants. He flipped through and noticed immediately that it was filled with numbers. He held up the notebook so Adam could see it. “This is pretty strange.”

Adam grunted his agreement as he opened a drawer, but then his face lit up, and he smiled at Rick. “Bingo. I think I just hit the Mother Lode.” He laid his find on the bedspread. There were two envelopes, one stuffed full of money, the other addressed to Leslie Mendez and marked Return to Sender. There was also a deck of cards and another piece of paper on which someone had written seventeen words.

Rick read through the saying twice. This one was different from the paper they'd found on the body but made little sense. He picked up the envelope addressed to Leslie Mendez and looked at the back. It was still sealed. "What do you think? Open it?"

"Unless you've suddenly developed x-ray vision, it's the only way we're going to know who she is."

Rick slit the envelope open with Adam's pocketknife, read the letter, then handed it to Adam. "Looks like Leslie Mendez was his ex-wife. And from the tone of that letter, I'd say Styles was still in love with her."

"More like obsessed," Adam said absently as he read the paper with seventeen words again. He motioned for Rick to take another look at it. "This must be some sort of code. What do you suppose this guy was into?"

Rick read the words slowly, committing each one to memory. "Do you suppose this could be a poem? It doesn't rhyme, but it seems to have a certain syntax. Whatever it is, it's one of the few clues we've got."

"And the deck of cards?" Adam asked, gesturing to the pile of items on the bed.

Rick spread out the cards slowly and carefully as he studied each one. "I don't know. Maybe he was a big card player."

Adam shook his head in disbelief and looked down at the items on the bedspread. He winced as he surveyed the paltry assortment of evidence. "So this is it?" he said, "We have an envelope stuffed with over two thousand dollars in cash, a faded photograph of a woman we assume to be his ex-wife, a letter that was returned to him by said ex, and a deck of playing cards. What's more, we seem to be missing a vital piece of evidence—his cell phone."

"I agree that we don't have much. But we also have these two pieces of paper with what looks like—for lack of a better term—some sort of little poem. And this," Rick said as he dropped the notebook on the bedspread.

Adam raised an eyebrow. "Some poetry and a bunch of gibberish. We could really use some sort of key to know what we're dealing with."

Rick flipped through the pages, and his eyes widened as a pattern began to emerge. "Adam, maybe these are bank account numbers."

"Can you look into that? And maybe try to see if those two poems mean anything. While you're doing that, I'll do a background check on Leslie Mendez. Maybe I can turn up something helpful."

"Sure." Rick checked the time, noting they'd been in the room for about twenty minutes. "Let me make a call to Marquetta. Alex is probably there to help, but I may need to get home and help Marquetta with the baby. I can always do some research later tonight."

"What do you want to do about the munchkin? She'll probably be hearing about this through the rumor mill in no time."

"I know. I'm not happy about that. I'll try to keep a lid on it." Rick said. "Let's get out of here and figure this thing out."

At the sound of a knock on the door, Rick did a quick check. Deputy Kama was visible through the window at the front of the room. "It's Amy."

"Sheriff must have taken control. If I ever get the mayor to approve another deputy, we might actually be able to keep control of a crime scene."

When Adam opened the door, Deputy Kama said, "They've secured the area, and forensics is doing their thing. You'll probably have company up here soon. The ME is Doc Turner again."

"Excellent," Adam said. "You may be getting another guest, buddy. Do you have any rooms available?"

"We're full up, as usual," Rick said. "Unless we have a no-show this afternoon. Three new guests are coming in, so if Patricia wants a room, she'd better pray for a cancellation."

"Oh, well," Adam said, then he looked at Amy. "Why don't you go home and get cleaned up, Deputy? Meet me back at the station. We've got work to do."

"Thanks, Chief. I can't wait to get out of these clothes."

"Come on, Rick. Let's go see Doc Turner. Maybe she can tell us something about our victim."

"We can only hope," Rick said as the door slipped closed behind them. "We can only hope."

10

ALEX

I SHOVE MY PHONE INTO my back pocket and bolt down the stairs. I gotta think of a good excuse for Mom so she doesn't start grilling me about my plan to see Veronica. It needs to be solid so I can make my escape without raising any red flags. Sometimes I swear she can read my mind and knows everything I'm up to. I totally believe her when she says we're soulmates. Pulling this off is gonna be super hard. Unless maybe she needs something at the market? That might be a good start.

I take a deep breath and push through the butler door, hoping I haven't been gone too long. I'm surprised to find her sitting at the island with the baby cradled in her arms. She's cooing to him softly, and my heart melts a little. I wish my real mom had done that when she had me, but that's not the way she was. The last time I saw her, she told me she just wasn't mom material. I get it. I guess. Maybe.

My throat is tight, and I give Mom a weak smile.

"Oh, Sweetie," she says. "Are you thinking about your biological mother again?"

And there it is—the soulmate thing. I swear she can totally read my mind. "It just kinda comes on at times." I pull in a sharp breath. It clears my head a little, and I ask, "How's Baby Jack doing?"

"He's been quiet since you took those towels up to the Jib Room. I take it you and Mr. Rhymes had a nice conversation?"

I snicker. See? She totally has me nailed. "He's super nice. Hey, do you need anything at the store?"

"Looking for a reason to get out of the house? I know. You're probably itching to get out of here. I should be hearing from your dad pretty soon. Tell you what. It's going to be two hours before dinner, so if you want to go outside to play or do something in your room, it's fine with me. Oh, and what about the diapers I asked you to get this morning?"

Awesome! I don't have to lie. Or even fudge the truth. "I'll take my bike, do some other stuff, then go get them."

"Don't be gone too long. Okay? I could use some help with dinner."

I start toward the door, then run back and give her a hug, making sure not to disturb our little opera singer. "I love you, Mom."

She smiles and shifts the baby into a more comfortable position. "I love you, too, Sweetie. Now, go out and have some fun."

The shed where we keep my bike is not far from the French doors at the back of the kitchen. It only takes a few minutes to ride to the Seaside Cove Inn. Between the two Seaside Cove Police cars and the sheriff's cars, the street is lit up like Christmas. Flashing red and blue lights are everywhere. I stop to watch what's going on. I don't see my dad or Chief Cunningham, but Deputy Kama is talking to a sheriff's deputy. There's also a woman kneeling down next to a body near the dumpster. I recognize her as Doc Turner. There's still no sign of Veronica.

Suddenly, a hand grabs my arm and yanks on it. For a second, I freak out. The last time someone grabbed me like that, it was a horrible man who wanted to kill me. The image only lasts a second, then it's gone.

"Alex, come on. I don't want to be seen."

Thank goodness. It's Veronica. She looks like she's trying to disguise herself as someone else. She's tucked her hair up under a baseball cap and is wearing big sunglasses and an oversized sweatshirt.

"What's up?" I ask.

"I can't be seen here, Follow me!"

She sneaks off toward an old oak tree. The way she does it kind of reminds me of one of those silly cartoon characters. For real? Anybody can see her right now. I park my bike on the sidewalk and join her behind the tree. When I look at her, I can see how worried she is. She seems almost frantic as she peers around the tree using a pair of binoculars.

"You totally came prepared," I say. She's gonna be an awesome friend. Assuming she doesn't do any more of those embarrassing sneaking-around moves.

Veronica takes a deep breath and lowers the binoculars. "They're my uncle's. I had to steal them from his closet."

"He doesn't know you're here?"

"Duh." Veronica makes a face, kinda like she's sorry she texted me. "Do your parents?" she snaps.

Right. I wasn't exactly honest with Mom when I left—and I feel awful about it. I look across the street. Now I'm the one who's being super lame. I'm totally blowing this with my new friend, and I so don't want to. "I see the forensics team got here."

"Is that who they are? What are they doing?"

"They're securing the crime scene and looking for evidence. There are only a few little markers, so there must not be much. See the woman kneeling by the body? That's Doc Turner. She's the ME." When Veronica gives me a funny look, I add, "That's the Medical Examiner. They all have to come here from San Ladron."

"Wow. You really do know about this stuff." She doesn't sound so nasty anymore.

"Yeah, well, I've been through it a few times. And Doc Turner stayed with us the last couple of times she was here. Her husband doesn't like her driving the road back to San Ladron at night. It can be kinda treacherous."

Veronica rolls her eyes and looks like she's just swallowed something icky.

"Do you get carsick?"

She ignores my question and looks through the binoculars across the street. "So what do you think they're finding?"

"I dunno." From this far away, it's super hard to tell. I don't mind answering her questions, but I don't want to be treated like an information source, either. We watch for a few minutes, and it's actually kinda boring. It's a lot more fun doing the investigating than it is watching someone else do it.

"Hey, Alex?" Veronica says absently as she stares through the binoculars.

"Yeah?"

"Is there anything to do in this town? Like, for a date?"

She's asking me? I'm thirteen. The only dates I've been on are school dances. And even then, Robbie, he's kinda like my boyfriend, is clueless. "Why? Do you have a date?"

Veronica sighs dramatically and rolls her eyes again. She's super good at that.

"You can't tell anyone, okay? Especially not your parents."

"Cross my heart," I promise, tracing an 'X' over my chest.

"I met this guy," Veronica's voice drops to a whisper. "He's local. We keep running into each other down at the harbor."

My pulse picks up a little, and I realize I'm holding my breath. Is this what it's like to talk about boys with a girlfriend? I clap my hands together. "That's awesome! Have you guys gone out yet?"

"No," Veronica grumbles. She looks down at her hands. "He's super shy. Sweet. I don't want to say his name. I don't want to jinx it or anything."

"Oh, come on! You're killing me!"

Veronica screws up her face, turns away from me, and raises the binoculars again. "Not cool. Not with that going on."

"Sorry," I mutter. "My bad." Talk about awkward. Veronica is like hot one second and cold the next. And she's gonna be super cold in about thirty seconds.

I take a breath, step out from behind the tree, and look across the street at my dad, who's got his hands on his hips and a scowl on his face.

Oh, yeah. We're so busted.

11

RICK

OF ALL THE THINGS RICK expected to find at a fresh crime scene, his daughter wasn't one of them. Then again, given Alex's fascination with crime, he knew he shouldn't be that surprised. "Adam, there are many skills I've mastered in life—from brewing a decent cup of coffee in a newsroom to running a successful business. I've been an investigative journalist and doggedly chased down leads just to break a story. But the one skill I haven't figured out yet is how to keep my daughter from one-upping me. I'll be right back."

Rick strode across the street, leaving Adam and a sheriff's deputy behind him. He could almost feel their smirks as he walked. He knew he should be mad at Alex, but the truth was he was proud of her. She was precocious. And growing up with a fierce sense of right and wrong. Both traits he'd wanted her to have. He guessed maybe he had done okay in the dad department after all.

Even though Veronica had tried to disguise herself by changing clothes and wearing dark glasses and a hat, Rick had no doubts as to who Alex's companion was. There was no mistaking that red hair, even if most of it was hidden by a Dodgers baseball cap. The large pair of binoculars hanging from her neck looked oversized and awkward against her slight frame.

When Veronica started to walk away, Rick called out, "I know where you live, Veronica."

The girl hung her head and didn't answer him, but Alex, ever the optimist, came forward and used her most positive tone on him. "Hey, Daddy."

"What are you two doing here?" Rick demanded, doing his best to sound irritated.

"I've never seen a real police investigation, and Alex said I should come along," Veronica answered, raising her head and looking him straight in the eye.

Alex did a double-take. Rick saw two possibilities—Alex was shocked that she'd been ratted out, or Veronica was lying. "Well, Alex?"

Alex launched into an explanation about how she had gotten wind of a possible homicide in the area and how they'd come down to investigate. At best, the explanation felt flimsy. She appeared ready to add a detailed explanation of how she'd heard about it when Rick cut her off with a wave of his hand.

"Save it for later." He said gruffly, knowing she'd have plenty more stories to tell at home. "Right now, I want you two to be moving along." Veronica hung her head and slowly crossed her arms over her chest. Taking pity on her, he added, "Let the police handle this, okay? No more sneaking around. Now, scoot."

The girl nodded and started to walk away, but Alex grabbed her arm and pulled her back in for a hug. "Come on," she said softly. "I'll walk with you."

When they were a few feet away, Rick called out to Alex. "Hey, kiddo, remember, your mom asked you this morning to pick up diapers at the market. Don't forget. Okay?"

Alex flashed Rick a thumbs-up, but he wondered if she would remember. He considered making a stop himself just in case, but decided against it and returned to where Adam stood. He watched Alex and Veronica as they walked, Alex pushing her bike while Veronica alternately waved her hands in the air and shot an occasional glance over her shoulder.

He had so many questions about them being here. How had they heard about the murder so quickly? Had Veronica called Alex right after he'd told her and her uncle? That would explain a lot. It also made him wonder why she might have done that.

Adam gave Rick a thumbs-up as he approached. "Your little girl is growing up, buddy."

"That she is." He said with a proud grin. Turning his attention back to the tree where the girls had been spying, he stroked his chin and spoke hesitantly. "The problem is her new friend. I don't trust her. And I'm definitely not a fan of Alex hanging out with someone who's four years older."

"I hear you. And I agree. If you want my opinion, Veronica Campbell is trouble. I'd keep an eye on her if I were you."

"Agreed. You know, Adam, there was something fishy in what Veronica said. She blamed them being here on Alex. She said Alex contacted her and said she wanted to see what was going on. But for them to both be here this soon, Veronica would have had to have been coming here anyway."

"And you think she came here to see our victim?"

"The thought crossed my mind."

Adam pondered Rick's comment, then said, "Look, Rick, this is Nancy Drew we're talking about. You know her better than I do. She's a brave young woman, and she's fascinated by criminal investigations. I'm not surprised at all that she showed up here."

Wagging a finger at Adam, Rick disagreed. "How did she hear about it? At first, I thought it was the grapevine. But the more I think about it, what makes more sense is that Veronica knew Styles had been murdered before I told her and her uncle."

"How do you figure?" Adam asked.

“I never mentioned where the murder took place, yet she knew where it was. The only thing she didn’t have was a partner in crime. Someone to help her.”

“Someone like Alex. Okay, but why would Veronica want to get involved in a murder investigation? I mean, what could she gain from it?”

Rick had been wondering the same thing. He squared his shoulders. “She might have wanted to see how things were going if she knew Styles was dead before you and I did.”

Leaning forward and locking his gaze on Rick’s, Adam said, “Are you seriously thinking Veronica Campbell had something to do with this?”

“It’s possible.”

Adam blew out a slow breath. “This is not like you, buddy. You’re always very methodical. You don’t jump to conclusions.” He paused, and a self-satisfied smile formed on his lips. “That’s usually what the munchkin does.”

“Don’t remind me. I’ll tell you one thing. Since Veronica Campbell walked into the B&B, I’ve felt like my life has been thrown off balance. I’m trying to make sense of it all, but I just can’t.”

“You’re right about one thing. It feels like the pieces aren’t fitting together yet. I think we agree there’s more to this situation than meets the eye. For now, though, let’s focus on our murder.”

“It looks like Doc Turner’s about finished. Might as well start there.” Without another word, they crossed the parking lot to where the medical examiner stood. Rick had so many questions rattling around in his head. He hoped Doc Turner would be able to give them some answers.

Patricia Turner was balancing herself against the hood of Adam’s 4x4 as she pulled off a pair of disposable shoe covers. She gave Rick and Adam a friendly smile as they approached. “I can tell you this much right off, Chief, you've got yourself another homicide. Four shots to the chest. Someone wanted this guy dead. And they wanted it bad."

"Four shots? Isn't that unusual?" Rick asked.

"Very," Adam said. "It tells me our shooter was quite upset with Mr. Styles."

"Could be," Doc Turner added. "But don't forget that there are other factors to consider. What was the intent of the shooter? How close were they? And was your victim moving—maybe he was trying to back away when he was shot. Preliminarily, it looks like there was no gunshot residue, so the shooter was probably at least six feet away. Sorry. I'm not being much help here."

Adam's face looked grim. Rick didn't blame him. They had so little to go on. On top of that, between being perpetually short-staffed and getting married in just a few weeks, Adam was swamped.

"Anything else you can tell us?" Adam asked.

"Unfortunately, nothing more at this time." Doc Turner paused and then added softly, "But maybe the techs will come up with something for you. Looks like Gigi's about done with her sketches, too."

A petite Hispanic woman with delicate features looked at them and said, "You're right, Doc. I just finished."

"Thanks, Gigi. That's it, Chief. We'll get the body out of here, clear the scene, and give the owner his parking lot back."

"So I gather you won't be needing a room this time, Doc?" Rick asked.

"I was hoping, but I called Marquetta before I left town, and she said you guys were full up. Too bad. My husband's been itching to come back."

"He loves it here."

"What Greg likes most of all is Marquetta's cooking and the chance to indulge his sweet tooth."

Gigi, the tech they'd been talking to, returned. She'd removed her protective clothing and looked like a different person from head to toe. Her dark hair had been pulled back into a neat ponytail and hung midway down her back. She had on a Rolling Stones tee shirt and jeans. Rick probably wouldn't have recognized her if he hadn't seen her transformation.

"Ready to roll, Doc? Van's loaded, and we're all set to go."

"You bet." Doc Turner gave Rick and Adam a final smile. "Gotta go, guys. Fortunately, I was able to catch a ride with Gigi today, and I'm not missing my ride back home."

After they said goodbye, Adam said, "Shall we go give Ray the good news? Maybe he won't be quite so grumpy."

"Don't count on it," Rick snickered. "Ray doesn't need a reason to be grumpy. It's just a natural state of mind for him."

12

RICK

"SO THAT'S IT, RAY?" ADAM growled. "You don't know anything about this Gideon Styles other than he rented a room from you?"

Ray's response wasn't exactly what Rick had expected. Not after he'd almost-willingly turned over the room key to Adam. In fact, Rick had hoped Ray wouldn't return to his obstructionist MO. He'd been wrong. Ray planted his hands on the counter, smirked, and said, "What are you going to do, Adam? Arrest me for not knowing the comings and goings of my customers? I try to keep everything on a business level. Unlike some places where they insinuate themselves into their customer's lives."

Rick bit his tongue to avoid getting dragged into an insultfest. Unfortunately, there was a bit of truth to the obvious swipe at the B&B. It didn't matter. Rick would rather be overly friendly than determined to obstruct justice.

"Watch how you play the ignorance card, Ray. You never know when it might come back to bite you."

Adam spun on his heel and headed for the front door. Rick followed. When they were well away from the door, Rick asked, "You think he really knows something?"

"Of course he does." Adam smiled. "Getting information out of Ray is always a long shot. It makes no sense to waste time prying it out of him when there are other ways to bring him in line."

"So why'd you even try if you knew what would happen?"

"I just wanted to jerk his chain to see what he would do. I'll let Madame Mayor know so she can remind him he's on a short leash. Ray will talk. It's all a matter of pushing the right buttons."

"Seems ridiculous to have to go to such lengths to get the truth," Rick said as he pulled out his phone and looked at the message he'd received while he and Adam were butting their heads against the wall with Ray. "Hmmmpf. Looks like Marquetta and Traci are one step ahead of us. Marquetta says I should bring you home for dinner. She and Traci have figured out a menu. You in?"

"Are you kidding? Of course, I'm in. If those two are planning something, I can't wait to see what it is. Those two might be thick as thieves, but I'll bet the food's going to be great."

Rick snorted. "There you go, buddy. At least you'll get fed."

Adam clapped Rick on the back and laughed. "Just to show you what a great guy I am, I'll even give you a ride."

"Your generosity knows no bounds."

Upon arriving at the B&B, Rick opened the front door and stepped into the foyer. Silence so commanding it almost felt like a living entity that demanded respect took over. It was as if time itself had paused. Leo and Lily Carmichael, newlyweds who had checked in the day before, had stopped midway down the stairs, where Leo had pulled Lily in for an enthusiastic kiss.

Turning, Rick raised his finger to his lips, not wanting to startle the newlyweds or break the spell of silence but was too late. The door slammed shut, the couple jumped apart, and Lily nearly took a spill down the stairs. She regained her balance when Leo grabbed her by the arm to steady her.

In his short time at the B&B, Rick had seen couples handle their urges in different ways. Leo and Lily, married only three days, were amongst the more demonstrative ones. With Leo standing about six-foot-two and Lily a petite five-three, they were quite the contrast.

Lily smacked Leo on the arm and giggled. Her face, which was filled with freckles, flushed bright pink. "I knew that was a bad idea!"

"Babe, it's never a bad idea to kiss you." He gave Lily a roguish smile, which sent her into another fit of giggles.

"No worries, you two," Rick said. "We were just passing through. Are you on your way to dinner?"

Lily grabbed Leo's hand and pulled him down the stairs. "We were thinking of going to the Crooked Mast. Marquetta said the food is really good."

"She's absolutely correct. Enjoy yourselves. I'd suggest walking. It's nice enough out that it will be quite lovely. It's just down past the roundabout."

Adam followed Rick to the kitchen. The room buzzed with activity. Marquetta and Traci had split the center island into thirds. Marquetta was chopping vegetables—onions, peppers, and mushrooms—in her section. Traci was working on pepperoni. And Baby Jack's bassinet took up the rest.

After they exchanged greetings, Rick said, "We saw the honeymooners on our way in. Maybe I should say we caught them in the act—again. They're supposed to be on their way to the Crooked Mast for dinner. I hope they make it."

Marquetta laughed. "Those two. They're in the top ten on my Guests in Heat list."

Rick's jaw dropped, and he stammered, "You have a…"

"Mr. Atwood, I do believe you're blushing," Marquetta winked at Rick, then returned to chopping. "Those two are so obviously in love. I hope they make it to dinner because I called Ken and told him to give them one of his best tables."

"I was just thinking of doing that," Rick said. "You've got everything covered. It looks to me like we're having pizza?"

"Yes. The dough's been rising for a little over an hour. We're almost ready to bake."

Rick scanned the assortment of vegetables. It looked like enough to feed a small army. "How many pizzas are you making, anyway?" Rick asked as he reached into the bassinet and let his son grab his finger. "Hey, buddy."

"Three," Traci said. "We figured at a two-to-one ratio—you each get two pieces for every one of ours, we needed three pizzas to be safe. Plus, there's Alex. She has a healthy appetite, so she's kind of a wild card."

"Speaking of Alex, why isn't she down here helping?"

Marquetta raised her hands to indicate that she didn't know. "About two hours ago, I told her she could go outside and play. I never dreamt she'd be gone this long."

Rick checked the time on the old grandfather clock. He straightened up, absently letting the baby play with his finger. "Two hours? That's about the time she was trying to spy on our crime scene. She was with Veronica."

"Veronica?" Marquetta said with a frown. "Alex never said anything about meeting up with her."

"And Veronica tried to blame their appearance at the crime scene on Alex. She said Alex texted her and asked her to meet at the Inn."

"Alex never even hinted that she knew about the murder. I swear, Rick. I'm beginning to think Alex's new friend is a bad influence."

"I'm convinced of it," Rick said. "Maybe we should go look for her."

"Rick, Seaside Cove's a safe town," Adam said. "She'll be fine."

"Adam, if this town's so safe, why are we investigating another murder?"

"Point taken, but you know what I mean. Why don't you text her? Tell her to get her butt home."

Marquetta came and stood next to Rick. She placed her hand on his arm. "Adam's right. We should give her a chance to come home on her own, but just with a little encouragement. Later tonight, we can talk with her about appropriate friends."

That all sounded like solid advice, but the cat was already out of the bag. Now that Alex was getting a taste of having older friends, it would be harder to rein her in. He knew he couldn't watch her every minute of the day, which meant he had to let go at some point.

"Okay, we'll talk to her at dinner." He pulled out his phone, sent the message, then took a deep breath. "I have a bad feeling about Veronica Campbell."

"So you've said, buddy. While you're doing the research on the connections between Styles, Tyler Winkle, and his niece, I'll run those background checks. I'm sure we can get to the bottom of this and still keep the munchkin out of trouble."

Rick's phone pinged with Alex's reply. "She's on her way. She said she lost track of time."

Traci, who'd been quiet through most of the conversation so far, chirped. "That's what happens when you're having fun."

Marquetta put her hands on her hips and gave Traci a look that said, "You're not helping."

Traci grinned back. "I'm trying to be optimistic."

"That's my girl, always looking on the bright side," Adam said as he went to her and slipped his hand around her waist.

Rick rubbed his temples, feeling the pressure of too much to do in a short span of time. "Marquetta, how much time do we have before dinner? Maybe Adam and I could get a little of this research out of the way while we're waiting."

"Sure. Why not? It's going to be about thirty minutes before dinner's ready. Do you want to go upstairs?"

Adam looked at the butler door, a smile on his face. "Assuming we don't have to push past any more lovebirds necking on the stairwell."

Rick rolled his eyes. "You're not helping, either. We should at least get started."

As the door to Rick's office closed, Rick breathed in the ever-present sense of quiet and solitude that always permeated the space. "I hated this room the first time I saw it. Now, it feels like a refuge."

"From what I understand, that's exactly what Captain Jack wanted."

"And a quiet place to nap," Rick said as he settled into the chair that had once belonged to his grandfather. "Right here, in this very chair."

"And Markie would nap over there on the couch. I've heard it before, Rick. Come on, we don't have much time."

Rick opened the cover of his laptop and brought up a browser window. "Let's begin with this supposedly famous bakery."

He did a search, clicked on a link to a two-year-old post in an online magazine article about the top 100 bakeries in the US, read part of the article, and looked across the desk at Adam. "This is not funny. The Secret Ingredient, owned by Maxine Campbell, is number four on this list, right behind Dominique Ansel Bakery in New York, Tartine Bakery in San Francisco, and Levain Bakery in New York. I can't believe it's actually true."

Adam came around the desk and started reading over Rick's shoulder. "According to this, Maxine Campbell was a master baker who had been creating unique recipes for over two decades using the finest ingredients from around the world. What put the bakery in the top ten is the chocolate she used in the desserts. Imagine that. And here I thought chocolate was chocolate."

"Apparently not," Rick replied. "That tracks with what Tyler Winkle told me. It sounds like their Flourless Chocolate Brownies were what set them apart. I guess that's why she named the bakery The Secret Ingredient. Okay, so this whole big deal about the secret family recipe must be true. Let's see if there's anything about her death."

Rick opened another window and brought up an index of newspaper archives. "In the old days, I used this all the time for background research. These days, it seems I just use it to track down murder suspects. Here we go. This is from a San Diego paper in 2014. Have a seat and listen to this. The headline reads, *Local Bakery Owner Tragically Shot in Robbery, Shooter Still at Large.*"

In a shocking incident that has left the community reeling, Maxine Campbell, owner of the world-renowned The Secret Ingredient, was fatally shot during a robbery on Monday. The bakery, a local institution famed for its Flourless Chocolate Brownies and other pastries, has been a heartwarming symbol of our city for generations.

Maxine Campbell, 38, was known not just for her exquisite baked goods, but also for her warm spirit and philanthropy. She was a beloved figure who touched countless lives through her bakery. Her sudden and tragic loss has left a void in the community that will be hard to fill.

The robbery, reportedly perpetrated by an unidentified drug addict, took place when Campbell was on her way to make a bank deposit at the end of the day. Despite the presence of multiple witnesses, the shooter managed to escape before the police arrived at the scene. The authorities are currently investigating the incident, but the shooter remains at large.

Campbell's family is grappling with their grief while also seeking justice for their loved one. "Maxine was more than just a baker; she was a mother and a pillar of the community," said her brother, Tyler Winkle. "We won't rest until justice is served."

The family urges anyone with information about the shooting to come forward. "Someone out there knows something," Winkle continued. "We plead with you to help us find the person who did this."

Despite the tragedy, the family vows to continue Campbell's legacy. "My sister poured her heart and soul into this bakery," Winkle stated. "We owe it to her to keep her spirit alive."

As the investigation continues, the community mourns the loss of a cherished local figure. A candlelight vigil is planned for later this week outside the bakery. In the face of this horrific event, the community's unity and determination to seek justice for Maxine Campbell shine through.

The family asks for donations to be made to local drug rehabilitation centers instead of flowers. "If we can prevent even one more family from experiencing this pain, then it will be a fitting tribute to Maxine," Winkle concluded.

Rick studied Adam from across the desk. "What do you make of that? This doesn't sound anything like the Tyler Winkle we met today."

"You're right about that. None of this makes any sense. If Tyler wanted to carry on his sister's legacy, why would he sell the bakery? Why would he have met with some guy to sell the family legacy? And why did the guy he met with suddenly turn up dead? I don't know what's happening, but we'll keep digging until we find out."

An alert popped up on Rick's screen. He clicked the little box and read the message. "I agree completely. And, by the way, my daughter just showed up. Let's see what she has to say for herself."

13

ALEX

I'M IN DEEP DOO-DOO. Mom was worried sick about me, and my dad is gonna be angry because I showed up at a crime scene and then went off the grid for an hour. Mom says he's upstairs with Chief Cunningham. Oh, man, when he shows up, it's gonna get ugly. I just know it.

Mom's already told me three times how glad she is that I'm safe. But she also wants answers, and I can't lie to her. She'll totally see right through it. And if that happened, it would totally break her heart. I can't do that to her.

I scrunch up my face, and for the millionth time, say, "I'm sorry, Mom. I didn't know I was gonna be gone so long."

"Sweetie, I know you're growing up, and I know you'll want to do more things outside of the house, but this isn't the way to do it. You need to be honest with your Dad and me and tell us where you're at and who you're with."

My stomach is churning with guilt. She's right because something could have happened to me, and she'd never have known. Mom pulls me into a hug and whispers, "I love you, Sweetie, don't ever forget that."

Traci's kinda watching us as she shreds mozzarella and Parmesan cheeses. She's gonna be an awesome mom someday. I know it in my heart. The butler door bursts open and my dad and Chief Cunningham are standing there looking at me. I am so dead.

"Alex, you have some explaining to do." My dad's voice is super stern. This is like the worst it's been in a long time. He's really mad.

My insides are shaking like crazy. All this thinking about how worried they got and what I did is making me so overwhelmed. And then, my face is hot, and the room gets blurry. It's so unfair. I did this to them, and I got lied to by Veronica.

The next thing I know, Mom's wrapping her arms around me. She's warm and soft and comforting. I can almost feel her heart beating along with mine, like she's telling me that everything will be okay. But it won't. It can't. Not until I tell her.

"Veronica lied to me," I blurt.

Mom's got her hand on my back, and she's rubbing it, pulling me into her and breaking down any defenses I thought I had. I was gonna deal with this. I was gonna be strong.

"What did she lie to you about, Sweetie?"

I sniffle, then pull back from Mom. It's time to do this. The right thing. No matter how mad my dad gets. "Daddy, I swear that I didn't text Veronica. She texted me and told me to meet her at the Inn because there'd been a murder."

My dad comes over, puts a hand on my shoulder, and gives it a squeeze. It's not as warm as Mom's, but it still feels kind of good. Does this mean he's not mad at me after all?

"We believe you, Alex," he says in a gentle voice. "Both Adam and I are convinced Veronica knows a lot more than she's letting on. Now, why don't you tell us what really happened?"

I take a deep breath. "After we left the Inn, me and Veronica walked back to Marina Park. We sat and talked, and then I walked back with her to her house. She said there was something she wanted to show me. Daddy, the reason she wants the secret recipe is because she wants to start a food blog and open a new bakery. She thinks all she needs is the one recipe to get rich."

My dad and the chief look at each other. The chief says. "That's pretty unrealistic, but that's her big secret? She wants to start a business?"

"Part of it. She told me all about her mom's death. How her uncle never forgave himself and how the cops didn't find the killer. That's got her super angry. It's all bottled up inside like she's ready to explode. She blames her uncle for everything. That's why she's always so angry with him."

"Excuse me," Traci says. "I hate to interrupt, but is it okay if I put the pizzas in the oven? Do you want me to wait?"

Awesome! "No! Don't wait! I'm starving!"

My dad smiles at Traci and gives her a thumbs-up. "Sure. Go ahead." He rests his hip against the center island and looks at me. "What about Gideon Styles? Did she say anything about how he fits into this?"

"For sure. She knew that her uncle met with him before. That's another reason she's so mad at him. She says she told him what she wanted to do, and he just told her she was being childish."

"Not exactly the caring and concerned brother he sounded like in the news story we read," my dad says.

I can feel my brow pucker. "What news story?"

Traci and Mom start gathering silverware, plates, and napkins. Mom picks up Baby Jack's bassinet and takes it to the back of the kitchen, where she lifts him out and starts to feed him. The first time she did that, it was like, whoa. But now, I get it, my baby brother's gotta eat. Right?

"Hey, kiddo, finish your story."

"I don't think she's being childish," I say, feeling kinda angry about the whole thing. "If Gideon Styles did everything she says he did, she might be right."

My dad shakes his head. He looks confused. "Right about what?"

"She didn't actually say it, but it sounds like she thinks he's the one who killed her mom."

My dad and Chief Cunningham exchange another look. I don't know what it means, and I don't think they're ready to tell me yet.

"It would make sense," I say.

"It would be a good motive for revenge," my dad says.

The chief clears his throat. "We need to find out more information before we can make that leap."

My dad nods in agreement. "Alex, how strongly does Veronica believe this?"

"One thousand percent."

My dad scratches his ear, then rubs his chin. His forehead's kinda wrinkly like it gets when he's worried about something. "And do you think she might have acted on those feelings?"

"She threatened him. She, like, told me that. But do I think she could kill him? No way."

"When did she make this threat?"

It feels awful telling on my friend like this, but she's not really my friend. She's just been using me 'cause she heard I was good at solving murders. "At the Rusty Nail. Just before she fell into the planter."

"Did you hear her make the threat?"

"No, she told me about it."

"I see," my dad says. He's got that faraway look in his eyes he sometimes gets, and I can see him mentally connecting dots that put Veronica in the middle of the murder.

"She didn't kill him!"

"You're sure?"

"She couldn't do it. She's not like that."

My dad pauses and watches my face before he says anything. "Okay. For her sake, I hope you're right. We all know that if she did kill Styles, her life as she knows it will be over."

He looks at Chief Cunningham, and the two of them exchange another look. This time I don't have to guess what it means: they're worried about Veronica. I am, too. "Do you think maybe her Uncle Tyler killed that guy?"

"As Adam will be sure to remind me, it's too soon to tell. We need more evidence. But this background information is a good start."

I look away because there is something else bugging me. "Do you think Gideon really did kill her mother?"

"I'm not sure. But if Veronica is right, it could certainly be a motive for murder."

I take a deep breath and force myself to look back at him. "There's something else I didn't tell you."

Chief Cunningham gets a funny look on his face. I guess he hears something in my voice that's got him worried now. "What did you leave out, Alex?"

"Veronica only wanted to be my friend because she heard how I helped solve some of the other murders in town."

Mom's hand goes to her heart. I can see the pain on her face. My dad closes his eyes for a moment. "So you're saying that she's been using you."

"I dunno. Maybe." Why should I lie to myself anymore? She's like four years older than me. Kids her age don't want anything to do with kids my age. My face is warm, and my nose is all stuffy. "Yeah," I confess. "That's totally why she wants to be my friend. She wanted me to help prove that Gideon Styles killed her mother."

The room is quiet for a long time while everyone takes this in. Chief Cunningham finally breaks the silence. "Alex, I'm sorry."

"Oh, Sweetie," Mom murmurs.

My dad's eyes are sad, and I can tell he feels my pain. "Are you angry with her, kiddo?"

"For sure. It makes me super mad. I hope when I'm older, I'm not like that."

The chief is nodding to himself, and he's grinning. "I have an idea. Rick, you're not going to like this, but it might be the best way to extract the truth from Ms. Campbell and her uncle."

My dad's shakes his head and buries his face in his hands. "No, Adam. I know exactly what you're thinking. There's no way."

"It's probably going to happen anyway."

I scrunch up my face and look at both of them. "What? I don't get it."

"Alex, I have an undercover assignment for you," Chief Cunningham says. "How would you like to spy on Veronica Campbell and her uncle for me?"

Just then, the timer on the stove goes off, and Traci calls out from across the room, "Pizza's ready!"

14

RICK

RICK LISTENED TO THE SOUNDS of the old house. Subtle creaks and moans whispered in the background when the wind coming in off the ocean broadsided the back wall. For more than a hundred years, the house had stood like a sentry looking out over the Pacific Ocean. It was at times like this that Rick thought about the difficulties he'd faced in his life.

He was not a man to back down from a challenge. He'd broken major stories about murders, drug kingpins, robberies, and God knows what other kinds of crime in his former life as a reporter. He'd taken over the Seaside Cove B&B after his grandfather died and turned the business around. And now he was stepping up for his once-again-new role as the father of a newborn. But with Baby Jack wailing in his arms at midnight, Rick found himself up against a formidable opponent.

Watching Marquetta desperately try to sleep, her brown hair splayed across the pillow, he told himself he'd survived this same time in Alex's life. In fact, he'd survived that one mostly on his own because Giselle had been gone nights. Marquetta was the exact opposite. She'd been up with Baby Jack most of the evening and much of last night. The solution seemed obvious. Marquetta deserved a break, so Rick stuffed a blanket into the bassinet, packed up his son, and padded quietly out of their bedroom, hoping desperately his wife could get a few hours of sleep before their day began again.

Inside his office, Rick attempted every trick in the book to soothe the baby. He rocked him, shushed him, even tried singing a sea shanty Marquetta said Captain Jack hummed when he ran the B&B. But nearly an hour later, Baby Jack was still fussing. It was then Rick realized the crux of the problem—a diaper change was overdue.

Why did it have to be the one thing he'd left behind? The diapers were in the master bedroom. Whatever possessed him to think he could get away without them? He knew better. And now, he had a dilemma. Should he try to get them and risk waking Marquetta? No, waking her was not an option. Rick didn't consider himself cowardly, but he also didn't consider himself foolish. Happy wife, happy life. He didn't know what the opposite was, but he didn't want to find out. So, he did what any resourceful B&B owner would do—he improvised.

He slipped out of his office and went to the coffee and tea station in the hallway. Quietly, he opened the bottom doors and pulled out all of the dishtowels. He winced as he looked at the stack of pristine, white cotton cloths with a blue stripe running down the center. "Sorry," he whispered. "I'm desperate." Realizing what else he was missing, he cursed his bad fortune. He didn't have wipes or anything to clean up with. With no other alternatives, he grabbed the pitcher of water and returned to his office. He cleared his desktop, grabbed the roll of duct tape he'd left lying on the corner nearly a week ago, and got to work.

Under the light of his desk lamp, Rick laid out one towel to use as a pad. He definitely didn't need to ruin his mahogany desk. It had been Captain Jack's pride and joy. And now he was using it as a changing table? Yes, he was desperate.

He laid Baby Jack on top of the makeshift changing station, unfastened the diaper, and slowly pulled it down. He used another towel to cover up the little boy, having learned the hard way that baby boys had a tendency to sometimes 'enjoy the moment.' Using the pitcher and another of the towels, Rick was able to do a reasonable job of cleaning up the mess. He tossed the old diaper and the cleanup towel in the trash can, pulled the plastic liner from the can, and tied it closed.

"You're doing great," Rick whispered to himself. "And you, little buddy, are doing great, too."

Baby Jack cooed and smiled up at Rick. It took several tries, but Rick finally managed to fashion a makeshift diaper using the dishtowel. He grabbed the roll of duct tape and did his best to secure his handiwork. Baby Jack seemed amused by the whole ordeal, gurgling and kicking his tiny legs. Once the operation was complete, Rick took a deep breath and gave himself a mental pat on the back. Not bad for a middle-of-the-night emergency changing. He gently placed the baby back in his bassinet, a proud smile spreading across his face. "How's that, buddy?" he whispered.

Baby Jack cooed again, then reached up. Rick looked at the roll of duct tape in his hands. "Okay, sure, why not?" He placed the roll of tape in the baby's hands and smiled when Baby Jack cooed again, then closed his eyes and drifted asleep. Exhausted, Rick covered the baby with a blanket and then placed the bassinet on the floor and flopped down on the couch. No sooner had his head hit the decorative pillow than Rick felt himself surrendering to exhaustion and closed his eyes.

At five, Rick felt someone shaking his arm. "Hey, buddy, just five minutes," he murmured. He felt himself again slipping back to sleep. After all, why not? The baby was still quiet, and he was still exhausted. A second later, he jerked awake when someone jabbed him in the ribs. He muttered a groggy, "Ow."

Opening his eyes, he saw Marquetta standing over him, her arms crossed over her chest.

"What was that for?" he asked.

"Rick Atwood! You'd better have a good explanation for this." Marquetta demanded. "What have you done to our baby?"

Suddenly wide awake, Rick sat up straight and looked down at the bassinet. He blinked twice as he tried to focus. The baby was right where he should be. All the pieces were there—the dishtowel, the duct tape, and the blanket. They just weren't where they were supposed to be. The dishtowel was poking out from under the blanket, which was bunched up at the foot of the bassinet, and Baby Jack wore something resembling a crown. Unfortunately, the crown was made of duct tape, and it was firmly affixed to his head."Uh, buddy, how did you do that?"

"Well…" Marquetta demanded.

Rick picked up the bassinet. "It's a long story."

He carried the bassinet to his desk and set it down. When he turned to face Marquetta, she was standing right in front of him.

"Why is he not wearing a diaper? And why did you put duct tape on his head?"

Rick broke into a sheepish grin. "Like I said, it's kind of a long story. Could we go downstairs and get some coffee? I'm dying here. Over coffee, I'll tell you about the great diaper adventure of last night."

"And what about the baby? Are you just going to leave him like that?"

"I guess not. But he seems happy enough."

"Rick!"

"Okay, okay. He probably should be changed first. You get the coffee, I'll take care of diaper duty and, um, remove the crown."

After changing Baby Jack's diaper, Rick gently put him back in the bassinet and took him downstairs. On his way to the kitchen, he spotted Leo Carmichael standing in the dining room, who was admiring the garden just outside the window, which was now aglow in the dim morning light.

"Leo, is there anything I can get you?"

"Java, Rick. I start every day with a big mug. Black. Marquetta said she's working on it."

Rick juggled the bassinet in his arms and gestured with his head at the baby. "Sorry. We got a bit of a late start this morning. This little guy had one of those fussy nights."

"No worries. I'll be in that boat soon enough."

"Where's Lily? Will she want coffee, too?"

"No. She's already doing yoga out back on the patio. She likes to get started before the sun rises."

Rick considered the night he'd had and tried to imagine how someone could have gone through what he had and then gotten up at the crack of dawn to do yoga. He could almost hear Alex's voice in his ear telling him it was an epic fail. Right now, he needed caffeine to get his brain moving. "Enjoy it while you can, my friend. These little guys have a way of changing everything."

15

ALEX

MISS REDMOND IS MY MOST favorite teacher ever. She totally knows how to engage the class. Today, we're learning about the solar system and how it was formed. Usually, I'd be listening to her every word, but today, I've got a lot to think about. I hope I've got the Veronica situation under control. I'm also trying to figure out how to get Miss Redmond together with Mr. Rhymes.

When my phone vibrates in my back pocket, I realize I totally spaced out today. I should have shut it off. Now, my butt's vibrating, and Miss Redmond is looking right at me. Rats. It's probably a message from Veronica. I never should have texted her this morning.

"Alex, do you have a question?"

Miss Redmond is looking at me over her glasses. That is so not good. My face turns bright red.

"No ma'am. I just forgot to turn off my phone." I stammer before I put it on Do Not Disturb.

Miss Redmond looks kind of irritated as she shakes her head and goes back to talking about Mars.

Halfway between Jupiter and Saturn, I come up with a plan. But first, I have to make sure Miss Redmond doesn't have a boyfriend. For the next twenty minutes, I feel like I'm gonna pee my pants. I've got such an awesome plan in mind.

When Miss Redmond excuses us for lunch, my best friend Sasha comes and sits at the desk next to mine. "Alex, come on. I'm starving."

For Sasha, that's like two bites. "In a couple minutes, okay? I gotta talk to Miss Redmond for a minute. See ya' out there?"

"I'll save you a seat." Sasha, who's into dance and crazy kinds of yoga, gets up and heads for the door. One of the boys is kinda hanging out, and he starts talking to her when she gets outside. I feel a little jealous as they walk away.

I gotta do this. I gotta ask now before I lose my nerve. Miss Redmond is straightening the papers on her desk. Today she's got her awesome blonde hair pulled back in a bun. She looks super hot, and I can't wait until Barrington Rhymes sees her.

"Miss Redmond?" I get up and walk towards her.

"Yes, Alex?"

"I'm sorry about my phone going off in class. It kinda took me by surprise."

"It's okay. Just don't let it happen again."

"I won't." I look down at her hand. Awesome! She's not wearing a ring, so she's not engaged or anything. What do I say? Talk about awkward. "Sasha looks like she might have a boyfriend soon."

Miss Redmond smiles. "I'm sure she will. And you. You like Robbie Sachetti, don't you? He'll figure it out soon enough."

Oh, man. She knows how much I like Robbie? My face gets all hot. That's super embarrassing. Or maybe not? That's what I need, right? "What about you? Do you have a boyfriend?"

"No, I don't. And you should know I don't discuss my love life with my students."

My pulse speeds up. This could totally work. "Why not? You're really pretty. And you're super cool. You should totally have someone."

She gives me that polite smile again. "Thank you, Alex, but for now, I'm married to my job and my students. That's enough for me."

That's sad. We're only around for a few years, and then we graduate. I have to get her together with Mr. Rhymes. "We have a guest who's staying at the B&B. He's really nice."

"Thank you, Alex, but no." Her voice is firm but still calm. "I don't do blind dates. Now, you should go to lunch. Before Sasha thinks you abandoned her."

Right. Got it. I'm gonna have to up my game. No problem.

I find Sasha sitting on one end of a table with a bunch of girls at the other end. The boy who was talking to her is sitting at a different table with a bunch of his friends. I sit on the other side of the table so I'm facing Sasha.

She watches me with a suspicious look. "Why did you take so long?"

"Miss Redmond wanted to talk to me about something." I try to sound casual so Sasha won't suspect anything. "So what's up?"

"No way. You're planning something. I can tell. I know you, Alex."

I give her an innocent look. "Me? What would I be doing?"

"You've got some kind of operation going. I know it. Spill."

"Okay. We've got this guest staying with us. His name is Barrington Rhymes, and he's super nice. I thought maybe he'd be a good match for Miss Redmond. They'd be perfect for each other!"

Sasha rolls her eyes. "C'mon, Alex. A blind date? No way. Miss Redmond's not gonna go for that."

My shoulders slump, and I lean my elbows on the tabletop. "Yeah, you're right. She just said the same thing."

A few seconds later, I see Miss Redmond walking toward the teacher's lounge. She's carrying the lunch bag she brings to school every day. It's got a lot of pretty tropical flowers on it, and it kinda looks like a purse. Just outside the lounge, she stops to talk to our principal, Mr. Thompson. He's kinda round, married, and has three kids.

But as the two of them chat, I get an idea. There might be a way to make this work after all. And when Miss Redmond laughs at something Mr. Thompson says, my plan comes together.

I look across the table at Sasha and give her a big grin. "But she might go for it if she doesn't know it's a blind date." Oh, yeah. This is totally gonna work.

16

RICK

"SO YOU IMPROVISED A DIAPER in the middle of the night, huh?" Adam said as they approached the entrance to the Seaside Cove Inn.

"I was desperate," Rick grumbled. Between the diaper debacle and the lack of sleep, Rick felt like he was hanging onto his good humor by a thread. "And you—you didn't help any by asking Alex to help on this case."

"I'm telling you, buddy, I wouldn't have done it if I thought for a second there was any real danger. But you know as well as I do that she'll probably get the truth out of Veronica and her uncle faster than we will."

"I still don't like it," Rick grumbled, but his expression softened when he thought about how happy Alex had been for the rest of the night. "I guess I have to face the fact that she's determined to help whether we green-light her or not."

"That's right. And besides, this way, you'll get reports from her, and she won't be hiding anything."

"At least she's in school this morning, so I know she's safe. How did I let you talk me into this?"

"Because you know that if you don't do it this way, Nancy Drew will just go underground."

They entered the lobby of the Seaside Cove Inn, and Rick felt the drab beige walls closing in around him. Ray Villari stood behind the counter and returned their greeting with something almost resembling a smile. He had paint chips spread out on the counter before him.

"You're here to see Maggie, aren't you?" Ray picked up a chip and held it out to them. "What about this color? Maggie says we should do some painting here. These are the colors she recommended."

"I like it," Rick said. "I think it will help brighten the place up a lot."

Ray's chin puckered as he put the chip off to the side and away from the others. To Rick's amazement, once again, Ray almost smiled. "Yeah. It'll brighten things up. She should be in either 211 or 223 right now."

As they walked out the door and into the gardens surrounding the pool, Rick asked, "What got into him?"

"Maggie Sullivan. She had to quit a few years ago so she could take care of her parents. They're both getting up there in years. Her mom had dementia, so it was doubly hard. Her mom passed a few months ago, so it's just Maggie and her dad. Maggie came back to the Inn about the time you stole Lydia away."

The lush garden around the pool was filled with the brilliant greens of palms and ferns. If the rest of the Inn looked like this, it could give the B&B a run for its money. And if Maggie Sullivan was going to help Ray make this place nicer, they might actually steal away a little business. "I hadn't heard that," Rick said. "I didn't know Lydia leaving was going to put Ray in such a bind."

Adam pointed at the second-floor walkway. "Looks like the door to 211 is open. Don't worry about Ray. You did him a favor. He's always had a fondness for Maggie."

"It sounds like a crush to me," Rick said as they followed the path along the pool.

They climbed the stairs to the second floor and took the walkway to Room 211. A robust woman with sun-kissed skin and auburn hair smiled at them when Adam knocked on the open doorway.

"Hey, Adam! How are you?"

"Good, Maggie."

When Adam made the introductions, Rick was surprised by how strong and calloused Maggie's hands were. She held her back straight even as she rested her shoulder against the door she'd propped open. "What brings you here? The murder?"

"Like you didn't know," Adam snickered. "What can you tell me about Gideon Styles?"

The little laugh lines around the corners of her mouth and eyes tightened into a grimace. "Not much. There was nothing unusual in his room when I cleaned. He kept to himself for the most part. Except for that woman."

"What woman?" Rick asked.

"I only saw her once. She was walking away from Mr. Styles's room."

"Are you saying she was actually in his room?" Adam asked.

"That, I don't know. I'd just come from the laundry room on the first floor when I looked up and saw her. She was walking away from his door. For all I know, she's also a guest and was on her way to the stairs. I didn't think much of it at the time."

Adam wrote down what Maggie said. "What did she look like?"

"Nothing special. Just an average woman, I guess. Mid-forties, maybe? Dark, almost black hair. She was wearing a tank top and jeans when I saw her."

"Would you recognize her again if you saw her?"

"Of course. I'll text you if you want. By the way, you should also talk to Bella. She might've seen something."

"Will do. Do you know where we can find her?"

"She had to leave. She's got a two-year-old daughter, and she had to take her to the doctor. I think she's planning on coming back this afternoon."

After finishing the conversation with Maggie, Rick and Adam returned to the office. While Ray still seemed to be riding some sort of emotional high, he was no more helpful than he'd been the day before. By the time they were climbing into Adam's 4x4, Rick was convinced they really only had one option for now.

"Adam, I think we need to take another crack at Tyler Winkle."

"I agree. Was just thinking the same thing." Adam started his vehicle and drove them to the Winkle home.

As the 4x4 rolled to a stop in front of the old Craftsman, Rick again noticed how inviting the front porch looked. Stretching across the width of the house, it looked like the kind of place you could spend hours sitting and talking with friends.

Rick did a double take as he realized the front door had been left wide open. "I don't think I'd do that if I'd just been burglarized."

"Neither would I," Adam said as he cut the engine. "Let's go see what's going on. I'll go first, just in case."

Raising both hands in front of him, Rick said, "Be my guest."

The porch creaked in the same spot it had the day before, but other than that one stair, it felt solid. Rick stood behind Adam, peering over his shoulder so he could see inside the house.

Tyler Winkle was bent over an end table, rearranging knickknacks. A small white trash bag lay nearby on the floor, but it looked like it contained only a few small items. At the sound of Adam's knock, Tyler straightened up and smiled.

"Hello!" he exclaimed. "Company! Come on in, please." He stepped forward and waved them inside.

As they entered the house, it struck Rick as odd that Tyler hadn't shown any sign of recognition. Rick's muscles tensed involuntarily as he prepared for the worst.

When Tyler extended his hand and introduced himself, Adam shook his hand, but a dark cloud seemed to drift over Adam's face at the lack of recognition. And when Tyler smiled broadly, Rick's gut twisted with a distant memory. Glancing around, he saw none of the chaos he'd observed yesterday. The lamps had been righted, the knickknacks were back in their places, and the papers that had been strewn about were gone.

"We met yesterday, Mr. Winkle. I'm Rick Atwood. I spent close to an hour here with you and your niece talking about the burglary and the damage to your house. Are you feeling okay?"

"You did?" Tyler blinked back surprise. "I mean…we talked for an hour? Wait! What burglary?"

"Of your family's secret recipe," Rick said slowly, deliberately. He cocked his head to one side and eyed Winkle. What was going on here? Was this an act?

Tyler did a double take and looked down the hall in the direction of his bedroom. "Our recipe's been stolen?" he gasped. He spun on his heel and ran down the hall and into the bedroom.

"I hope this isn't what I think it is," Rick muttered.

"He's certainly got my curiosity up," Adam said and took off after Tyler.

They found him kneeling in front of the safe in his bedroom gaping inside. He had the door open and was frantically going through the contents.

"It's gone!" he whimpered, tears streaming down his face. "My family's secret recipe for chocolate is gone! Who would do such a thing?" His hands shook as he shuffled through the contents of the safe again.

As Tyler frantically sorted through the few items in the safe, Rick felt certain this was something he'd seen before. He recalled a story he'd worked on long ago in New York. It was only one way he could think of that Tyler's behavior made any sense. "Tyler?"

The man looked up. He still had tears streaming down his cheeks. He croaked, "Who would do this?"

"Tyler? Where's your niece?"

"She had school today."

"And what day is today?"

"You don't know?" Tyler scoffed. "It's Tuesday. Why?"

"No, Mr. Winkle," Adam said. "It's Wednesday."

Rick nudged Adam and spoke quietly. "Adam, I think this man has had a TGA."

Adam shook his head and raised his hands. "What's that?"

"Sorry. I once did a story about a guy who had this happen. It's called Temporary Global Amnesia. If I'm right, Mr. Winkle has lost the last twenty-four hours. We need to get him to a doctor. Fast."

17

ALEX

I'M STANDING OUTSIDE MISS REDMOND'S classroom, trying to slow my racing heart. It was three years ago that I was playing matchmaker for Mom and Dad. I was only a little kid then and didn't realize what a rush it was. I just wanted Marquetta as my mom. But this, today, is next level. Who knew playing matchmaker could be such a cardio workout? Anyway, deep breaths, Alex, deep breaths. I step inside, clutching my history book like it's a lifeline.

I don't have much time before class starts, but for now, Miss Redmond's back at her desk, and she's alone. I gotta do this now, or I'll have to wait until after school.

"Miss Redmond?" I say, trying to sound casual. "I need some advice."

She looks up from her desk, surprise lighting up her blue eyes. "Sure, Alex. What's on your mind?"

"Well," I start, trying to keep my voice steady, "I've decided to get into this whole healthy eating thing. You know, less junk food, more green stuff." I pull a face, hoping it comes across as genuine. I totally want her to think I'm disgusted by junk food and not about ready to double over from the knots in my stomach.

Miss Redmond's eyebrows shoot up her forehead like they're trying to escape her face. "Really, Alex? That's wonderful!"

"Yeah, I figured it was about time," I reply, shrugging like it's not a big deal. I pause, trying to act like something just occurred to me. "I always see you carrying your lunch. I'll bet you always eat healthy. Do you get your groceries at the Seaside Cove Market?"

Her eyes crinkle as she laughs, "You know it's about the only place in town if you want fresh produce."

"Right. So what's a good time to shop there? When do you go?"

"I always go when I get off work. I grab something fresh for dinner as I'm walking by." She frowns and gives me a suspicious look. "Marquetta is supposed to be an excellent chef. Are you saying she doesn't cook healthy meals for you?"

Uh oh. I didn't think of that. "Oh, no," I stammer, feeling my cheeks heat up. "She does. But you know how it is when you're a kid. Sometimes you just want something different."

Miss Redmond gives me a knowing smile. "Well then, Alex, I suggest going to the market on your way home from school. And talk to your mom. I'm sure she'll be happy to help you learn how to cook whatever you pick up."

I'm super relieved when the other kids start to come back in from lunch. "Thanks, Miss Redmond," I say as I take a step back. "I'd better get to my seat." As I return to my desk, I want to do a fist pump. Operation Green Smoothie is on!

I'm anxious for the rest of the afternoon because I wanna get home and talk to Barrington Rhymes. All I have to do now is convince him to go grocery shopping with me. That shouldn't be too hard. Right? I also realize I didn't read Veronica's message from earlier. Rats.

When the final bell rings at the end of the day, we all bolt for the door. I thank Miss Redmond on my way out, then while I'm walking with Sasha, check Veronica's message.

"Who's that from?" Sasha asks.

"Oh, this girl I'm kinda helping. Hey, Sash, she wants to meet me down at the harbor. Can we talk tonight?"

Sasha looks kinda hurt. Her brown eyes are glistening, and I feel awful. We always ride our bikes together and talk.

"This is super important, Sash. It's kind of a case I'm working on."

"Oh. Okay. Well, see ya' round, Alex."

I feel awful as I watch Sasha wheel her bike away. She's been my best friend since I got to Seaside Cove, and I feel like I'm letting her down. But my dad and Chief Cunningham want my help. Sasha will come around after this is all over. I'm sure of it.

I ride my bike to the marina, where Veronica is pacing along the dock. She glares at me when she sees me. "Where have you been? I've been waiting for, like, forever."

"Sorry. I just got out of class."

Veronica rolls her eyes. "Whatever. I need your help. My uncle is playing these stupid games. We have to find out what he's up to. You're good at that kind of stuff, right?"

Is this gonna be it? The big reveal of all the secrets Veronica's been hiding? On the other hand, I don't even know what Chief Cunningham wants to know about Veronica and her uncle. He didn't say exactly what he wanted me to do, but maybe this is kinda what he had in mind. "Yeah, I can totally help you out."

"Awesome. Stop by the house and get him to tell you why he's pretending to not remember anything. I want to know what his game is because I'm going to sue for emancipation."

Wait. What? Her uncle doesn't remember anything? And what's this about emancipation? Isn't that when kids decide they want to be an adult early? Holy cow. I'll bet the Chief will want to know about this. "What do you mean your uncle lost his memory?"

Veronica rolls her eyes. "When I got up this morning, the house was almost all cleaned up, and he was acting like nothing had happened."

"I told him the house looked way better than yesterday, and he asked me what I was talking about. I knew he was messing with me, so I left."

"You didn't talk to him about it?"

"No way. There's no talking to my uncle. He's got his mind made up on everything." Veronica's eyes fill with tears. "My Uncle Tyler is really mean to me, and he won't let me do anything I want. He makes all the decisions for me, and he's stolen my inheritance."

"Do you wanna go see him now? Maybe we can talk to him and get some answers."

"I can't go."

I look around. There's nobody here. "Why not? We're totally alone."

Veronica shakes her head. "I don't want him to know I'm here talking to you. He'll get suspicious. Besides, I'm meeting somebody."

"Really? Who?"

"None of your business. It's a secret for now."

"Is this that boy you mentioned? You said there was someone you liked."

Veronica rolls her eyes. "Whatever. He comes down here sometimes in the afternoons. You can't be here when he shows up."

"Why not?"

"Because we're not like official yet."

I get it. She wants to keep this a secret. Kinda like Operation Green Smoothie. I don't want anybody to know about that, either. "Okay. Got it."

Veronica smiles. "You're pretty cool, Alex. We can talk later. Okay?" She walks away before I can answer.

Sure. Whatever. I grab my bike and head back up to the roundabout, then I turn left toward the B&B. But instead of going home, I park my bike near the benches overlooking the marina. If Veronica won't tell me who she's seeing, all I have to do is watch to find out. Easy peasy.

18

RICK

RICK VOLUNTEERED TO CANVASS THE neighborhood for witnesses who might have seen someone entering or leaving the home while Adam escorted Tyler to a local doctor. Though reluctant to accept that he needed medical attention, the overwhelming evidence that he'd forgotten an entire day finally won out.

According to Adam, the best place to start asking questions was across the street with Mrs. Maynard. Apparently, the woman was notorious for her love of daytime soap operas and her aversion to neighborhood drama but was also an incurable busybody who loved to spy on her neighbors.

As Rick approached the house, he noticed the rust-colored draperies swish closed. He gave an inward chuckle. "Looks like you were right, Adam," he murmured.

He knocked lightly on the door and waited. When the door creaked open, a woman wearing round spectacles perched precariously on the bridge of her small nose peered at him through the opening. The glasses magnified her keen blue eyes. If Adam was right, those blue eyes missed nothing.

"What is it?" she asked, her tone laced with annoyance. Her skin was weathered and wrinkled. She had thin lips that practically disappeared when she pressed them together.

"Mrs. Maynard? I'm Rick Atwood. I run the Seaside Cove Bed & Breakfast."

"I know who you are. What do you want?"

"I'm working with the police and investigating a break-in," Rick began, flipping back a stray lock of hair from his forehead with a quick, unconscious movement of his hand. "Right across the street. Yesterday. Did you happen to notice anything unusual?"

Mrs. Maynard hesitated, clearly torn between her desire for privacy and the tantalizing pull of revealing what she'd seen. "Well…" she began, glancing anxiously over her shoulder.

When the old woman turned, Rick noticed a pair of binoculars on a side table against the wall just inside the door. Binoculars were the equivalent of professional spycraft in neighborhood terms, which meant Mrs. Maynard was not only a busybody, but adept at keeping tabs on the comings and goings of her neighbors. Keeping his tone encouraging, as if he were coaxing a kitten out of hiding, Rick said, "It would be a tremendous help to our investigation if you could recall even the slightest detail."

"I did see a woman leaving the house."

Rick perked up. It was a start. "Can you describe her?"

"She had dark brown hair."

"Anything else?"

"I don't want to get involved." Mrs. Maynard started to ease the door shut, but Rick put up his hand.

"Please, Mrs. Maynard. We need all the help we can get."

"My show's coming back on," she grumbled.

"Police business," Rick said, trying to make it sound exciting. "Isn't that more important?"

"Fine. I was tending to my garden," she said defensively.

"I saw it on the side of your house. It's lovely. You have some beautiful roses."

"My late husband never liked them. After he passed, I decided it was high time I planted something I liked."

Rick smiled and reminded himself that honey, not vinegar, got better results. Even so, he hoped this wouldn't turn into an afternoon-long discussion. "You've certainly done a wonderful job with them. So, were you tending your roses when you saw this woman? Was she leaving the house?"

"I don't want to judge, but she was dressed rather…slutty. I thought at first that man had brought in a—I can't even say it."

Rick nodded attentively and tried to sound encouraging. "I agree with you. That would be terrible. He has a young niece."

"A niece?" Mrs. Maynard perked up, leaning forward on her antique cane. She was obviously pleased to have a new tidbit for her neighborhood archives. "I thought the girl who lives there was his daughter."

"Sadly, her mother is deceased. He's now her guardian," Rick replied, hoping their apparent rapport gave him the green light for more questions. "Can you be more specific about what the woman was wearing?"

Mrs. Maynard's nose wrinkled in distaste. "She had on a skimpy tank top and jeans that were far too tight for decent wear."

"I see."

"I wasn't particularly surprised because the man's niece dresses far too old for her age. I don't know why he doesn't do something about it! Letting her run around half-naked all the time."

"Exactly," Rick said, keeping his tone encouraging. "What else can you tell me? Did you see Mr. Winkle?"

"No. He came home later. That's when I realized the woman must have been in the house on her own. I assumed she had a key."

"Did you see anything else?"

Mrs. Maynard shook her head and glanced over her shoulder, her temporary interest in gossip appearing to fade. Rick thanked her and turned to leave. He couldn't help but check over his shoulder as he walked away. He spotted Mrs. Maynard's faded strawberry-blonde hair through the window just before the drapes swished closed.

After spending the next half hour going door-to-door, all he had were conflicting stories. Mrs. Maynard had seen a brunette; another neighbor had seen a woman with red hair. Another swore there had been no one in or out of Tyler's house the entire day.

With his canvassing done, Rick called Adam to check on Tyler. "The doc is doing a physical exam right now. But you could do me another favor. I got a call from Maggie. She says Bella Rodriguez is back at work. Can you go talk to her?"

"Sure thing. Keep me posted about Tyler's condition. Okay?"

"Roger that."

At the Seaside Cove Inn, Rick considered going through the front door but chose the back entrance instead. He'd have a better chance of talking freely with Bella if Ray didn't even know he was here. Rick paused as he passed the spot where Styles had died. Another death. Why? He pulled himself away, took the right into the courtyard, and almost walked into a maid's cart. The petite woman pushing the cart had dark hair tied up in a loose bun and was dressed casually in a tee shirt and jeans.

"Are you Bella?" Rick asked when she acknowledged him.

"Yes, how can I help you?" The woman's brown eyes mirrored the warmth of her voice.

Rick introduced himself and asked if he could talk to her about Gideon Styles.

"Oh, Maggie said you or Chief Cunningham would want to talk." She shot a look in the direction of the office. I guess Ray won't mind —too much."

"I'll have Adam talk to him if he gives you any trouble. Can you tell me anything about Gideon Styles?"

Bella shook her head. "He was a real loner kind of guy. I only saw him a few times. I never heard any noise from his room, either."

"Maggie said something about a woman walking by his door. Do you know if she'd been in the room?"

"Oh, yes. She was inside. For sure. I saw her come out."

"Do you know who she was?"

Bella shook her head. "I don't remember seeing her around here before or since. She was wearing a tank top and jeans when I saw her."

"Dark hair?"

"Yes. Shoulder length." She frowned and placed her hand just below her shoulder blade. "Maybe a little longer."

"Is it possible she's a guest here?"

"It could be." She paused, then added, "The funny thing is, I haven't seen her since. We're in the rooms most of the day, though, so we don't see very many guests."

"I tell you what. If you do see her, would you call Chief Cunningham or me? We'd definitely like to talk to her if she's still here."

"I sure will, Anything else I can do?"

Rick shook his head. "No, you've been a big help." He gave her a friendly smile and, knowing he now had a network of spies watching, walked away feeling a little closer to solving the mystery of who this woman was and why she'd been in Gideon Styles's room. He also wanted to know why she hadn't been seen since. They had to keep digging.

As he walked through the gardens surrounding the pool, Rick paused and squinted at the sky. A flight of birds was making lazy circles against a backdrop of bright blue. The sun shone through the wispy clouds, creating a tranquil scene. He smiled and reminded himself that there was beauty in every situation—even if it was sometimes hidden beneath layers of mystery.

The Seaside Cove Inn lobby was empty when Rick walked in. The front door was propped open, allowing a gentle onshore breeze to drift through and create an almost inviting atmosphere. Rick tapped the bell on the front desk and waited until Ray appeared from the back room.

"What can I do for you, Rick?"

"I was just wondering if you remember a woman with shoulder-length, dark hair checking in recently," Rick said. "She might have checked in about the same time as Gideon Styles."

In typical Ray fashion, his jaw tightened. "Why do you ask?"

Really? What part of murder investigation did Ray not understand? Rick explained the situation with the mystery woman. To Rick's surprise, Ray didn't grumble but stroked the stubble on his chin thoughtfully. "So this will put me in good with Adam if I help you?"

"Yeah, Ray, I'm pretty sure it will."

Ray fingered the stubble again. Could it be he was actually thinking about answering? Rick could only hope. He waited as Ray tapped on the keys to his computer. A few seconds later, he turned to Rick and gruffly said, "Nope. Nobody I can recall."

Really? That was it? *Nobody I can recall?* Ray was just being a jerk—again. "What about at your coffee bar? Do you remember seeing Styles there?"

"You know how they are. They come and go so fast. I think he might've been there, but I'm not sure."

"Or this mystery woman? Dark hair. Tank top. Jeans."

"For crying out loud, Rick. That describes half the women who check in here."

Rick had hoped for better information, especially when Ray asked about getting in good with Adam. But, as usual, talking to the man was like talking to a wall. “Thanks, Ray,” Rick said. “I appreciate your help.”

Not that Ray had actually been of much help. But, unlike his competitor, Rick really didn’t like confrontational relationships or burning bridges. Whoever this mystery woman was, they probably wouldn’t need Ray to find her anyway. As Rick had learned long ago, there were always ways around a roadblock. Sooner or later, they’d find this woman. They’d find out why she’d been in Styles’s room. And that might tell them why she was so hard to find.

19

ALEX

I HAVE AN AWESOME VIEW of the harbor and Veronica from Marina Park. From here, I can see her, but she's never gonna notice me.

I gotta admit, I'm curious about Veronica's life now. I wish I had my dad's old binoculars. And a snack. Maybe a bag of Cheese Puffs. Oh, yeah. Cheese Puffs. I wince. Miss Redmond would totally not approve.

Veronica's still pacing. Her red hair is glowing like a beacon in the afternoon sun. She's staring out at the harbor, and I can't help but wonder what she's thinking about. This mysterious boyfriend of hers? Her uncle?

She pulls out her phone and starts texting like crazy. My heart skips a beat. Could she be talking to her boyfriend? As I wait, I can't help but feel a twinge of guilt. Am I crossing a line? Spying on her like this? Maybe if we were actually friends. But I'm totally sure now that she's just using me. Maybe to get away from her uncle? Could be. But I shake the feeling off because Chief Cunningham asked me to do this. Besides, this is Seaside Cove. If you're not snooping, you're not living. Right?

I smile to myself when a guy shows up at the roundabout. I don't recognize him. The guy has sandy blond hair and looks like he's in super good shape. He's wearing worn-out jeans and a T-shirt with some saying on it. He's too far away to read what it says. When he gets down to the harbor, Veronica looks like she's gonna burst. She's standing there with her hands clasped in front of her and a huge smile on her face.

They start to walk together. They're talking about something as they walk out toward the end of the dock. Bummer. I wish I could hear what they were saying. It surprises me that they're not holding hands or anything. Wow. I never thought Veronica would be so shy around a boy. Rats. This isn't doing any good at all.

I pack up my stuff and walk the rest of the way home. It's time to make some notes about what's happened.

September 12

Hey Journal,

Operation Green Smoothie is a go! I got Miss Redmond to tell me when she does her grocery shopping. Now, all I have to do is get Barrington Rhymes to 'accidentally' bump into her at the store. I mean, how hard can that be, right?

And guess what else? I'm actually making progress with Veronica! Being friends with her is kinda like trying to be friends with a cactus. You never know when it's gonna stick you! LOL. Anyway, I'm doing what my dad and Chief Cunningham want and getting closer to her. I also found out who her boyfriend is. I don't know his name, but I'll bet Mom knows.

Gotta go talk to her now before she starts on dinner.

xoxo

Alex

I find my mom right where I thought I'd find her, in the kitchen. She's got some music playing in the background, and Baby Jack is asleep in the bassinet. The crockpot is steaming away on the counter. It smells like heaven.

"Hey," I whisper as the butler door closes behind me.

Mom whispers back, "Hey, Sweetie. How was your day?"

I fill her in about what I saw at the harbor and then ask her if she knows anything about Veronica's new boyfriend.

She raises her eyebrows and looks at me. "Is this for Adam?"

"Yeah. Maybe. I dunno if the chief needs to know about him or not."

"Fair enough. From your description, it sounds like Quincy Knox. He's Isabelle's nephew."

I blink at her. "How do you know that?"

Mom shrugs and gives me a sly smile. "Isabelle told me she suspected her nephew was seeing someone."

Sheesh. Why isn't Chief Cunningham having my mom help him instead of my dad? She's better than a CIA spy. "What else do you know about him?"

"He went away to law school and just came back to help Isabelle run the shop because she's having more medical problems."

"Is that 'cause of the brain tumor? I heard it's gonna get her sooner or later."

Mom sighs. "You're right. It is. Anyway, Quincy's a lovely boy who grew up here. After he graduated, he went to law school. When Isabelle's health started going downhill, he volunteered to put his schooling on hold and came back to help her at the pet store."

"He gave up being a lawyer? To help his aunt?"

"I know, Sweetie. His motives might not have been completely altruistic. From what I've heard, he was having a little trouble in law school. And besides, Isabelle has made him the beneficiary of her will. She doesn't have anybody else, so it's kind of a win-win. So Veronica is the girl he's seeing? Oh, goodness."

"It looked like she was super excited to see him."

"I hope he knows what he's getting into. I'm convinced that girl is deeply troubled."

"Maybe they'll be good for each other. You know, kind of like making the two halves whole."

"Look at you, all grown up. You could be right. So did you discover anything else that might help Adam?"

I tell her about Veronica's plan to sue for emancipation. When I finish, she shakes her head.

"Veronica may be right about her uncle, but I just can't figure it out," Mom says.

"Figure out what?"

"It sounds like the poor man blames himself for his sister's death. He sold a thriving business to move him and his niece here. Why? The only thing I can come up with is that he thought it would help Veronica. But instead, it looks like it drove them apart. Think about it, Alex. Why would somebody sell a profitable bakery chock full of family history? It certainly wouldn't be for the money. There had to be another reason. Why don't you put on your reporter's hat and do a story on him for *The Cove Talkers Newsletter?*"

I feel like my head is gonna explode. I never thought of that. Mom's brilliant.

"Maybe you should talk to him," Mom suggests. "He might open up if he feels like someone is listening."

I'm feeling an odd sense of determination. This might not be exactly what Chief Cunningham had in mind, but maybe I can figure out why Veronica's uncle did what he did and make a difference in their lives. Talk about giving me a warm fuzzy feeling inside.

"That's an awesome idea. Thanks, Mom!" I start to turn away, but she stops me.

"Not so fast. You're not going anywhere today. You are hereby recruited for kitchen duty or for bathing your baby brother. Take your choice."

Dinner. Rats! I got so caught up with Veronica that I forgot to take Mr. Rhymes to the market. Maybe I can set it up for tomorrow. "I'll do dinner. What are we having?"

"I've got pulled chicken in the slow cooker. You'd just have to make some rice and saute the vegetables."

"On rice? Not on buns?"

"We're out, and this is a little healthier."

Has she been talking to Miss Redmond? Oh, well. I can do sauteed veggies and rice in my sleep. And then I can tell Miss Redmond about it tomorrow. As I take out vegetables for dinner, I make a mental list of questions to ask Veronica's uncle when I see him. Maybe his story will help me understand Veronica's situation. And who knows? It might even help me solve the murder before my dad and Chief Cunningham. Oh yeah, totally awesome.

20

RICK

THE SALT-LADEN AIR FILLED Rick's lungs as he walked toward the Seaside Cove Marina. The earthy scents of washed-up seaweed and fish grounded him as he prepared for the task ahead. The marina, once a bustling hub filled with fishermen, was now mostly occupied by sailboats bobbing serenely in their slips while seagulls squawked overhead. The clanking of rigging echoed like a nautical symphony, punctuated by the approaching hum of a small boat's outboard motor as it puttered into the harbor. The atmosphere was peaceful yet alive, a comforting contradiction that mirrored the town's charm.

"Afternoon, Rick!" Joe Gray called out as Rick passed the pristine houseboat that served as the office for Gray's Sailing Charters.

"Hey, Joe. I'll be back right after I talk to Jennifer. I'll see you in a few minutes."

"I'll be here," Joe said with a wave of his hand.

Rick continued along the dock until he reached the Ugly Worm Bait and Tackle Shop, psyching himself up for a visit with the fiery-haired Jennifer Martin. Stepping inside the bait-and-tackle shop was like stepping into a world where the old and new peacefully coexisted. Fishing rods of all shapes and sizes lined the walls while assorted tackle jingled softly in the sea breeze wafting through the open door. The other half of the shop was taken up by trinkets the tourists seemed to love. Barely a day went by that one of his guests didn't return from a stroll down here with some Seaside Cove memento.

At the counter stood Jennifer, her red hair gleaming under the shop's fluorescent lights. Her brown eyes sparkled with curiosity as she pushed her short mop away from her face.

"Hey there, Rick, what brings you to my humble establishment?"

"I'm just doing some digging, Jennifer. You know how it is."

Jennifer shifted her weight and supported herself against the counter. She crossed her arms and regarded Rick with obvious interest. "Oh, I'm all ears. Do tell." She gave him a slightly crooked, impish smile.

"I'm wondering if you've seen my daughter down here lately."

"Your daughter?" Jennifer said, her voice suddenly thoughtful. "No, I can't say as I have." She paused, then cocked her head at a stack of boxes in the corner. "As you can see, I got in an order this morning. I've been busy in the shop most of the day. Is something wrong?"

"No. Nothing wrong. It's just that she's been hanging out recently with an older girl named Veronica Campbell."

Jennifer's right cheek tightened into something resembling a grimace. "How much older?"

"I believe Veronica is seventeen."

"Oh, my. At her age, that's a big difference." Jennifer paused and pushed her hair behind her right ear. "Veronica? You know, I think my daughter might know her. You want me to text her?"

Rick didn't want Alex to think he was checking up on her, but on the other hand, he wasn't comfortable with Adam's belief that having Alex spy on Veronica and her uncle was a safe activity. "Would you mind?"

Jennifer shook her head. "I never mind texting Cecelia." She pulled her phone from her back pocket, sent a quick message, and then laid the phone on the counter. "Should only be a minute. You know these kids. They can't live without their phones."

Before Rick could answer, Jennifer's phone bleated twice. He read the message display upside down and could make out that it was, indeed, a message from Jennifer's daughter.

"Yup, she knows her, alright. Cecelia says she's, and I quote, all screwed up because of her mom's murder."

"Did she say anything else?" Rick asked reluctantly.

"No, but she's working at the Crooked Mast right now if you want to talk to her."

"I just may do that." Rick thanked Jennifer and departed with a wave of his hand. As he stepped outside into the bright sunshine, he wondered what he would find out when he talked to Joe Gray. Joe was like Ethel Maynard without the binoculars or drapes. Joe was all eyes and ears and happy to sit on the deck of his houseboat to watch the goings on.

The weathered boards of the dock creaked under Rick's feet as he walked. The sun's rays glinted off the windows of Joe's houseboat, in front of which stood a small portable pale blue-and-gray sign for Gray's Sailing Charters. As usual, Joe puttered around the houseboat. Today, that involved sanding the handrails in preparation for a fresh coat of varnish. When he saw Rick, he waved again.

"You mind bringing in the sign when you come onboard?"

"Not at all." Rick picked up the sign as he passed, amazed at how light it was. When he was on board, Joe thanked him and asked what brought Rick down to the harbor.

"I'm doing a little snooping. Alex has been hanging out with an older girl, Veronica Campbell. I wondered if you'd seen them together."

"Ah, the Campbell girl. Wild one, that one, from what I hear."

Of course, Joe had heard something. And it didn't sound good.

"What have you heard?" Rick asked, suspecting Joe would regurgitate whatever was circulating around the rumor mill. He was, after all, the practical head of the local gossip group that congregated most mornings at Crusty Buns for coffee and muffins.

Joe clucked his tongue and shook his head. "She's been in some trouble in the past. Got caught with stolen property." He lowered his voice a notch. "I heard the police busted her for drugs, too."

Not wanting to fuel the rumor mill more than this visit alone would do, Rick gave Joe a noncommital, "I see. Anything else?"

"Well, I did see Alex with her a little while ago. Maybe thirty minutes or so? Right over there." Joe pointed toward the entrance to the docks.

Rick wanted to kick himself. If he hadn't gotten caught up at the Inn, he might have arrived while Alex was here. "So I just missed them. What were they doing?"

"Girl stuff. Just talking. It did look like Veronica chased Alex away at one point. I think it was because she was meeting a boy."

"Veronica? She has a boyfriend?"

Rick's breath caught. It was too soon for Alex to go down that path. Alex's crush on Robbie Sachetti was one thing—it was still perfectly innocent. But Veronica would know older boys. Boys who might want something other than friendship. "Was there just the one boy?"

Joe raised his hands with his fingers splayed. "Oh! Sorry! I didn't mean to alarm you. It's not like Veronica was introducing her. She wanted this one all to herself, I think."

"So this is Veronica's boyfriend?"

"Based on what I saw, I think so. She had that look when girls get all googoo-eyed. You know?"

"Thank goodness Alex isn't there yet. But she's getting close. I'm not looking forward to that day, Joe. Did you recognize him?"

"Sure. Quincy Knox. Isabelle's nephew. Nice kid." With a chuckle, he added, "Been a long time since Angela and I had to deal with that stage. We had two girls, you know. One went boy crazy in sixth grade, and the other waited until almost the end of high school. You never can tell. You've got my sympathies, Rick. It'll give you gray hairs for sure."

"You're probably right."

"Quincy's a little old for Veronica, in my opinion. I sure hope he knows what he's getting into with that girl."

Rick blew out a slow breath. "You're the second person today to tell me that same thing. Anything else?"

"Not much. They walked a little. Talked, then they left separately. Didn't even kiss or anything. Might be a little too soon for that sort of thing."

Rick thanked Joe and asked him to call if he saw Veronica again. When he left, he felt a sense of hope. Just like with Penny Feeney, he had eyes watching for her. With luck, it would only be a matter of time before he could unravel the mystery of why she'd befriended Alex in the first place.

21

RICK

RICK'S THOUGHTS WERE A MAD whirlwind as he walked away from the Seaside Cove Marina. The more he learned about Veronica Campbell, the more he felt sure she was destined to live a life shrouded in whispers and sidelong glances. For some crazy reason, he felt he should try to change that. He took a last look at the marina and turned right, intending to go to The Rusty Nail, the place where all the drama had begun.

But as he passed The Crooked Mast, he decided to take Jennifer Martin's suggestion and talk directly to her daughter, Cecelia. He knew Cecelia was a level-headed kid, and she'd been working as a hostess at The Crooked Mast to help pay for college. Why not see what one of Veronica's peers thought of her? With luck, he'd get plenty of detail.

Upon opening the front door, Rick was engulfed by a warm, welcoming aura. With rough-sawn planking for accents and large floor-to-ceiling windows along the west wall, it was hard not to be awed by the interior of the otherwise nondescript building. And then there was the view from most tables that looked across the street at the marina, the ocean, and the horizon beyond. It was simply spectacular, and one he, Marquetta, and Alex enjoyed immensely.

Cecelia, her dark hair pulled back in a loose ponytail, greeted Rick from behind the front podium with a bright smile. They exchanged pleasantries, and then Rick explained his concerns about Veronica and Alex. Cecelia listened attentively, her young yet wise eyes reflecting understanding far beyond her years.

"Like I told my mom, I don't know Veronica that well. What I do know is mostly second-hand. She seems to keep to herself a lot. Most of the new kids just fit right in, but I've heard she resents being here. I guess she thinks she's better than Seaside Cove."

"Do you know why she'd want to be friends with Alex? I'm surprised because of the difference in their ages."

"Honestly, it is weird. But Alex has this reputation as a good detective, and when Veronica heard about it, I guess she started asking questions."

Rick's gaze narrowed. Despite his determination not to look overly concerned, he felt his brow furrow. "What kinds of questions?"

"You know, like, what cases had she solved? How could she contact her? That sort of thing. It was like she wanted to hire her or something."

It took a few seconds for the shock to subside. When Rick recovered, he asked, "You mean, as a private detective?"

"For sure," Cecelia's ponytail bobbed enthusiastically.

This was not good. Alex had already told him that Veronica believed Styles killed her mother. Given Alex's interest in solving murders, the thought of her having anything to do with Maxine Campbell's death was frightening. What kind of mess had Adam gotten Alex into? "Did Veronica say anything in school about her uncle?"

"Plenty." Cecelia went on to tell him much the same as he'd heard elsewhere. At the end of their conversation, Rick was convinced his worst fears were justified. Veronica was attempting to use Alex for her own purposes, and the supposedly safe assignment Adam had given her might be fraught with danger.

Unfortunately, Cecelia hadn't heard anything about Veronica and Quincy Knox being a couple. As worried as he was for Alex, he also felt strongly that one of those two was in for heartbreak. He just didn't know which one.

After leaving The Crooked Mast, Rick walked along Front Street, past Ocean Surf, where Dennis Malone had his usual racks of sale merchandise in front of the shop, and to The Rusty Nail. The peaceful atmosphere stood in stark contrast to the turmoil in Rick's mind.

Sally Costas was a phoenix who had risen from the ashes. After her husband's death, she'd raised their two children and taken control of the Rusty Nail, turning it into a town staple. Fiercely independent, her energy seemed to have no apparent limits. The incident with Veronica having a meltdown in her restaurant was bound to have left an impression, and Sally would certainly have lots to say. The question was, what did he want to know? Certainly, he hoped Sally could shed some light on Veronica's erratic behavior. But more than that, maybe she'd seen what had happened out front. He was curious how Veronica had so easily sucked Alex into her web.

His choice of wording sent a chill down Rick's spine. Was he really thinking of Veronica as a black widow? Parental worry gnawed at him, and it was making him crazy. The stakes were simply too high. He had to talk to Adam about the situation and get him to rescind his request. His daughter's safety was his priority even as he delved deeper into the questions of who killed Gideon Styles and who stole Tyler Winkle's secret recipe.

Sally greeted Rick just inside the front door. She cradled a small stack of menus in front of her, treating them like they were a precious cargo. "Afternoon, Rick."

"Hey, Sally. How are you?"

"Chipper as ever. And busier than all get out." She paused, looked beyond Rick at the closed door, and made a face. "You're alone and kind of early for dinner. I'm assuming you're here to ask questions about what happened the other day."

"Right choice. I actually have several questions."

"Fire away."

"Let's start with what happened inside the restaurant. I've heard that Tyler Winkle was meeting with Gideon Styles. What can you tell me about the meeting?"

"You know what? You want to talk to Di. She was the server, and she overheard something you'll want to know about." Sally raised her hand and motioned for one of the servers, a petite woman with short, wavy hair, to join them.

"What's up, boss?" The woman asked as she approached.

"Di, have you met Rick Atwood? He runs the Seaside Cove B&B and does some consulting with the police when they need a little expert advice."

"I think you're overstating my role a smidge, Sally," Rick said sheepishly. "Anyway, we haven't met before."

Sally shook her head as they introduced themselves. "Hard to believe in this little town. Anyway, Rick's got some questions about the lunch meeting you were telling me about."

Diane, or Di, as she liked to be called, rolled her eyes. "Oh. Piece of work, that one."

"Which one?" Rick asked.

"Not the guy with the bakery. That's Tyler, right? No, the other one."

"Gideon Styles?"

Di frowned, then shook her head. "That's not the name on his credit card. It was Russell Caraball. I remember the name because I've got a cousin with a similar name. My cousin is Russell Carstairs."

Rick said, "I didn't see this one coming. Styles had an alias? Did the card go through?"

"Sure. No problem at all."

The story sounded similar to one he'd worked in New York. A man had assumed more than a dozen personas, all with their own credit cards, bank accounts, and IDs. If that was part of Styles's game, how many aliases did he have? "Did the card look like it had been used a lot?"

Di did a double-take before she answered. "Come to think of it, no. It looked brand new."

"Does that mean something?" Sally asked. "We don't care what credit cards our customers use. If the card can be authorized, we're good with it."

"If Styles had two identities, why wouldn't he have more?" He told them about the New York story, then said, "Why he used a different credit card here is kind of a mystery. And why the second card wasn't in his wallet when we found it near the body raises even more questions."

"I don't know about a missing card, but he might have pulled this one out by mistake," Di said. "He was getting his wallet just as the girl started going off on him. He looked kind of flustered when he pulled it out."

"And once he'd handed you the card, what could he do? Say, oops, that's not me. Sounds like Mr. Gideon Styles was a conman, pure and simple." Rick paused, thought back to the crime scene, then mused, "So why didn't we find multiple IDs in his room?"

Sally and Di both gave him blank stares. Rick grimaced and shook his head. "Sorry. I was just thinking out loud." Trying to regroup, Rick looked again at Di. She had almond-shaped emerald green eyes that sparkled with curiosity. A smattering of freckles dotted her nose and cheeks. It gave her a look of pure innocence, but Rick suspected she'd gotten plenty tough in her line of work. "You mentioned Veronica making a scene. What can you tell me?"

"I think everybody in the restaurant heard it," Sally chuckled. "Let me tell you, that girl knows how to get loud."

Di laughed along with Sally. Her smile revealed a small gap between her front teeth. She looked at Rick and added, "I've seen and heard some crazy things working in restaurants, but quite honestly, I was embarrassed for the way she was acting. She aired more dirty laundry than I go through in a month!"

"Like what? Anything you can recall might be helpful for the investigation."

"She basically accused her uncle of being in cahoots with this Styles or Caraball or whatever his name is. After she got going, it got ugly. She claimed that not only had her mother promised her the business, but so had he. He got pretty flustered and said he'd only told her he'd consider it. When she called him a liar, he said this was exactly why she couldn't be trusted. He called her irresponsible. That ticked her off even more, and she claimed he just wanted to keep her under his thumb. She threatened to sue him for emancipation, and then she was going after him for fraud. That's when she stormed out. He looked super upset and followed her."

"Wow," Rick said. "All that? All with a roomful of people around them?"

"Oh, yeah. Like I said, it got ugly. Then, while her uncle was outside with her, this Styles guy places a phone call." Di looked back to her tables, seemed satisfied that everything was still under control, and turned her attention back to Rick.

"Did you hear any of it?" Rick asked.

"All I heard was him telling somebody to work fast."

The break-in, thought Rick. Had he been giving somebody a signal to go ahead?

"Does that help?" Di asked, her nose wrinkling as she awaited his answer.

“More than you know.” Rick finished the conversation with Di, who excused herself and returned to work her tables. “She was very helpful, Sally. Thanks for connecting us. Is there anything else you can tell me?”

“Oh, yeah. Let me tell you what happened outside. But first, let me get these people seated.”

22

ALEX

I've got the skillet on the stove and the bottle of olive oil out. All I have to do now is finish washing my hands. While I'm doing that, I look across the room at Mom's old grandfather clock. It's only taken me about fifteen minutes to get everything ready. Easy, peasy. I have time before I have to start cooking. Maybe even enough time to run up to my room and do a little research on Veronica.

On my way through the living room, I spot Barrington Rhymes sitting on one of the couches. There's a notepad on his lap and a pen poised in his hand. He looks lost in thought.

"Hey, Barrington. What are you working on?"

He looks up, smiles, then raises the notepad. "A haiku." He sounds like he's super enthusiastic.

"A what?"

"It's a form of Japanese poetry."

"Oooh. I love poetry."

His eyes light up, and he shifts position so he's facing me. "Haikus are a specific type of poetry. They have three lines with a 5-7-5 syllable count. It sounds easy, but finding the right words can make it very challenging."

Maybe I should have told him that I love reading poetry, but I've never actually tried writing it. I'm feeling a little awkward, so I say, "We've studied sonnets in school."

"Ah, yes, Shakespeare. A bit verbose for me. The Japanese are much more succinct. Especially if you're a purist. That's my preference. I like sticking to the original form rather than the more relaxed styles."

I have to admit, if Robbie wrote a poem for me, I'm sure I'd like it no matter how many rules it broke. But Robbie isn't into poetry. I'll bet Miss Redmond is. Oh, snap! That's it. "Can I see it?"

"Why not? It is about your town. Or, rather, its setting." He hands me the notepad so I can read what he's written.

His writing is super neat. And he's right. The poem isn't long at all. But there's something about it. The more I think about it, the more I realize it's surprisingly deep.

Golden sun rays dance,
Sea waves whisper, gleaming bright,
In blue, serene joy.

The words paint a vivid picture. A sunny day near the sea. It's the sort of calm I feel down at the harbor. Somehow, that little poem stirs something deep inside me. I read it again and discover a new layer in the simple structure. Miss Redmond would love it. "That's awesome."

I think he kind of blushes a little. Like maybe he's embarrassed by the compliment. "Thanks. A haiku is an illustration of the power of words. The art of haiku is something truly beautiful."

Oh, yeah, this guy is gonna be perfect for Miss Redmond. "So how'd you learn about these…"

"Haikus?"

"Yeah, that. Have you been to Japan?"

He chuckles and gets a faraway look in his deep blue eyes. "Oh yes, several times. It's a beautiful place, filled with history and tradition. I've always been fascinated by it."

He starts talking about his travels. His voice and words give me visions of ancient temples surrounded by lush greenery, bustling city streets illuminated by neon lights, tranquil gardens where time seems to stand still, and cherry blossoms that paint the sky pink. He talks about the people, their warmth, their discipline, and their dedication to preserving their culture.

"But what fascinates me the most is their poetry," he says, his eyes gleaming with excitement. "Sorry, I get carried away. Especially when I'm talking about haikus."

"Like this one?"

"Exactly. Haikus are a form of expression that captures the essence of a moment in just 17 syllables. My travels in Japan deepened my appreciation for them. There's something magical about how much emotion and imagery can be packed into such a concise form."

"Wow. That's awesome."

His fingers drum on the armrest of the couch. "I've been longing to go back. There's still so much I'd love to explore. And well, it would be truly special if I could share that experience with someone."

Oh, yeah! He's perfect. "Like a girlfriend?"

"Well, yes, I suppose. Or even a good friend. Sharing experiences often makes them more meaningful, don't you think?"

"Totally." My mind is already racing with ideas. If Operation Green Smoothie works, his wish might come true. I hand the notepad to him and notice how he seems lost in thought. "Hey, you said you liked Seaside Cove, right?"

"I do. It's a nice little town."

"Would you like to learn more about it? Maybe see how the locals do stuff?" Uh oh. I almost said how they shop for groceries. Talk about boring. And sounding lame.

"I love doing that sort of thing. Getting to know the places I visit is a passion of mine."

My heart's pounding a million miles a minute. Am I really gonna ask this? It's the only way to get him together with the future Mrs. Barrington. "Maybe tomorrow afternoon, after I get off school, we could go grocery shopping?"

He blinks hard. "Excuse me? You want me to go to a supermarket?"

"Yeah. We don't have any big chain stores or anything. It'd be like going to Japan and seeing what kinds of stuff they have on the shelves. That can tell you a lot about the people. Right?"

"I suppose." His voice trails off, and he looks down at the notepad.

I gotta do something before he says no. "It's a great way to learn more about Seaside Cove. All the locals shop there, so you'll get a real taste of the town."

He kind of makes a face. "I don't know, Alex. I'm not really a 'grocery shopping' kind of guy."

"You probably shopped in Japan. Right?"

"Well…yes."

"This would only be a little different. Think about it. It'd be epic! You could even pick up some ingredients to make sushi. Or better yet, find something new to try!"

He drums his fingers on the armrest of the couch a little more, then frowns as he looks at me. "You're not going to let this go, are you?"

"My dad says I'm super persistent."

"Alright, Alex." A smile tugs at the corners of his mouth. "Let's do it. Let's go grocery shopping."

"Awesome! You won't regret it. I promise."

"Somehow, I already do. But I'll go with it."

"Are you going out for dinner tonight?"

"Yes, I have a reservation at the Crooked Mast."

"Awesome. It's a great place."

"So I've heard." He looks at his watch, closes up the notepad, and adds, "In fact, I should be heading out."

"No problem! Enjoy your dinner." If Operation Green Smoothie works, he might want to go there again tomorrow night—with a date.

I don't have time to check out Veronica, but that's okay. It's feeling like Operation Green Smoothie is gonna be a total success. I can't wait until Miss Redmond sees Barrington. They're totally gonna fall in love!

As I fire up the stove to start the veggies, I realize I'm humming *Here Comes the Bride*.

23

RICK

At the mention of customers, Rick looked to his side and saw an older couple waiting patiently. Sally told the couple they'd be seated right away, then motioned for one of her waitstaff to escort them to a table. When she looked back at Rick, his gaze locked onto hers. The ambient noise of The Rusty Nail faded into a distant hum, the clatter of dishes and buzz of conversation merely a soundtrack to their exchange.

"Rick," Sally began, her voice steady and serious. "Unfortunately, I have to divulge a secret to give you the whole story. I hope you'll pretend to be surprised when the big moment comes, but Alex has been trying to make money. She wants to buy you and Marquetta a first-anniversary gift and has been working as a courier for some of the local merchants."

"Excuse me? How did I not know about this?"

Sally gave Rick an embarrassed smile. "We were all so taken by what she was doing that we agreed to keep her secret."

A warm glow spread through Rick's chest, a mixture of pride and surprise. His little girl was working to buy him and Marquetta a first-anniversary gift? But the internal warmth was quickly overshadowed by a pang of guilt. She was only thirteen. Should she really have to worry about such things?

"She delivered an order to the store the day Veronica fell," Sally continued, her clear blue eyes filled with concern.

Thinking about the timing of when Alex and Veronica had shown up at the B&B, everything suddenly made sense. Rick's heart pounded in his chest. "Let me guess, Alex was delivering right when this whole argument took place."

"Pretty much. Alex showed up to deliver what I'd purchased from Howie's Collectibles just as the argument was ending. Veronica rushed past her, and Alex went out the door after her. Veronica's Uncle Tyler had started to unload on your Mr. Styles when there was a big gasp from the front section of the restaurant."

"Is that when Veronica fell?"

"Yes. Several of our guests later said they actually saw Veronica fall into the planter. From what I've heard, it sounds like Alex called out to her, and that's when she fell. Her Uncle Tyler must have heard the commotion at the front of the restaurant because he rushed out to help." Sally grimaced, and her eyes filled with sadness. "The poor man was trying to care for his niece, but it only upset her more. All his trying to help did was start another argument. I went through something similar with my youngest daughter when she was the same age."

Rick swallowed, his throat dry. He hoped he and Alex never got into that situation but could picture the scene all too well. In this case, he could see Tyler, his face flushed with anger and guilt, facing off against Veronica, defiant and hurting.

"And then Gideon Styles showed up. I realized how dangerous the situation looked, so I ran outside with my cell. I was going to call Adam, but it all happened so fast."

"What did?"

"Veronica had another meltdown, and her uncle turned on Styles and got into his face. He said that he was tired of him changing their deal and messing with their lives. That's when things got really ugly." Sally's gaze never left Rick's face as she took a long breath and shook her head.

"Uglier than what sounds like a knockdown, drag-out argument? What did Tyler do, threaten to kill Styles or something?"

"Actually, that's exactly what happened. Styles said the bakery had been going downhill ever since Tyler's sister's death. And then Tyler threatened him. He said he was going to bury Styles. Rick, I don't want to make any trouble for that poor family, but he looked like he was angry enough to kill."

Rick's mind raced, his thoughts tumbling over each other. Who killed Styles? Tyler? Veronica? Both had made threats…and how many others had threatened Styles? "Gideon Styles seemed to have a knack for making enemies. I wonder how many others wanted to kill him?"

"Glad I only have to deal with customers who complain about their meal not being cooked properly. You have my sympathies."

"Thanks." Rick let his gaze drift around the bustling restaurant. The waitstaff was rushing around, ferrying plates of seafood to the patrons, their faces, a blur of concentration and cheerfulness. The rustic charm of The Rusty Nail, so comforting and welcoming, hardly seemed like a place where a motive for murder might surface.

"You're keeping busy, Sally," he commented, forcing a smile.

"We always are," she replied. "I don't know how I'd do it if I had to help Adam, too. You deserve a medal."

"I'd settle for a reprieve from murder," Rick sighed. "Is there anything else you can tell me?"

"That's all I can think of. Please, don't tell Alex I told you about her delivery gig."

"No problem. I'll keep it a secret. But, just so I know, are there any other stores besides Howie's Collectibles that she's delivering for?"

"Traci at the Bee's Knees is the only other one I know of. But your daughter is quite the hustler. It wouldn't surprise me if she's talked a few other merchants into the same sort of thing."

Rick left The Rusty Nail and headed for the Bee's Knees. He'd wanted to talk with Traci, anyway. He wouldn't let on that he knew about Alex making deliveries, but the mention of the shop had given him an idea about how he might find the mystery woman from the Seaside Cove Inn. This town had a heck of a gossip mill, so why not make the most of it?

The familiarity of Seaside Cove's tree-lined streets comforted Rick as he walked the few blocks to the downtown. The vibrant foliage whispered of untold stories as a cool breeze rustled the leaves above. He wandered down the sidewalk and once stopped to watch a squirrel dart up a tree.

Soon enough, the quaint and colorful storefronts of Main Street were in front of him. The stores, once dual-purpose buildings with storefronts downstairs and residences upstairs, were now strictly commercial. The Bee's Knees was nestled between Scoops & Scones and Isabelle's Pet Shoppe.

The cheerful yellow and blue color scheme of the Bee's Knees fit in perfectly with the rest of the brightly painted downtown. While it was possible Traci would levy a barrage of questions at him, he felt confident he could fend off most of them. He climbed the stairs and walked past the display of candles and knickknacks. The soft tinkling of a door chime announced his arrival.

A warm, inviting aura that was as comforting as it was captivating greeted Rick. The air was perfumed with an irresistible blend of fragrances, from the sweet allure of vanilla to the refreshing zest of citrus. After exchanging greetings with Traci, Rick launched into one of his reasons for being there.

"Traci, I'm looking for someone. Has Adam mentioned a woman with dark hair who seems to like tank tops and jeans?"

"No, and he'd better not!" Traci shot back playfully. She winked and laughed. "Actually, I haven't seen my fiancé since last night. He was so exhausted that he dropped me at home and went back to his place. Is this woman part of the case?"

"She's been seen in two locations now. The first sighting was near Tyler Winkle's home—the house that was burglarized. And the other sighting was at the Seaside Cove Inn near the room of our murder victim."

Traci's eyes widened. "Showing up like that's pretty odd, right? Tank top and jeans, you say? That's a pretty popular way for tourists to dress, but are you talking about the woman Old Biddy Maynard is calling a tramp?"

"The same one," Rick said, holding back a smile at the questions forming in his head. Did he have a nickname, too? As for Mrs. Maynard, of course, she'd talked. His interview with her had probably been the highlight of her week. Maybe the year. "I didn't realize you were friends with Mrs. Maynard."

"I'm not. I heard it from Francine, our illustrious mayor and chief gossip," Traci smirked. She laughed, then began to sing softly, "The wheels of the mill go round and round, round and round."

"Enough!" Rick shook his head and failed at trying to keep a straight face.

"Believe it or not, Adam started the whole thing," Traci continued, her eyes twinkling with mirth. "We were casually discussing the local gossip mill, and he suddenly started making jokes about it. You know Adam, he can be a natural comedian when he's not being serious. And before I knew it, he was singing that old nursery rhyme."

"With a twist. Odd, I've never known Adam to be very funny."

Traci giggled. "Well, to be fair, you've never been in a bubble bath with him, either. I hope."

Rick cleared his throat. "Uh…no. Never have, never will. But our police chief likes to inject a bit of humor into the mundane, huh? I'll have to keep that in mind."

Traci cast a glance at Rick, her laughter subsiding. "On a serious note, if that's the woman you're talking about, it's possible she was here in my shop."

"Could be. What can you tell me about her?"

"She bought a vanilla-scented candle. And she paid cash. Oh, wait. She had a bag from Bound to Please. There was only one book in the bag, so that's where she put the candle."

"Looks like I'm headed to the bookstore next. Thanks, Traci."

"Rick, do keep me posted about this woman. If she's causing trouble around here, it's something we all should be wary of."

"Will do. And please, Traci, you do the same. Let me or Adam know if you see her again."

As Rick descended the stairs, he thought about his last words to Traci. That was how they'd find this woman. Get the entire town looking for her. She wouldn't stand a chance. Not against this town's gossip mill.

24

ALEX

THE ANTIQUE CLOCK ON THE wall fills the room with its soft tick-tock, tick-tock as I set the table, laying out the silverware just the way Mom likes it. My dad's gonna be here any minute. That's what we're hoping, anyway. Mom still hasn't heard from him, and neither have I.

After a few minutes, we agree that he's gonna be late. We try not to let the disappointment bring us down, but without him here, it feels like there's a shadow over everything. Even the white tiled backsplash doesn't seem as bright now.

When we're sitting down for dinner at the island in the kitchen, Mom says, "I hate it when your dad is late like this. I worry about him."

I push a piece of sauteed zucchini across my plate. I don't wanna talk about downer stuff now. It's only gonna make us both miss my dad more. "At least you got Baby Jack's bath done early."

"I know. How was your day, Sweetie?"

"Good. Hey, Mom, what do you think of Mr. Rhymes?"

"He's a nice man. Why do you ask?"

I shrug. "No reason. Just curious."

She puts her fork down and gives me the Mom stare. "Alex, you're never 'just curious.' What are you up to?"

"Oh, nothing."

"Don't try and stonewall me, young lady. I know you, and you're planning something."

There's kind of a long silence while I try to think of ways out of this. I messed up by saying anything. But I was thinking of asking her opinion anyway. So what the heck? Why not just throw it out there? "I think Miss Redmond would be a good match for Mr. Rhymes."

Mom picks up her fork and pops a carrot into her mouth. As she chews, I can practically see the wheels turning. "Where is this coming from, Alex?"

I hesitate and fiddle with the hem of my cloth napkin before I look at her. "I just think they'd be good together."

She sighs again, this time, softly, and sets down her fork. The glow from the overhead lights makes her look kind of worried. Her voice is gentle but firm when she says, "Alex, it's not our place to interfere in other people's lives, especially when one of the people is one of your teachers."

Baby Jack gurgles from his high chair. He's got no clue as to what we're talking about, but his innocence is a nice distraction. Mom's words hang over my head like smoke, clouding my thoughts and tugging at my emotions. In a way, she's right. I never thought about how bad things might get for me in school if it turns out I'm wrong about her and Barrington Rhymes. And what if he dumped her? I'd feel awful. A knot of disappointment forms in my stomach. In a way, I know Mom's right. What if I mess this up? But what if I make two people happy?

"Mom, I had it right with you and Daddy. Look at how good that worked out!"

"You've got me there, Sweetie. I truly do love your father. And you. But just because you got lucky once doesn't mean you can predict the same outcome for other people. Even if it feels like it would be a good match, it's not up to us."

I let out a slow breath and mumble my agreement, but then I confess. “I’ve already got a meeting set up.”

“You what?” Mom’s jaw drops as she gapes at me.

“Well, I kinda asked Mr. Rhymes to go grocery shopping with me tomorrow.”

Mom shakes her head. “Is that when Miss Redmond goes?”

“Yeah. She said she stops at the market on her way home from work.”

“Alex, I really do think you’re making a mistake. But I’m also sure you’re convinced you know best, so I’m not going to belabor the point. However, don’t be surprised if this backfires on you.”

Talk about a downer. All I can say is that Operation Green Smoothie better go smoothly! We get quiet for a while and eat our dinner. Finally, Mom breaks the silence.

“Alex, I’ve been wanting to talk to you about Veronica.”

Uh oh. Now what?

“I’m concerned about the age difference between the two of you. I’m also worried about you becoming involved with a crowd that’s too old for you.”

“It’s not like that at all. I thought Veronica was nice at first, and it was cool having someone her age pay attention to me, but she’s super selfish, and I don’t even know if I like her anymore. The only reason I’m still hanging out with her is because Chief Cunningham wants me to get him information. Plus, you suggested I write a story about her and her uncle for the *Cove Talkers Newsletter*.”

“Actually, I’ve changed my mind. I think you should stay clear of both Veronica and her uncle.”

I shrug. “But I promised Chief Cunningham I’d get information on them.” And if Veronica’s right about Gideon Styles killing her mother, this could be an epic story. “Mom, I’m just pretending to be friends with her. I don’t want to be her real friend.”

"Sweetie, real friend or not, these people worry me."

"I'll be careful."

"You always say that." She gets a worried look on her face when she says, "Okay. I don't want to be telling you who you can and can't see, but I think we should talk to your dad. Maybe there's some middle ground. I know Adam doesn't want to put you in danger, so maybe we can come up with a plan that keeps you safe, and you both get what you want. Just be honest with me. Let me know when you're going to see her. Okay?"

Staring at the last of my veggies, I know she's right. "Okay. I get it. Some of the kids at school are saying the only reason she started being nice to me is 'cause she wanted me to find something she could use against her uncle."

"That's cold, but I can see there's something else bothering you. Come on, Sweetie. Tell me the truth. What's really going on?"

I blow out a short breath. "It's gonna sound lame, but she's bossy."

"You mean she tells you what to do?"

"Yeah. It's like she's my actual boss, and I'm supposed to do whatever she wants. When we were at the marina, she chased me off 'cause she was gonna meet her boyfriend. I'm not even sure he really is." My shoulders slump as I realize how much better my life would be if I wasn't dealing with Veronica and her drama.

"Do you want me or your dad to talk to Adam? We could tell him you're no longer comfortable hanging out with her."

The words pop out of my mouth before I can even think of what to say. "No!" If I don't do this, then Chief Cunningham might not want my help in the future. I don't want him to think I'm just a big baby. "I can handle it. It won't be that much longer anyway."

"You do what you think is right," she says finally. "But remember, if this becomes too much and you don't want to continue, all you have to do is say the word."

Right. What? That I'm afraid? I can just hear the mean kids at school chanting—Alex is a chicken. That is totally not happening.

25

RICK

RICK TOOK THE MOST DIRECT route to the entrance of Bound to Please, a mad dash between cars across the street. The sun, which now hung low in the sky, cast a golden glow on the front of what had become an instant favorite of his when it opened a few months earlier. The first time he'd been in the charming bookstore, he'd fallen in love. The only problem was that each trip to the store resulted in another in-depth conversation about books with the shop's owner, Arthur Bennett.

The soft tinkle of a vintage brass bell combined with the comforting scent of paper and ink greeted Rick. The faint notes of sea salt carried in on the coastal breeze blended seamlessly with the bookish fragrance. A smile crept onto Rick's face as he breathed in the mixture. As usual, Arthur Bennett sat behind the counter, his full attention taken up by a book.

"Hey Arthur," Rick called out, his voice echoing lightly in the cozy space.

Arthur looked up, his round spectacles sliding down his nose. His hazel eyes twinkled with warmth. "Ah, Rick! Just the man I was hoping to see."

Of course. Arthur probably had about a dozen new books for the library at the B&B. Unfortunately for Arthur, today was not a day to be buying books. Rick approached the counter and tried to sound official. "I'm not here to make a purchase. I'm here on police business."

"Oh? Well, we can talk about that in a minute." Arthur's eyes danced with excitement. "I've just received a first edition of Hemingway's *The Old Man and the Sea*. Thought you might be interested."

Despite his mental preparations, the news sparked Rick's interest. He always had been a sucker for good literature first editions. Inwardly, he groaned. "You know me too well, Arthur." He extended his hand for the book.

As Rick gently inspected the cover, the binding, and the pages, Arthur prattled on about tourists and how they didn't appreciate good books the way they used to. "Nobody has time to enjoy these treasures the way they should. Most of them have the attention span of a gnat. They flit in, and they're gone before they even look around."

"I hear you, Arthur. That's one reason I like to keep adding to our library at the B&B. When they're in that environment, many people seem to disconnect from all the craziness of their everyday lives."

Arthur smiled knowingly. "I'm glad you understand what I mean. You should keep up the good work of spreading literature around. It's important for people to have time and space to slow down and appreciate the beauty of a story. Do you want me to bag that one up for you?"

Rick took another look at the book in his hands. He liked Hemingway, and the thought of having a first edition in his collection appealed to him. He reached for his wallet. "This isn't going in the B&B's library, though. This is going in my office."

"I've heard Captain Jack had quite the collection. Didn't he?"

"He did. Right now, I'm helping Adam on a murder investigation, but I'm sure I'll find time to read this once the case is over."

Arthur smiled, rang up the sale, and bagged the book. As he returned it to Rick, he thanked him for his purchase.

"Now, let's get to the reason I came in here. I'm trying to find a woman who bought something from you. She had dark hair and was probably wearing a tank top and jeans."

Arthur's eyes glazed over as he absently pushed up his round glasses. "Ah, yes. I remember her. She bought a copy of *The Sun Also Rises*."

"She bought a classic? That's not what I would have expected."

Arthur sat up straight and shook his head vigorously. "It wasn't just any copy. We're talking about an early printing of the Charles Scribner's Sons edition with an introduction by Henry Seidel Canby!"

Rick cursed himself for his lack of tact. Everyone knew about Arthur's passion for rare and collectible books. Clearly, he was excited about the book he'd sold to this mysterious woman. Even more surprising was that this woman might not only be a burglar but also a collector of rare books.

"Did you talk to her for long?" asked Rick.

Arthur shook his head. "No, not really. Why are you looking for her?"

"She may have information relating to the murder case I'm working on."

Arthur pulled back and gripped the countertop to steady himself. "You don't think she's the killer, do you?"

"Right now, we're just trying to compile a list of people who had contact with the victim, and this woman is on that list."

"I'd like to help, but I don't know her name or what room she's staying in at the Inn," he said.

"Wait. How do you know she's staying at the Inn?"

"She made a comment about how dingy the rooms are. I knew she wasn't talking about your place. I've heard the B&B's rooms are quite immaculate. She seemed like the kind of person who would appreciate the nice touches you have. Quite honestly, it surprised me when I learned she wasn't staying at your B&B."

Rick quickly paused and mentally rewound what Arthur had just said. He asked, "How do you know she'd appreciate those touches?"

"It was her jewelry. It looked very high-end."

Interesting observation, thought Rick. There was only one problem. Arthur was a bookworm, not a jewelry expert. "Can you tell me anything else about her? Anything at all?"

Arthur looked lost in thought as he tapped his jaw with his finger. After a few seconds, he said, "She had a very distinct perfume. It smelled like lilacs."

Rick smiled. Now, finally, he was getting somewhere. Perfume might not seem like much, but it provided another detail. He might find this mystery woman yet. "Thanks, Arthur. You've been a big help. I've got what I need."

"Good luck finding her," Arthur said as he reached for his book. When his fingers touched the cover, a smile spread across his face, and he seemed to disconnect from the physical world in favor of a fictional one.

As Rick stepped outside, he spotted Traci locking up across the street. He quickly decided to talk to her again and made another dash across the street between cars. He caught her at the base of the stairs to the shop.

"Hey, Traci. I've got one more question for you. Arthur says this mystery woman was wearing expensive jewelry. Did you notice what kind of jewelry she had on?"

Traci thought for a moment, then her blue eyes lit up. "He's right! It did look valuable. She only wore one piece, though. It was a necklace made of antique gold. It had intricate patterns etched around a blue diamond centerpiece. Judging by the way the diamond sparkled in the light, it looked like it was perfectly cut and polished."

Caught off guard by the detailed description of the diamond, Rick blinked, his eyes widening in surprise. A pause hung in the air before he leaned back and let amusement flicker across his face. When he mustered a response, the words were drawn out in playful disbelief, "Wow. That's pretty specific."

Traci winked at Rick. "It was a stunning piece."

"Okay. One more question. Did you recognize the scent of her perfume?"

"Sure. Lilacs. It's very distinctive. I don't see how that's going to help you, though. It's not like I could tell if it was a designer perfume or anything."

"No, but it's not a common fragrance. Right?"

"One of my big sellers with candles is lilac scented. But, in perfume, you could be right. Now I'm curious. How are lilacs going to help you find her?"

"Two words," Rick said with a smile. "Maid service."

Traci blinked in confusion. "I don't understand."

"Arthur thinks this woman is staying at the Seaside Cove Inn. All we have to do is talk to Bella and Maggie and see if they can tell me if any women who use lilac-scented perfume are staying there. Also, the book she bought from Arthur will probably be in her room. It's a rare edition, so she's not likely to be carrying it around."

Traci's eyes widened in understanding. "That's sneaky. Adam's going to love that."

Rick felt a little flush of satisfaction at the compliment. "It's worth a shot. Right? I'll call Adam on my way home. Who knows? I'm feeling better about finding her."

Traci wished Rick luck with the search and then walked toward her house, which was only a few blocks away. As Rick returned to the

B&B, he called Adam and explained his idea for finding the mystery woman.

"Unfortunately, both Maggie and Bella have probably gone home now," Adam said. "Why don't you let me call them both tonight? And by the way, you were right about Tyler Winkle and the TGA. The doctor confirmed that his loss of memory is legitimate. Since he won't be of any help, I have another lead I'd like you to follow."

That was disappointing. Just when he was getting close to an answer, Adam wanted to take over. On the other hand, he didn't have any authority, and if they were making contact after hours, it made sense for the man with the badge to do the calling.

"Okay, what do you want me to do?"

"I think I've found Leslie Mendez, Styles's wife."

"Really?"

"I've left messages at her work, but she's not calling me back. I thought maybe if you called, you might have better luck."

"What's she do?"

"She's an ER nurse."

Rick stopped walking, huffed, then blurted, "What exactly do you expect me to do, fake a heart attack?"

"I'm sure you'll figure out something. I'll text you the number."

26

RICK

DESPITE A LONG DAY OF chasing down leads for Adam, Rick couldn't get over how energized he felt. He held Baby Jack in his arms, a stupid grin forming on his face as he watched Marquetta and Alex work together. They'd already whipped up a quick dinner for him, and now they were working on what Alex referred to as the most important meal of the day—dessert. He gazed at the seafoam green wall and let the baby shift position in his arms, then held out his little finger so Baby Jack could grab on.

"This is one of his favorite toys right now," Rick said proudly as he looked up at Marquetta.

Marquetta rolled her eyes. "Don't kid yourself. He seems to like anything that wiggles." As she patted the last of the strawberries with a paper towel, she turned her attention to Alex. "Hey, Sweetie, how are you doing with the chocolate?"

Alex pulled the glass bowl from the microwave, gave the dark chocolate a stir, and said, "Done! Yum! Chocolate-covered strawberries!"

"Alright, Mr. Atwood. You're being called into action. I have to feed the baby while you help Alex. Your task is simple. Grab one of those berries, dip it into the melted chocolate, and then let the excess drip back into the bowl. After that, it goes on the baking sheet. Repeat, and do not eat any of them. Do you think you can follow those instructions, or should I have Alex supervise?"

Rick pulled himself off his stool, which had started to feel pretty darned comfortable after the day he'd had, and handed the baby over to Marquetta. "You're a tough one, General. But I think you'll find I'm trainable, and you won't be disappointed in my work." He made a face and added, "I hope."

"Oh, brother. Tell you what, Sweetie, you're in charge. You know what to do. If your dad messes up, you have my permission to reprimand him."

"Awesome!" Alex's blue eyes twinkled with excitement as she pointed to the bowl. "Get to work, Recruit!"

Rick smiled at his daughter, then dutifully picked up a strawberry and did as he'd been told. As he and Alex dipped the berries, Marquetta nursed the baby and told him about her day at the B&B. It was a well-needed change from mystery women, burglaries, and murder.

Though he'd been able to deflect answering her questions about the case so far, when Alex asked this time, he knew he was out of excuses. He told her and Marquetta about the task Adam had given him.

"So Chief Cunningham is making you find a way to contact this Leslie Mendez because she won't respond to phone calls or messages?" Alex said. "That sucks."

"Yeah, kiddo. It kind of does."

"Do you want help?" Alex's eyebrows arched up, and a smile spread across her face.

"You've already got too many irons in the fire, Sweetie," Marquetta said.

Alex dipped the last strawberry in the chocolate, then looked up and said, "I know, but I think I can help."

Rick ruffled her hair, thankful once again for having the opportunity to think about something else. "What are you up to, kiddo?"

"Not much."

"Don't let her kid you, Rick. She's playing reporter, matchmaker, and detective in addition to being a big sister and helping me."

"Reporter? About what?"

"Mom said I should write a story about Veronica's uncle for the *Cove Talkers Newsletter*. It can be my cover for Chief Cunningham's assignment!"

Rick fixed his gaze on Alex. "I have strong reservations about you investigating Veronica and her uncle, Alex. The more I hear about both of them—"

"Daddy, it's okay. I get it. I've been thinking about it, and I'm not even sure I want to meet with them in person. It sounded like a good idea at first, but it might not be the safest thing to do."

"Oh," Rick said, unsure of what else to say. This was a first—Alex being worried about her safety. She really was growing up. "If you want, I'll tell Adam I've put my foot down and won't allow you to be involved."

Alex shook her head. "I didn't say that. I wanna finish the job, but I'm gonna try to be smart about it."

"Sweetie, I'm positive that Adam isn't going to want you doing anything you're not completely comfortable with doing. If you want to back out, I'm sure he'll understand."

"Your mom's right. I can tell him we'll have to find another way to get information out of Veronica and her uncle."

"No! It's my job! My decision. Right?"

Alex's dark blue eyes flashed, and Rick's concern for her safety went to war with his desire to ensure she grew up strong and confident. Finally, he found a mental middle ground. "I've always said you should be able to make your own decisions. I'll back you up. Whatever you decide to do. And if you want my help, just let me know."

"I'll think about it," Alex said with a heavy sigh.

Rick supposed that was the best he'd get for now and suggested they dive into dessert. After finishing, Rick retreated to his office and fired up his computer. While he waited for it to finish, he dialed Adam's number. When Adam answered, he said, "Hey, buddy, I'm just giving you a heads up. You should be aware that Alex isn't completely comfortable with the assignment you gave her, but she's determined to follow it through."

There was a long pause, after which Adam said, "What do you want me to do about it?"

"Nothing, for now."

"It could be tricky. But I could find a way to pull her off without actually doing it if you want me to."

"No. Don't do that. I agreed with Alex. She should be able to make her own decisions. I'm letting you know because you're the man in charge. And by the way, I'm starting on your Leslie Mendez request."

"Rick, if it's too much."

"It's fine. Tonight, I'm just doing some background checking. My goal is to find out what I can about her divorce from Gideon. I'll let you know what I come up with."

Rick navigated to the newspaper archives he'd used so many times in the past. His search for Leslie Mendez produced an enormous list of results. "Need to narrow that down," he muttered.

Restricting the search to newspapers in the Sacramento area did the trick. His heart pounded as he read through the first article, which was in an independent paper for a small neighborhood outside of

Sacramento. When he saw the byline, he smiled to himself. "Why, Mick McCormick, you old dog. What have you been up to?"

No good, apparently. Even the title, *The Downfall of a Power Couple*, sounded like it had been stolen from a tabloid.

In the world of academia and medicine, the marriage of Gideon Styles and Leslie Mendez was nothing short of a sensation. But beneath the glamour and intrigue lay a story of betrayal, heartbreak, and an alleged affair that tore apart a once-enviable union. This is the inside story of the highly publicized divorce between Styles and Mendez.

Gideon Styles, a former college professor turned broker dealing in inventions and trade secrets, and Leslie Mendez, a dedicated and passionate nurse, first crossed paths in a college classroom. Their love story began controversially, with Styles, then 41, falling for his 19-year-old student, Mendez.

After a scandalous start, which saw Styles lose his job and Mendez get suspended, they tied the knot in 1994. "It was a whirlwind romance," recalls a former colleague of Styles who requested anonymity. "Gideon was swept up by Leslie's youth and vitality, and she was enamored with his intellect and charisma."

However, their happiness was not to last. Over the years, cracks began to show in their relationship, with Mendez eventually describing Styles as "narcissistic and uncaring." Rumors swirled about Styles's gambling habits and his on-again, off-again relationship with a woman named Penny Feeney. It was this alleged infidelity that reportedly led to their separation.

Rick stopped reading and read the last lines again. A woman named Penny Feeney? On-again, off-again? Could it be the woman he'd been trying to find? He made a note of the name before finishing the last paragraph of the article.

The couple's assets before the divorce included a lavish home where Styles hosted poker parties and an undisclosed amount of money from Style's business. Legal proceedings have been initiated, and the stage is set for a bitter battle over the division of assets.

When he finished, Rick sat back and read the article again. This time, making notes to pass along to Adam. Styles was a gambler, a philanderer, and dealt in trade secrets. Maybe there were far more suspects than he and Adam had originally thought. Finishing his notes, Rick clicked on a link for a story that was dated later than the first one.

The legal battle over the Styles-Mendez divorce was a spectacle, with both sides hiring top-notch lawyers. However, the court eventually sided with Mendez. According to court documents, Mendez was granted the majority of the couple's assets and properties.

Following the divorce, Mendez continued her fulfilling career in nursing, providing care and compassion to those in need. She remains wary of relationships but finds satisfaction in her work. "Leslie worked hard to build a career and life for herself, and it wouldn't have been fair if Gideon's actions jeopardized that," shared a close friend of Mendez.

Reflecting on their tumultuous relationship, a friend of the couple said, "It's a tragic tale of love lost, a reminder that not all that glitters is gold. They had everything - youth, charm, success - but in the end, it wasn't enough to keep them together."

This saga serves as a poignant reminder of the complexities of love and the price of fame.

* * *

Recalling his conversation with Arthur Bennett about the mystery woman, a smile tugged at the corner of Rick's lips. "I think I've just killed two birds with one stone."

He checked the time, saw how late it was, and locked up his office. In the morning, he'd tell Adam what he'd found. However, now, it was time for bed.

Quietly slipping under the covers, Rick was surprised when Marquetta snuggled up next to him. "Did you find what you were looking for?"

He turned, drew her in close, and whispered, "Yes. And she's right in front of me."

27

RICK

BARRINGTON RHYMES DRUMMED HIS FINGERS on the tabletop as he gazed up at Rick. The man had a smile on his face that wouldn't quit. "I can't get over this. You were an award-winning journalist before you became the sole proprietor of this beautiful B&B?"

"I was," Rick said. "If my grandfather hadn't left it to me in his will, I'd still be in New York chasing stories and missing life."

"That's what I'd like to do," Barrington said.

"What? Miss life?"

Barrington snickered and ran his fingers through his chestnut hair. "No. Stop missing it. By the way, the Eggs Benedict is fabulous. I've never had it with smoked salmon and avocado. My compliments to the chef. I've been in some great restaurants, but your little B&B can hold its own with any of them."

Rick picked up the empty plate, told the man he'd relay his compliments to Marquetta, and then asked, "So what are you working on?"

"Oh, your daughter was asking the same sort of question. I like to write haikus. Sticking to the traditional syntax is my favorite mental challenge. This one's kind of personal. Hopeful, I guess, actually." The man blushed, then added, "Dare to dream. Right?"

"It's the only way to live," Rick said. "Can I read it?"

"Sure. Why not?" Barrington handed Rick a four-by-six inch notecard.

Summer's sun caress,
Her laughter, a sweet sea breeze,
Love blooms, heart's undress.

"If I didn't know better, I'd say you're in love."

He held out his hand and took the card back from Rick. "Smitten, for sure."

"Anyone I know?"

Barrington shook his head. "Sorry, but I've heard about the rumor mill in this town. I don't want this out before I say something to her."

"No worries. I get it. In your shoes, I'd probably do the same. But good luck. I hope it works out the way you want it to." Looking across the room, Rick saw that Leo and Lily Carmichael were engaged in a playful debate over a crossword puzzle. In the short time they'd been at the B&B, their bickering and the occasional stolen kiss in the hallway had become as much a part of the B&B's ambiance as the antique furniture and seaside views.

Leo held up one finger to indicate a timeout to his new bride and called out to Rick, "Hey, Rick, can we get some more coffee over here?"

Grabbing the pot, Rick went to the table and began refilling Leo's mug. "How's our honeymoon couple this morning?"

"Ready for another day on the road," Leo said.

"Where are you headed to?"

"San Francisco," Lily said enthusiastically. "I love everything about the City, from the street art to the restaurants to the foggy mornings."

Leo reached out and hooked his little finger around Lily's. "And don't forget the coffee, babe."

"He's determined to turn me into a coffee drinker." She leaned toward Rick, held her hand to her mouth so Leo couldn't see her lips, and whispered, "Don't tell him, but I hate the stuff."

"I heard that," Leo pronounced.

Lily blew her husband a kiss. "I know. Don't worry, babe. If you add enough chocolate and sugar to it, I love any coffee!"

After filling Leo's mug, Rick held the pot over Lily's. She held up her hand. "No. I'm good."

"Then I hope you two have a lovely rest of your trip. If you'll excuse me, duty calls. Looks like the town's police chief wants a table."

"Do you have a few minutes to talk?" Adam asked as Rick approached.

"I will in about thirty minutes."

"Oh? Are you closing then?" Adam asked innocently.

"Pro tip, Adam. You're a terrible liar. I'll tell Marquetta you're here. I assume you want your usual?"

"Sounds good to me."

Rick went to the kitchen to turn in Adam's order. On his way, he passed Lydia, who was carrying two plates stacked with blueberry pancakes.

"Those sure look good," Rick said as they passed each other.

"Dios mio! I can't wait to try them!"

Indeed, thought Rick. Neither could he. And in twenty-nine minutes, he could. He went back to the kitchen and told Marquetta that Adam wanted bacon and eggs with the house-fried potatoes. She snickered, made a comment about predictability, and said it would be ready shortly.

When Rick returned to the dining room, he found Adam sitting at a table next to Barrington Rhymes. He also noticed that Adam was looking over a photocopy of the little poem they'd found on Gideon Styles's body. The instant he saw the words, he felt like a fool.

"That's a haiku!" Rick blurted.

Adam screwed up his face. "A what?"

Barrington shifted sideways so he could peek at the paper. "You're right." Chuckling, he said, "Most Westerners don't know what they are." He went on to explain the five-seven-five syntax and then asked if he could take a closer look.

Life's candle flickers,
In death, the heart quiets,
Silence, a soft nightfall.

As he read, he shook his head. "This one doesn't stick to the rules. Notice how the second line and third lines both have six syllables. This is either a mistake, or it could be whoever wrote it doesn't care about the syntax." He paused, read the words again, then pointed at the paper. "Look, if you swap the words death and silence, it conforms to the traditional syntax."

"And it makes a little more sense," Rick said.

"I still don't see what this tells us," Adam said.

Barrington stroked his chin as he reread the words. "I'd say it means you're dealing with an artist, a poet, and someone who's created their own unique form of expression. Perhaps, someone who might read Hemingway."

"Really?" Adam asked. "You got all that from a few words on a piece of paper?"

"It's just a guess." He quickly added, "Sorry, gentlemen, but I've got a meeting this morning. Good luck with your search." He stood, started to walk away, then turned back to face them. "You know, there is another possibility. That mistake might be unintentional. Just a thought." He waved, then left the dining room.

"Interesting development," Adam said. "Our killer could be a rogue Japanese poet who likes to break the rules."

"Don't forget the, or not, part of that," Rick snickered. "We'll be closing down in about ten minutes. I'll see if your breakfast is ready and let you enjoy it before we get into what I discovered last night."

After retrieving Adam's order from the kitchen, Rick made a last call for coffee refills before the dining room officially closed for cleaning. By eight-thirty, Adam was the only one left, so Rick talked to Lydia, asked her to finish the last of the cleanup, and went to the kitchen for the plate of blueberry pancakes Marquetta had prepared for him.

Sitting down opposite Adam, Rick stretched from one side to the other. "Man, some days are tougher than others."

"You're probably not sleeping as well as you should. Happens to me, too, when we're working on these cases. Mess up those sleep patterns, and life gets tough the next day. So, what did you find out?"

Rick simultaneously added syrup to his pancakes and recapped his research from the night before. As he talked, Adam made notes in the little pad he pulled from his breast pocket. When Rick finished his recap, Rick cut off a wedge of the pancakes and popped it in his mouth.

The warm and juicy blueberries added a sweet-tart burst of freshness and fruitiness to every bite. The berries provided a lovely contrast to the soft, sweet pancake batter. The drizzle of maple syrup Rick had added not only gave the pancakes a little extra moisture but also an extra layer of sweetness accented by a hint of caramel-like flavor.

"You look like you're in heaven," Adam said as he rested his chin on his knuckles.

Rick enjoyed the final burst of flavor, then said, "I am."

"Sorry to interrupt your little bit of food love, but we do need to keep on this. So Styles and his wife were considered a power couple?"

"I wouldn't put much stock in the tone of the piece, but the facts seemed solid. And if it's correct, this Penny Feeney could possibly be our mystery woman."

"Now you're sounding like the munchkin. Why, just because this woman broke up his marriage years ago, would you say she's our mystery woman?"

"Other than the fact that they had what sounds like a volatile relationship with plenty of ups and downs, I have nothing. But I can tell you this. I wrote stories about enough crooks for the paper to see a pattern in those types of relationships, especially when you're dealing with organized crime. They can last a very long time."

"Okay, but how's that prove anything about this Penny Feeney?"

"It doesn't. But, what will prove it one way or the other is what we're going to find out from the maids at the Seaside Cove Inn. As I was traipsing all over town yesterday, I stopped at Bound to Please. Arthur told me about a woman—a tourist—who wore lilac-scented perfume and bought a copy of *The Sun Also Rises*. We can ask Maggie and Bella if they've noticed either of those things in a guest's room. If they have, we have our mystery woman."

"Nice," Adam said with a smile. "I like it. So what are we waiting for?"

Rick stabbed another piece of his pancakes. "Me, to finish my breakfast."

"Not a problem." Adam picked up a fork, stabbed a large slice of pancakes before Rick could stop him, and moaned. "You're right. These bad boys came straight from heaven."

28

ALEX

I'M SITTING IN THE BACK corner of the classroom, twirling my pencil around my fingers 'cause after school Miss Redmond is going to 'accidentally' meet Barrington Rhymes at the market. Nothing can stop Operation Green Smoothie now!

I study the faded world map on the wall. Japan. It's like, halfway around the world. And Miss Redmond knew all about it when I talked to her this morning.

I got here super early just so I could ask her about Japan. When I asked her what she'd want to see most, she said it was the Cherry Blossom Festival. She says it happens during the school year. I think that would be a bummer because we'd lose her for a couple weeks. But…

Cherry blossoms. That would be super romantic. Maybe someday, I could go there. I can just picture me and my boyfriend walking along under the trees while they're all blooming and the air is filled with their scent.

Uh oh. At the front of the room, Miss Redmond is leaning against her desk. She's scanning us from behind her glasses. I nudge Sasha to get her attention. She's been doodling in her notebook, drawing a tree that's filled with cherry blossoms. Yeah, I totally told her what me and Miss Redmond talked about.

"Hey, Sash, that's awesome," I whisper.

Sasha smiles at me, then motions towards Miss Redmond with a flick of her eyes.

"Miss Redmond's cool. No worries," I whisper. "Operation Green Smoothie is a go."

Sasha raises her eyebrows. "Cool. You're sure?"

"Totally!"

Suddenly, Robbie turns around. His eyes meet mine. "Shhh. Alex, you're gonna get us in trouble!" It doesn't matter that Robbie's scolding me. I swear my heart skips a beat just looking in those dreamy blue eyes.

"No worries, Robbie. I've got it all under control."

Robbie rolls his eyes, clearly not buying it, then shrugs and turns around.

Sasha bursts into silent giggles beside me. "Smooth, Alex. Real smooth."

"Alex! Come talk to me for a minute." Miss Redmond's voice sounds kinda sharp. Like she's angry or something. She never gets angry. And once I set her up with Barrington, I'm totally gonna be her favorite student ever.

"Yes, ma'am."

Over in the corner, I hear Billy Thornton, "Ewww. Teacher's pet is in trouble."

I glare at Billy. I'd love to punch him in the nose. He's such a bully, but I bet he'd cry like a baby if somebody hit him. He makes me so mad I just wanna be the one to do it.

"Alex, what are you doing?" Miss Redmond asks.

I gulp and look at her. "Um. Nothing."

"You were supposed to be reading, and instead, you're talking to your friends. I'm disappointed in you. It seems that lately, you're not applying yourself."

"Yes, ma'am. I mean, no, ma'am." Uh oh. Maybe Billy's right. I might be in trouble.

Miss Redmond takes off her glasses and makes a face. After a long breath, she puts her glasses back on and looks straight at me. "I'm sorry, Alex, but if I let you do this, there will be others right behind you."

Oh no. No, no. She can't do this. "What about the cherry blossoms? What about Japan?" I stammer, "What about the market after work today?"

"Alex, I'm sorry. You're one of my best students, but I can't let you get away with talking and daydreaming in class." She stops and frowns at me. Her glasses inch up on her nose as it wrinkles. "What do you mean, the market?"

Uh oh. I am so dead. "I was gonna meet you at the market after school so you could show me some healthy options."

"I'm sorry if I mislead you, Alex, but I can't be having personal relationships with one of my students." She lets out a long, slow breath, like maybe it's torturing her to do it. "I'm giving you detention today. You'll be staying after with Mrs. Wallaby."

"Mrs. Wallaby?" OMG. She's like a hundred years old. And she smells. "Does it have to be her? Can't you keep me after? I promise I'll be good."

"Sorry, Alex, but I've got meetings all afternoon. Maybe you'll think twice if you're inclined to talk in class in the future. You may return to your seat now."

I'm in a total daze as I walk back to my desk. Everybody's looking at me. And Billy Thornton has a super big smirk on his face like he's better than me. He's had detention so many times that nobody even knows how many times it is.

I sit down and keep my attention focused on Miss Redmond. It's the only way I can keep myself from rushing across the room and punching Billy Thornton in the nose. Why not? I've already got detention. And Operation Green Smoothie just blew up. And my dad? Oh, my dad is gonna kill me. Right after he grounds me.

29

RICK

A FRAMED, CALLIGRAPHIC MAP OF Seaside Cove, a beautiful blend of art and cartography, hung on the wall of Rick's office. He could still recall the first time he'd seen it during his visit to meet his grandfather. At the time, he'd been ten and enthralled by the intricate artwork, the carefully crafted lines and delicate swirls that formed a mesmerizing pattern.

He hadn't caught the finer details, like the muted color palette, reminiscent of aged parchment and faded ink. Today, he treasured the map, its old-world charm, and the memories he had of the man he'd known only as Captain Jack.

The scent of leather and old books wafted in the air, creating an atmosphere of quiet contemplation. The map, one of those hidden-in-plain-sight-clues, had once held secrets that helped solve a murder. While Rick didn't expect to have the same kind of luck again, he was hopeful about their next step. In fact, he was positively upbeat. He looked across the room at Adam, who sat in front of Rick's desk.

Rick snickered as he said, "So you want me to call Mick McCormick and ask him what he didn't print in his articles about Styles and Mendez? And you think this will help us break the case?"

Adam's green eyes sparkled with determination. He tugged at his right ear, leaned back in his chair as though he'd been deep in thought, and said, "Yes. Exactly. You said you know the guy." He pulled out the small notepad from his pocket and gazed at Rick expectantly. "Ready?"

Rick sat at his desk and positioned a pen and a notepad with lined yellow paper in front of him. "Mick and I only worked together once when he came to New York to track down a lead for a story. I helped him out, so he owes me a favor. He's a good reporter, but he's also a no-nonsense guy."

Adam chuckled, running a hand through his blond hair. "Okay, fine. Don't beat around the bush. It's your call. Literally."

Rick couldn't help but feel a pang of nostalgia as he dialed the phone. His days as a reporter uncovering truths and chasing top awards seemed like a lifetime ago. In some ways, he missed the thrill, the chase. On the other hand, he was happy to exchange that for ice cream breaks at Scoops & Scones with Alex and Marquetta.

When Mick answered, Rick smiled at the memory of the gruff voice. "Pokerville Post."

"Hey, Mick, Rick Atwood. It's been a while."

"Well, well, R.J. Atwood. Last I heard, you gave up reporting to live in some fishing village on the West Coast. Seaside Cove or something like that?"

Rick chuckled. "Seaside Cove's not exactly a fishing village anymore. My grandfather left me his bed and breakfast. I'm now an innkeeper, divorced from Giselle, and remarried to the love of my life."

Mick's voice softened, and Rick could almost see his broad forehead furrow. "Good for you. Sounds like you're a lot happier than you were when we met. So, to what do I owe the honor?"

"I read the stories you wrote about Gideon Styles and Leslie Mendez."

"Wow. That's been years. Not exactly the caliber of stories you used to work on, but celebrity gossip helps pay the bills. What's going on with them?"

"Styles is dead," Rick said flatly.

Mick grunted. "Huh. Figures. Any idea who might have wanted to hasten his demise?"

"That's what we're trying to figure out."

"We?"

"My reporter background got me drafted as a consultant to the town's Chief of Police. I'm helping to solve Styles's murder. It's a long story, but I assist when there's a tough case. In fact, I'd like to put you on speaker right now."

"Wait, wait, wait. This old dog's having trouble keeping up. You? Consult with the police on murder cases?"

"That's right. Like I said, it's a long story."

"He's a big help," Adam chimed in, then gave Rick a thumbs-up.

After a long pause, Mick said, "And you've done this more than once?"

"Too many times. We seem to have more than our fair share of homicides," Rick said.

"Hmmpf. Imagine that." Mick chuckled, then said, "I can just see the slogan on the sign at the entrance to this little berg you're living in. Welcome to Seaside Cove, the little town where murder meets the sea."

Adam grimaced, then shot back, "It's not that bad."

"Really?" Mick scoffed.

"Okay, maybe it is," Rick confessed. "Can you help me out, Mick?"

"Can I write about this?"

Across the desk, Adam's shoulders slumped, and he whispered, "Sure. Why not?"

Rick passed along the message and followed up with the reason for his call. “I’ve read the stories, Mick, but what’s not in there? What didn’t you print? Let’s start with how a college professor got into the business of dealing in trade secrets.”

“It’s an interesting question. I never did find a defining event, but there was a pattern. Styles was a professor who had automatic authority by virtue of his position. He consulted periodically, especially with startups and inventors who were convinced they had the next big thing.”

Looking at the note he’d made, Rick thought he recognized a familiar methodology. “Are you saying he took advantage of his position?”

“I don’t think he did at first because he did help a few newbies transform their inventions into products they could take to market. But along the way, he realized there was a lot more money to be made by being the patent owner than by facilitating the process. Help someone get their patent; you get paid once. Own the patent, and you get paid over and over.”

“How much money are we talking about with these inventions?” Adam asked.

It took some time for Adam’s rationale to make sense, but from a law-enforcement perspective, Rick supposed it could be the difference between a minor offense and a felony. But from a practical standpoint, did it really matter? Rick didn’t think Styles was a man who would only break the law for large amounts of money. After all, the Secret Ingredient recipe wasn’t worth nearly enough to make him rich.

“Nothing on the order of the iPad or a self-driving car,” Mick said. “But the one that sticks out in my mind is a fitness tracker one of his clients invented a few years before those wrist doodads.”

“Apple Watch? Fitbit?” Rick asked.

"Yeah, those things. His client invented a sensor he could have sold to either of those companies, but Styles delayed his client's patent filing and then tried selling the invention to another company. Unfortunately for him, the company was also kind of shady and went bankrupt before they had a salable product. Styles cost his client, and himself, a ton of money because he got greedy."

"Was any of this ever proven in court?" Adam asked.

"You would have thought," Mick said. "But the inventor just disappeared into the woodwork, so to speak. Nobody knows exactly why. I tried talking to him, but he always refused to comment. I finally gave up because I figured he would never do anything about it."

"So Styles was nothing more than a crook?"

"In my opinion, he was an excellent conman. But I don't think he was as good as his girlfriend."

Rick shot a look across the table at Adam, who was writing furiously in his notepad. "Penny Feeney?" Rick asked.

"The one and only. They were on again, off again, but even when they weren't romantically involved, I think they might have worked together."

"Can you tell me more about her? Why didn't you include her in the story?"

"I couldn't prove anything, and my editor at the time wasn't willing to risk a libel suit." Mick laughed, the sound crackling through the receiver. "Of all the garbage he had me write, I was shocked when he drew the line on this one. What I can tell you is this. I always felt like Penny Feeney was going to be the death of Styles."

"What makes you say that?"

"Nothing concrete. But it was just a feeling. You know how it is. Sometimes, you have to follow your hunches."

"So you have nothing proving what you're saying about this woman?"

"Correct. But if you look at the number of times Feeney and Styles crossed paths, it only makes sense. Whether they're lovers or enemies, their paths keep crossing. I suppose that unless you can find something tying her to Styles's death, that's all it'll ever be—a hunch."

"It was the same thing with Leslie Mendez for a while from what I read in your articles."

Mick grunted a noncommital, "Maybe. But I think she was different. She truly was in love with Gideon. Penny Feeney, on the other hand—that wasn't love. It was more of an addiction. She wanted the fix, whether it was romantic or business. I'm not sure how much it mattered."

"I need to talk to Leslie Mendez, Mick. Our Chief of Police thinks she might be an ER nurse. Do you know if that's correct?"

"That's right. Contacting her at work is probably your best bet. I haven't been in touch with her in ages, but I could always call the hospital and leave a message. She'd get back to me when she had a break."

Adam began tapping his foot impatiently and checked his watch. "What hospital? The only number we had for her was Gold Country Realty. That's the number where I've been leaving messages."

"Her father runs that company and is very protective of his daughter. Especially after what she went through during the divorce. If you want to reach her, call the ER at Pokerville General. I'm sure she'll call you back."

30

RICK

SURROUNDED BY THE COMFORTING SMELL of leather and old books, his new acquisition of *The Old Man and the Sea* on his desk, Rick considered the irony as he repeated his name and phone number for the operator at Pokerville General. Their search for Leslie Mendez, instead of being done with online databases and searches, was coming down to good old-fashioned phone calls and humans passing along written phone messages.

As he disconnected the call, Rick's gaze flicked around the room. What had once been his grandfather's library was now his. And growing. For some reason, he'd recently decided to continue Captain Jack's legacy. It didn't hurt that he'd always had a fondness for Hemingway's writing. But until this minute, he hadn't really understood why the urge to build the library had come upon him.

"You know, Adam, I think I've figured something out."

"What's that? You've got another angle to find Styles's killer?"

"No. It has nothing to do with the case. I finally figured out why this urge came over me recently to add to Captain Jack's library."

Adam glanced around and frowned. "You mean your library."

"I still like to think of it as his. In any case, it's about engaging all the senses. A book like this…" He stopped, picked up the copy of Hemingway, and then laid it back down gently. "Something like that is tangible. You can see it, feel it, and even smell it. I think I'm hoping that Alex will someday develop the same sort of appreciation."

"To each his own," Adam said as he stood. "We should be getting over to the Inn."

"The woman I left that message with said Leslie might be going on her break any minute. Maybe I should try again before we go."

"Come on. The number you left was for your cell. That's the beauty of modern technology. You can take a phone call anywhere." Adam looked down at his notepad and then continued. "And since this sudden wave of nostalgia is washing over you and making you like the old way of doing things, we can canvass the Inn just like real gumshoes."

Rick pushed back in his chair, stretched, and stood, "You're a riot, Adam. Let's get moving."

Before they were out the door, Rick's cell rang. He checked the number, saw it was not a local call, and answered.

"Mr. Atwood, this is Leslie Mendez. You left a message that it was urgent I call you?"

The woman's voice held a tremor, betraying some sort of conflict. Rick wasn't sure whether it resulted from fear, suspicion, or something else. Was it possible she'd heard about her ex? "Thanks for calling me back so quickly, Leslie. And please, call me Rick. I'm sorry to be the one to tell you this, but your ex-husband, Gideon Styles, is deceased."

After a short stretch of silence, Leslie said, "Well, okay. How'd it happen?"

"There's no delicate way to say this, but, um, he was murdered."

"Hmmm. I'm not surprised. Given the life Gideon chose, it's no surprise something like this would happen to him." Leslie took a deep breath. "Why are you calling me? I haven't seen Gideon in over five years."

"Why do you say, given the life he chose?"

"Are you a detective or something? Why all these questions?"

"No, I'm not in law enforcement, but I am doing some work for the local police department. I'd like to put you on speaker with Chief Adam Cunningham of the Seaside Cove Police. Is that okay?"

"I guess."

When Adam was on the line, they exchanged greetings, and Rick asked his question again.

"Let's put all the delicacy aside, okay? Gideon was a thief. He stole people's work and tried to make money off the intellectual property he stole. Chief Cunningham, it wouldn't surprise me if Gideon was in your town to work one of his scams."

"You are correct, Ms. Mendez. There is a local man who was trying to make a deal with your ex-husband."

"Of course, it's classic Gideon. He loved going where the money was. He was also a gambler. His weekly poker games were part of what broke up our marriage. I'd come home from working a long day to find my house filled with smoke and smelling of beer. I hated everything about those games except the money."

"He won a lot?" Rick asked.

"Gideon never lost."

"Never? Are you saying that he cheated?"

Leslie stifled a laugh, then said, "Do you have any suspects in his murder?"

Adam's jaw tightened, and Rick knew he didn't want to release details of the investigation, but sometimes, you just had to prime the pump.

"There's a woman in town, dark hair, maybe a little above average height, with an athletic build. We believe she may have been here with your husband."

"Penny Feeney. Right? She was his girlfriend, on and off, during our marriage. I'd bet anything that's her."

"What makes you so sure?" Rick asked.

"Is she a suspect? Did she kill Gideon?" Leslie insisted, her voice trembling.

Adam, clearly unhappy with the way the conversation was going, shook his head and interrupted, "At this point in the investigation, we can't comment on any suspects or persons of interest."

"Leslie, in your opinion, would Penny have had a motive to kill your ex?"

"Gideon had a hold on her. She'd do anything for him. But sometimes, people reach a breaking point. I did."

"That's why you divorced Gideon? Because you reached yours?"

"Yes."

"What kind of hold did he have on Ms. Feeney? He wasn't blackmailing her, was he?" Adam asked.

"I suppose you could call it emotional blackmail. Gideon had this way of doing things. He'd ask nicely, and if you refused, maybe because what he wanted you to do was wrong, he'd apply more pressure. In the beginning, all he had to do with me was become very insistent. But as I got wise to his tactics, he started using little threats—I'll tell people you did this, or how much you like that."

How many times had Rick seen it in New York? A professional manipulator could find and then use your little secrets against you. "Did you get to the point where you became immune to the pressure?"

"Not so much immune as tired of it. I got fed up with the threats and his attempts to make me feel guilty when I wasn't even the one in the wrong. I finally recognized him for what he was. Who knows? Maybe Penny got fed up and decided to kill him."

"Then you think Penny had some secrets Gideon knew about and was willing to divulge?"

"Of course."

"Do you know what they were?"

"No. Sorry. Gideon was really good about hiding his private business."

Adam shifted in his chair, and Rick knew he was getting impatient with this conversation because it could easily turn into an emotional dump for Leslie. Rick held up a finger for Adam to be patient. He only needed another minute or two, and then they could continue their search at the Inn.

"Leslie, I only have a couple more questions for you. When was the last time you spoke to Gideon?"

"The last time I saw him was at the divorce proceeding. I guess you could say we spoke. He tried to butter me up by telling me that he'd learned his lesson and was done with Penny once and for all."

"And you didn't believe him?"

"Not for a second. I'd heard it too many times before to fall for it."

"I think I only have one more question. Do you know what kind of perfume she wears?"

Leslie snorted, then laughed. "Yeah, I know. I smelled it too many times in his shirts. Lilacs. She loves lilacs."

Across the table, Adam sat up straight and mimed applause. Rick gave him a thumbs-up. Now, they knew exactly who they were looking for. Rick thanked Leslie for her time. He closed by asking her to telephone or message him if she thought of anything else.

After letting Marquetta know he and Adam were leaving, they drove to the Seaside Cove Inn. On the way, they agreed that Rick would find Maggie and Bella while Adam pressed Ray to check his register to see if he'd rented a room to Penny Feeney.

Rick strolled through the Inn's lush garden surrounding the pool. Who would have thought such a picture-perfect oasis would be home to so much trouble? He stopped to scan the walkways and spotted the second-floor maid's cart. The first-floor cart was outside a room to his right. Though he really wanted to talk to the two women together, he didn't have time to round them both up.

Taking a side path, Rick wove through the garden to the first-floor cart. As he approached, Maggie Sullivan came through the open doorway and dumped a load of wet towels into a hamper.

"Hey, Rick." Despite the heavy load, Maggie's posture was perfectly erect. "What can I do for you? More questions?"

"I was actually hoping to get a few minutes with you and Bella together."

"Sure. Why not. I was about to take some extra towels up to her, anyway. Let me grab them, and let's go."

Rick offered to carry the towels, but Maggie refused, reminding him that she'd been doing this for many years and was no stranger to hard work.

When they reached Bella's cart, Maggie placed the towels on the shelf and then told Bella what she'd done: "Rick Atwood's back. He wants to talk to both of us."

Bella exited the open doorway and gave Rick an infectious smile. "What can we do for you?"

"Well, ladies, I'm trying to piece together something, and I need your help. We have some additional information about our mystery woman. It appears that she likes lilac-scented perfume, and she has a penchant for old books. Have either of you been in a room where you've seen either of those things?"

Bella's brows furrowed in thought, but then she seemed to recall something. "Yes, there is a lady who's staying in Room 207. That perfume is so strong that it lingers even when she's out."

"Excellent! Did you see an old novel in any of the rooms recently?"

Bella's eyes darted from side to side as she thought. "I think so. In the same room, actually. But I can't remember the title."

Footsteps on the second-floor walkway caught Rick's attention. Maggie and Bella perked up like a pair of birds on a wire, and Rick turned to see who was coming.

Adam flashed Rick a thumbs-up. "I got Feeney's room number."

"Me, too. Room 207." Rick said, then raised an eyebrow. "Ray was helpful for once?"

"Don't get used to it," Adam said resignedly. "I think he's having an off day."

"He's been having a lot of those lately," Maggie snickered.

Rick had no desire to know what Maggie meant, but he definitely wanted to see if their mystery woman was in her room.

31

RICK

MAGGIE AND BELLA BOTH SAID, "Chief Cunningham," in unison, and Rick was struck by the contrast between them. Maggie stood about six inches taller than Bella. And where Bella's hair was black and wavy, Maggie's had faded with the years to a soft auburn. And yet, despite their physical differences, they'd parroted their greeting with almost perfect timing.

"Bella, Maggie, nice to see you both again." Adam tipped his hat to the women and then turned to Rick. "I've got a problem. Some tourist wasn't paying attention to where he was driving and didn't see my deputy while she was directing traffic."

Gone was Bella's infectious smile, replaced instead by a look of horror. She croaked, "Is Amy okay?"

Rick noted Bella's familiarity and concern. It didn't surprise him that in a small town like Seaside Cove, the two would have crossed paths. Apparently, though, those paths had done more than just cross.

"She says she is, but to be safe, I'm required to take her to San Ladron and have her checked out at the hospital."

Rick's brows knitted together, and he shook his head in confusion. "How do you miss a cop in the middle of the street?"

"The wife was busy pointing out all the different colors on the buildings on Main Street, and her husband was just as entertained—until he heard a thud. Guy was completely oblivious until he looked in his rearview mirror. Now, of course, he's contrite as can be. The whole thing happened right near Scoops & Scones, so the mayor rushed out and took control of the situation. Traffic is snarled now. The mayor insists we get my deputy checked out, so I'll be playing chauffeur and waiting around the hospital for the next few hours. Can you handle this?"

Handle this? Which now involved dealing with a potential killer in a motel room? "Sure. Why not? I've been in this situation before. I don't relish the thought of dealing with this woman alone, but Amy is a good friend. And she's a good police officer. Yeah, I got it."

"Thanks, buddy. I owe you. Again."

As Adam walked away, Maggie whispered, "He owes you a lot, doesn't he?"

Rick snickered. "He does, but maybe it all balances out in the end."

Bella rolled her eyes. "Sounds like quite the bromance. Rick, I was headed to Room 207 if you want to check it out. We can go there right now. I don't think anyone would complain if you were to walk into a room while I'm cleaning."

"Don't look at me," Maggie said. "I've got no complaints. In fact, why don't I go keep Ray busy while you check this out?"

Rick flashed a grateful smile. "That would be wonderful." He turned to Bella and gestured for her to lead the way. "Let's get this done."

When Bella reached the door, she knocked and announced herself. After a few tense seconds with no answer, she knocked again. When there was still no reply, she opened the door and peeked inside. "Housekeeping!"

She pushed the door open and let Rick follow her inside. There were fresh towels in the bathroom and a half-eaten sandwich on the bedside table. Bella stood in the middle of the room and took a final look around. "I guess we just missed her."

"That's good news as far as I'm concerned," Rick said. "I'll make this quick."

He went to the nightstand on the left side of the bed and noted nothing on it. The drawer was also empty. The other nightstand was a completely different story. There, he found the book Arthur had told him about.

"This must be her," Rick said absently. He turned to tell Bella he'd be leaving but stopped when she held up a bottle of perfume.

"Lilac. This has to be the woman you're looking for. Right?"

"Put that back. I'm going to leave and—"

Rick stopped at the sound of his phone ringing. He checked the display and wondered why Alex's teacher would be calling him. Across the room, Bella had already put the bottle back and was going about her normal duties. He gave her a wave goodbye and answered on his way out the door.

"Hello, this is Rick."

"Mr. Atwood. This is Francesca Redmond. I'm calling to discuss Alex's recent behavior. Unfortunately, I had to give her detention today."

Alex? Detention? Rick stopped to take that in. "What happened?"

"Alex was being disruptive in class. I believe it's important for us to have a conversation, teacher to parent, to address this matter."

"Sure. Thank you for letting me know. I'm sorry, Miss Redmond. This has never happened before. Is this something we can talk about now? Or do you need me to come in?"

"I think you should come in."

"When?"

"Can you be here at three p.m.?"

Based on the tone of Miss Redmond's voice, it didn't sound much like a question. "Sure. I can be there." Murder investigation or not, Alex was always his first priority. Alex had tried his patience in so many ways, but never had she done anything disruptive in school.

He walked almost in a daze, still trying to process the news. Alex was having problems in school? Now, he had a real dilemma. In just over two hours, he'd have to meet Miss Redmond. He'd also promised Adam that he'd keep looking for Penny Feeney.

So what did he do now? There was nothing he could do until three. That meant he should stay focused on the investigation. For a second, he thought about sitting at a table in the pool area. Nothing conspicuous about that other than the fact that he was fully dressed and he'd be the only one there.

He did an about-face and returned to the open doorway just as Bella was closing up.

Bella's eyebrows rose, and her dark brown eyes watched him closely. "Did you need to get back in?"

"No, but is there someplace where I can watch the room without being seen?"

"Oh, for sure. Go down to the laundry room on the first floor." She went to the railing and pointed to a spot across the courtyard. "You see? It's kind of hidden behind some of the bushes, so you should be able to see the room from there. Nobody will notice you."

"Thanks, Bella. I appreciate it."

Rick went down the stairs and followed the path to what he hoped would be his hidden surveillance spot. He quickly realized that if he stayed just inside the doorway, he was hidden behind the bushes and could still clearly see the second-floor walkway. From here, he could watch for Penny Feeney to return and would never be spotted.

While he waited, he dialed Marquetta.

“Well, what a nice surprise,” she chirped. “I’m hearing from my husband in the middle of the day. Don’t tell me you’ve solved the case already.”

“No such luck. I’m actually calling because I got a call from Miss Redmond.”

“Frankie? Why?” Marquetta sucked in a breath, and her tone quickly escalated to what sounded like panic. “Did something happen to Alex? Is she okay?”

“She’s fine. But, the thing is, Miss Redmond says she gave Alex detention because she was being disruptive. Do you have any idea what she might be going through? Do you think it’s her relationship with Veronica?”

“I don’t know, Rick. I’m not so sure it’s Veronica. Lately, Alex has been concerned about Frankie. She wants to get her married. Alex might be trying to play matchmaker again.”

Rick groaned, the thought of Alex staging another of her operations causing a lump to form in his stomach. “Are you sure?”

“She hasn’t given me all the details. But she was asking some pointed questions. Do you want me to talk to her tonight?”

“Actually, I might want to do that on the way home from school. I have a feeling I’ll be asked to take her home.”

Marquetta chuckled. “You think Frankie’s going to release her into your custody?”

Rick felt another groan coming on. “Just what I need. A jailbird daughter.”

“I guess we’ll find out. Won’t we?”

“Yeah. We will. But right now, I have to get back to my surveillance.” He told her about the accident with Amy Kama and how Adam had asked him to see if he could find Penny Feeney.

”Adam really needs another deputy in addition to Amy,” Marquetta said.

"I know. But we all know the mayor won't let that happen as long as she's got me as a freebie."

"You know Francine, Rick. She can be a tightwad when she wants to be."

"Hey, I have to go. I might have just spotted our mystery woman."

"Be careful. Don't take any chances with her."

"I know," he said absently as he watched a woman climb the stairs to the second floor. She was attractive with cascading dark hair. There was a deceptive innocence about her. She was petite, yet she held a commanding presence. At the door to Room 207, she stopped and twirled a lock of hair as she surveyed the courtyard. Rick felt a sudden chill. Did that friendly smile of hers mask a life of crime and constant vigilance? He was about to find out.

He stepped through the open doorway and walked toward the stairs to the second floor.

32

RICK

RICK KNOCKED ON THE DOOR to Room 207, still unsure of what he would say when the door opened. But that didn't happen. Instead, the drapes in the window next to it swished apart, and the dark-haired woman he'd spied from the laundry room peered out at him.

He smiled inwardly, recalling how Ethel Maynard had done the same thing. Age, in this case, didn't matter. Cautious people were cautious. Something else he now knew about Penny Feeney. Since he didn't have a badge or an officer standing next to him to make this official, subterfuge felt like the only option. He'd have to fall back on his old reporter's skills of weaving stories to put subjects at ease.

The woman behind the window eyed him carefully, then spoke in a stern voice muffled slightly by the single-pane window. "Who are you?"

"Rick Atwood. Arthur at Bound to Please told me about you. I'd like to talk to you about buying the copy of *The Sun Also Rises* you purchased from him."

"I'm not interested in selling," she snapped, then slapped the drapes closed.

Rick knocked again, this time, more forcefully.

When she jerked open the door, she glared at him. "I said I'm not interested."

Keeping his voice low and reassuring, he did his best to look slightly sheepish. "I'm sorry to bother you, but we share similar tastes in literature, and I'd had my eye on the book. I should have bought it when I had the chance, but I dawdled around."

Penny Feeney was a contradiction, a mixture of strength and vulnerability. Her eyes were sharp, her posture defensive, but Rick picked up an undercurrent of fear. Standing opposite her, Rick averted his gaze from hers to avoid seeming too confident and focused on the threadbare carpet.

Though there was a hint of amusement in her voice, her arms remained crossed, and her body language, still closed off. "What do you expect to accomplish by coming to my motel room door and giving me a line like that?"

The sound of Rick's chuckle echoed in the small room. "I like to keep people on their toes."

She looked over her shoulder. Her gaze flicked past the dull and faded paint on the walls and seemed drawn to the book now lying on the scruffy bedspread. Despite their surroundings, there was a hint of curiosity in her expression.

"Well," he continued, "if you're not interested in selling it, I guess I'll just have to come clean."

Immediately, Penny was on guard. She stood straighter and scrutinized him. "Come clean about what?"

Taking a deep breath, Rick prepared to drop the bombshell. "I'm a reporter working for the San Ladron Times. I'm working on a story about the death of Gideon Styles."

Penny blinked, but then her eyes widened with shock. It took Rick by surprise when she laughed. It was a harsh, bitter sound. "You're joking, right? This is some kind of sick joke?"

Rick shook his head. He wasn't sure how much he should reveal, but his instincts told him to play dumb. Let her be the one to create the narrative, then blow holes in it later. "I'm afraid it's not a joke. Were you having an affair with Gideon Styles?"

Penny's laughter died in her throat. She stared at Rick, her eyes hard. "You're telling me you came here, pretended to be interested in some book I bought, so you could dig up dirt on me and Gideon?"

Excellent, Rick thought. She'd bought the lie. Rick pretended to wince. "It's not like that, Penny—"

"But it is, isn't it?" Penny interrupted, her voice rising. "You're like all the rest. You don't care about the truth. All you want is a juicy story."

"That's not exactly what I'm looking for. I told you, I'm working on a story about Gideon's murder."

"And you think I had something to do with it? Well, you're wrong. I didn't kill him."

"I know that," Rick lied. Good. They were past the 'who are you' stage, and she was fully invested in proving her innocence—whether she was or not. "All I want is the truth. That's why I'm here."

Penny watched him suspiciously, her brows furrowed. Finally, she ran a hand through her hair as though she were preparing to flirt her way out of this conversation.

Rick cut her off by stepping forward, which forced her to step back into the room. He kept his gaze steady. "How did you know Gideon Styles?"

"I didn't. Not really."

The blatant lie stopped Rick. Now what? He was obviously not going to get the truth out of this woman. He watched as she flicked a cascade of dark hair back over her shoulder. Rick cataloged the move as one of her possible tells. Hoping he had a way to tell if Penny was lying, he chose to play this subterfuge all the way through. "Multiple witnesses will put you in Gideon Styles's room."

"Fine!" She shook her head. "So I went into his room. Big deal. He propositioned me."

"Gideon Styles propositioned you?"

"What? You think I'm not attractive enough to have men want me?"

It was nearly impossible to miss the hard edge in her voice, and Rick's first thought was, vanity, oh vanity. He made a show of letting his eyes roam over her body. When he'd finished his overt assessment, he noted that she didn't blush. "Actually, I was thinking exactly the opposite."

A sly smile formed at the corner of her mouth, and she fingered her chin as she held his gaze. "That's right, he did. And I thought, why not? A little fun never hurt anyone."

Her direct attempt at flirtation caught Rick off guard, and, once again, he realized he'd underestimated Penny Feeney. He needed to ramp up his game if he was going to survive this round. "I see that you're wearing an engagement ring. What about your fiancé?" Rick pressed, crossing his arms over his chest. "He was okay with this?"

Penny laughed, a hollow sound that echoed around the room. "My fiancé is a stick-in-the-mud. Always working. Never has time for me. He was supposed to come on this trip, but work took precedence. As always."

"That doesn't sound like someone who'd be okay with his fiancée having a fling."

Penny's smile faded, and her gaze drifted away from Rick's. "He's not just a stick-in-the-mud. He's jealous, too. Overbearing. He's stalked me before. I've been scared, really scared. I filed charges against him once."

Rick watched her closely, noting how her hands shook slightly as she spoke. Oh, he thought, she was good. Very good. This woman was a master of charm and persuasion. “And yet you’re still planning to marry him?”

“I don’t know,” Penny admitted, her voice barely above a whisper. “We're taking a break.”

“Then why are you still wearing an engagement ring?”

“It keeps the riff-raff away,” she snapped. “Why do you care?”

Choosing to deflect rather than answer her question, Rick changed subjects. “Tell me more about Gideon. What did you know about him?”

Penny hesitated, her gaze flicking up to meet Rick’s. “What do you mean?”

“Like, what did he do for a living? Where was he from?” Rick asked, watching her reaction closely.

Penny faltered, then her eyes locked onto his, and the slight smile returned. “I don’t know. We didn’t have much time to talk.”

A rush of adrenaline coursed through Rick’s veins. His heart beat faster, his senses sharpened, and he now had a crystal clear picture of Penny Feeney. The momentary flush was as if he’d stepped into the eye of a storm, where everything around him moved in slow motion, yet he remained in control. It was time to exert some pressure and change the game slightly.

“If you and Gideon were having this impetuous affair, why weren’t you seen in public together?”

Penny laughed, a genuine, surprised laugh that lifted the tension and gave Rick a glimpse of the woman beneath the defenses. But then her laughter died away, and she was once again the guarded professional.

“Are you kidding? I couldn’t be seen with him. If word got back to my fiancé, he’d come after me.” She looked away, her hands clenching tight. “I had to be careful.”

"I see," Rick said. The truth was probably that it wasn't her fiancé who would come after her, but the police once they connected Styles to the break-in. He reached out to touch her shoulder. "Is your fiancé abusive?"

Penny recoiled, but her surprise was short-lived and quickly replaced by a determined look on her face. "Yes," she said firmly. "But I don't see what that has to do with anything."

"What's your fiance's name?" he asked, wondering if it might actually be Gideon Styles.

She barked out another laugh, then said, "No comment. I am not giving you that information."

"No problem. I can find it. I just thought you might want to save me some time. From what I understand, the police have a few suspects. At the top of the list is a man by the name of Tyler Winkle. Do you know him?"

Penny's eyes widened. It was only the second time during this conversation he'd been able to surprise her, but dropping Tyler's name had gotten a reaction. A big one.

"Well?" Rick pressed.

"No comment. This interview's over."

She reached up to grab the edge of the door as if she were going to slam it in Rick's face. He pressed his hand against the room number on the door.

"I'll go, for now. But this isn't over. I have plenty more questions." The door slammed as Rick walked away. He smiled to himself, confident that he'd gotten to Penny Feeney. The question was, if she'd killed Gideon, why was she still in town?

33

ALEX

I'M SITTING AT A DESK in the front row of Mrs. Wallaby's classroom. I wanted to hide out in the back, but she made me sit where she could keep an eye on me. Not that she's actually watching, she's actually half asleep. Ever since she told me my dad was coming to pick me up, I've had a sinking feeling in the pit of my stomach. He's gonna be totally unhappy with me. While Mrs. Wallaby kinda drifts off again, all I can do is sit here, pretend to work on my homework, and wait.

When my dad comes into the classroom, his face is totally serious. Mrs. Wallaby jolts awake when she hears him, looks at the clock, then tells him he can take me home.

"Hey, Daddy." It's super hard not to sound like I'm all bummed out. Especially when I am.

"Alex," he says. "I spoke to Miss Redmond. We need to talk."

Oh, man. He's super disappointed in me, and that makes me feel even worse.

"I can explain," I blurt out, but I sound like one of those crooks on the witness stand in the old movies. I'm guilty, and we both know it.

He raises a hand, cutting me off. "Not here, kiddo. Let's go home." He doesn't say a word on the ride back to the B&B. In fact, he hasn't said a word since he bailed me out of detention jail.

When he turns off the engine, I say, "Daddy, I'm super sorry I disappointed you."

All he says is, “Your mom and I would like to talk to you together. She’ll meet us in the kitchen.”

I lead the way, and when I see my mom, my heart breaks again. I never wanna disappoint Mom, and yet—I can see it on her face.

“Sit down, Alex,” my dad says.

He takes the stool across from mine and drums his fingers on the tabletop.

“Alex, I have to say that I was surprised when Miss Redmond called me.” He stops, takes a breath, then continues, “When I spoke to her at the school, she said you’ve been disruptive in class.”

I open my mouth to protest, but he holds up a hand. “She also said you’ve been asking her some personal questions. About whether she’s single.”

My face heats up, and I drop my gaze to the table. “I was just trying to help,” I mumble.

Mom leans forward and looks at me. “Sweetie, what did I tell you about playing matchmaker?”

“That it wasn’t a good idea.”

“Right.” She reaches out, puts her hand under my chin, and lifts it until I’m looking her in the eye. “I know how much you like Miss Redmond. But you need to focus on your schoolwork, not other people’s love lives.”

“And certainly not be disruptive in class,” my dad adds. “Which brings me to the big question. Kiddo, are you having trouble adjusting to the new baby? Are all the responsibilities of being a big sister getting to be too much?”

What? What’s Baby Jack got to do with…oh, they think I’ve gone mental.

Mom drops her hand to mine and squeezes. “Sweetie, if you need to talk because things are getting to be more than you can handle…”

All of a sudden, my face is hot, and I can feel the tears streaming down my cheeks. “I can’t believe you guys think I’ve gone crazy! No! It’s not Baby Jack. I was just—I thought that Miss Redmond and Mr. Rhymes would make such a perfect couple. They like so many of the same things.”

My dad looks totally lost. He looks at Mom, then at me. “What does our guest have to do with this?”

“Rick, I didn’t tell you because I talked to Alex and thought we’d worked it out.”

“Alex, you got lucky with me and Marquetta. I understand why you were trying to get us together.”

“What your dad’s trying to say, Sweetie, is that you had a personal stake in us forming a relationship. You’re not related to Miss Redmond. What you’re doing there is called meddling. And most people don’t appreciate other people meddling in their lives. Do you understand?”

“I messed up.” I hang my head, and a tear dribbles down my nose. Just before it drips off, I wipe it away. Now, Miss Redmond will never get together with Barrington Rhymes. And they’ll never see the cherry blossoms together or get to do anything else. I feel awful ‘cause I might have ruined everything. “I’m sorry. It won’t happen again.”

But if I’m the one who made the mess, I should fix it. Right?

My dad gets that look on his face he gets when he’s trying to make a hard decision. “Alex, I also want to talk to you about Veronica. From the beginning, I haven’t been comfortable with you having a friend who’s so much older. I’ll be talking to Adam about his request to have you spy on her and Tyler. Especially because I think he’s barking up the wrong tree.”

“You’re grounding me?” My jaw drops open. This is so not fair. “But Daddy!”

"No, Alex. I'm not grounding you. I just don't want you around Veronica anymore. I'm convinced that having you around her is part of the problem."

"Rick. We should talk about this."

My dad shakes his head. "No, Marquetta. I have to put my foot down. Alex is my daughter, and I have to put a stop to this."

"She's my daughter, too!" Mom explodes.

Whoa. Mom's face is super red, and she's got a fire in her eyes that says my dad struck a nerve. I've never seen her lose her cool before, and it's obvious she's totally not backing down on this.

My dad's face softens, and he reaches across the table to take her hand. "I'm sorry. That came out wrong. Of course, she's your daughter. What I should have said was that we have another suspect, and it's neither Tyler Winkle nor Veronica. There's little to be gained because Tyler has lost all memory of the day when Veronica fell in the planter."

Oh, wow. Nobody told me about the memory thing. Or another suspect. "He doesn't remember anything about the murder?"

Uh oh. I didn't even realize I said that. And now I'm the center of attention. Oh. So. Awkward.

After what feels like forever, my dad says, "The doctor believes some sort of stress or trauma caused Tyler to forget those twenty-four hours. Nevertheless, I don't think either of them committed murder. I also don't think there's much to be gained by trying to get information from them. That's why I'm worried about you being around Veronica. I see way too much downside to having you influenced by a seventeen-year-old."

Mom squeezes my dad's hand and takes a deep breath before she speaks. Her voice trembles slightly. "We need to protect Alex, whatever it takes."

I swallow hard. This is, like, huge. But I can see a way now to fix everything. Operation Epic Recovery is on!

34

RICK

AFTER CLOSING HIS OFFICE DOOR behind him and sitting at his desk, Rick planted his elbows on the desktop, rested his chin on his palms, and gazed around the room. He wanted to be done with Penny Feeney and her lies and leave the rest up to Adam. On the other hand, he didn't want to let her disappear before Adam could get to the Seaside Cove Inn. His next step depended on how long it would take Adam to get back to town. He placed the call and crossed his fingers as he asked the question.

Adam's sigh was loud enough to come through the background road noise. "Deputy Kama and I are just coming into Seaside Cove. She's doing fine, but the doc wants her to take it easy for twenty-four hours. This is definitely not good timing, but I have no choice. She has to take time off."

In the background, Rick heard Amy protest, but he knew Adam would remain unmovable. "Adam? Did the doc restrict her completely, or can she work in the office? Would that work?"

"I asked the same question, and he said no. He wants her to avoid reading and computer work. He also wants her to rest. Unfortunately, I don't see any way around this. I'll be dropping her off at her place in about fifteen minutes. Did you need me for something?"

Rick relayed what had happened with Penny Feeney. When he finished, he said, "Do you think you can make her stay in town?"

"I can warn her not to leave. But if she wants to disappear, you know how easy it would be. There's not much we can do to stop her. I think the best thing we can do is to investigate her background. If she has been involved in anything illegal or suspicious, that might give us some leverage. Maybe even a way to hold her. I know it's not ideal, but at least it gives us an angle of attack."

Adam was right. It was frustrating, but it was the truth. If Penny Feeney wanted to vanish, she could do it without much effort. So, what should he do next?

"She hasn't left town yet," Rick said. "That must mean she's staying in town for a reason. That might give me time to find this supposed fiancé of hers. I'm not sure what to make of that. Maybe I'll get some straight answers from him."

Adam agreed that getting the truth about her relationship and having a complete background were essential next steps.

"There's something else we need to talk about—Alex. She got in trouble at school today." After Rick explained the situation and reiterated his concerns, Adam agreed that it was best for him to tell Alex he no longer wanted her to be checking out Veronica.

"You were right from the beginning. Involving the munchkin was a mistake. I'll talk to her right after I go to the Inn. It was Room 207, wasn't it?"

After confirming the room number, Rick disconnected the call. He breathed in the quiet and looked around. This office was his spot to think, plan, and leave behind the stresses of the day. He hoped at least one of those problems, Alex being involved with Veronica Campbell, might soon be resolved. But in truth, he wasn't sure the problem would go away so easily. Based on the way Alex's face had lit up when she'd been asked to help, he was willing to bet he'd be dealing with the Veronica subject again.

As ready as he was to dig deeper into Penny Feeney's past, he also recalled Leslie Mendez's comment about Gideon having a hold on Penny. Was she right? Would Penny do anything for Styles? And if they were that close, would she show up as one of his friends on social media?

He brought up Gideon Styles's profile. Styles had nearly a thousand friends. And as Rick scanned the list of recent posts, extensive as it was, he saw a familiar pattern. Most of Gideon's so-called friends had never met him in person. But then, he found what he was looking for—a picture of Styles and Penny Feeney. They were arm-in-arm, posing for a selfie at what appeared to be some sort of party. The date on the post was the week before Styles had arrived in Seaside Cove.

Scanning the comments on the post, he found that not only had Penny liked the photo, but she'd commented on how good it was to be back together with Gideon. Rick printed a screenshot to capture the information, then followed the link to Penny Feeney's profile.

This time, he took a different path. He began with Penny's photos. By looking through those, he finally came to a group of photos of her and a man named Tom Reynolds. In one, they were kissing. In another, she was showing off a ring while he stood behind her. Perfect. He'd found the ex.

It took only a few seconds to come up with a phone number for Reynolds. The man was a consultant with a prestigious firm and had his business card posted on his profile. Reaching for his phone, Rick muttered, "Thanks for making it easy."

Tom Reynolds answered on the second ring in a deep voice with only his name. Rick paired the voice with the man's photo—crewcut, dark suit, and determined hazel eyes—and immediately categorized him as a natural-born leader. Someone used to making decisions quickly. He was also probably ambitious, driven, and competitive. Of all the people Rick had interviewed over the years, he'd come to realize his first impressions were most often correct. But if the man answered his questions, did any of that really matter? Rick followed his instincts and cut right to the chase.

"Tom, my name is Rick Atwood. I'm a consultant working for the Seaside Cove Police. I need some information about Penny Feeney."

There was silence on the other end. Rick could almost picture the man's surprised expression. "What did she do now?"

"You are her fiancé, is that correct?"

"No. That's been over for years. What is she doing, telling you we're still together?"

"She said you're taking a break, but she's still wearing a ring."

"Sounds like her. That ring cost me three grand. She refused to give it back, but I don't care. It's good to be rid of her. That woman is toxic."

"She also said that after your breakup, you were stalking her."

"Are you investigating her for something?"

"Possibly. Were you? Stalking her?"

"No. Never. You can check the court records. I had to get a restraining order against her to stop her and that no-good boyfriend of hers from harassing me."

"Are you referring to Gideon Styles?"

"Oh. You're familiar with him, too? Yeah, he's a piece of work."

Rick scribbled down notes, doing his best to record everything Reynolds said. "It appears they were here together in Seaside Cove. Do you know why they would have come here?"

Reynolds snorted, then laughed. "Mr. Atwood, I can tell you one thing. It wouldn't be because they were on vacation. I have no idea why they were there, but I wouldn't be surprised if they're up to no good. I just hope they don't cause too much trouble for you."

"Certainly, Gideon Styles won't. He's dead."

There was another long pause, then Reynolds responded. “Did Penny have something to do with it?”

“I can’t comment. I’m only trying to get some information.”

“I see. You got some. So, unless there’s something else, that’s all I know. Good luck with your investigation.”

Rick grimaced. Unfortunately, his instincts had been correct. Reynolds would only talk on his terms. So be it. Rick needed this man’s cooperation because he felt certain Reynolds knew something else.

“Alright. Just between you and me, she’s a person of interest in Styles’s murder. How would you characterize her relationship with Styles?”

“How would I characterize it? Fire and ice, Mr. Atwood. When I met Penny, she hated Gideon. He’d dumped her, and she was crushed. It took a few months to pick up the pieces, but gradually, it looked like she was getting over him. It was only about two months after I proposed that I noticed things starting to change. Penny was disappearing. She’d go out late at night, and she refused to tell me where she was. She wasn’t the same woman I had fallen in love with.”

“Do you think she was spending time with Styles again?”

“I know she was. I saw pictures of them together more than once. And then, the next thing I know, she was breaking off our engagement.” Reynolds paused for a few seconds before continuing. “I couldn’t believe it. Penny was…she was in love with him. In a way that nobody else seems to understand. It was like they couldn’t stay away from each other. Two moths drawn to the same flame.”

“Meaning?”

“Meaning they both loved the thrill, the rush of adrenaline, they got from living on the edge. It was a dangerous flame, and I wanted nothing to do with it.”

"Why did you have to get a restraining order against her? You said she was harassing you?"

"After the break-up, Penny began to follow me around. She would show up at my house in the middle of the night or call and hang up when I answered. When a valuable painting disappeared from my living room, I knew she had to have stolen it. I got a restraining order to keep her away, but I could never prove she stole the painting."

Rick sat back in his chair and considered the possibilities. "So you're saying she's an adrenaline junkie?"

"Yeah. I would call her that. Penny would do anything for a thrill. I'm telling you, man. Anything. And if Styles is dead, I wouldn't put it past her."

35

ALEX

SEPTEMBER 13

Hey Journal,

I got into a lot of trouble today. My dad had to pick me up at school and bring me home. I got chewed out for being disruptive in class. Okay, so I did kinda go too far, but I thought me and Miss Redmond were getting to be friends. I guess if she let me get away with stuff, she'd have to let all the other kids do it, too. Even Billy Thornton. Ugh. That makes me wanna throw up. Anyway, I've got a plan to fix everything.

I can still get Miss Redmond together with Barrington, I just need to keep it on the down low. I also wanna figure out what Veronica's up to. She's been so secretive lately about this boyfriend of hers. Even though Mom thinks its Isabelle's nephew, she's not a hundred precent on it. If I get lucky, maybe they're down at the harbor now.

I'm gonna have to be super sneaky to try to get to the bottom of things without anyone else knowing. It all begins with confirming whether Mom is correct about Quincy Knox being Veronica's boyfriend. Operation Epic Recovery is on!

xoxo,

Alex

—Hey Veronica, have you got time to talk?

—No. I'm busy.

—Are you at the harbor?

The answer that I don't get is all I need. That's totally where she is. She's got to be with her supposed boyfriend. It's time to do a little spying! All I have to do now is get the green light to leave the house.

When I walk past my dad's office, I can hear his voice. It's muffled, and I can't hear the words. That means Mom is probably in the kitchen alone. I go downstairs to find her. She's sitting at the island and has one eye on Baby Jack and the other on a piece of paper. It looks like she's making a list.

"Hey, Sweetie," she says when she looks up. "How are you doing?"

"I'm good." I walk over to her, wrap my arms around her and give her a hug. "I love you, Mom."

"I love you, too, Sweetie. What's up?"

I take a deep breath. "Can I go to the park for a little?"

"You're not meeting Veronica, are you?"

"Nuh uh. I just texted her, and she said she was busy."

"Oh. Has she decided you're too young for her?"

I shrug my shoulders. "I dunno." I'm not gonna tell Mom about my plan to spy on Veronica and her secret boyfriend. She'd send me back upstairs or put me to work if I did.

"What about Robbie or Sasha? Are they going to meet you?"

"Not today. I just want to get out for a little while."

She smiles at me. "You are growing up, aren't you? Ok. Just be back by dinner time. And don't wander too far away."

I give her a kiss and head for the door. My heart is racing with excitement. I'm one step closer to finding out what's going on with Veronica. I get my bike, and I'm at the park in no time.

It's empty, just like it usually is, so I can do whatever I want, and nobody will know. When I cross the park to the lookout, I see Veronica and her boyfriend walking out toward the end of the dock. I wish I had a way to hear what they were saying. After a few minutes, he pulls his phone from his back pocket and looks at the screen. He says something to her, then turns to leave.

Veronica stands there on the edge of the dock looking like a lost little girl. I feel a little sorry for her. She probably needs somebody to talk to. But for now, she's gonna have to wait. When her boyfriend gets to the roundabout, he continues up Main Street.

My heart races faster. Am I gonna do this? Oh yeah. Totally. I take one last look at the docks, see Veronica is still standing there alone, and follow the guy toward the downtown.

I walk my bike along the sidewalk on the opposite side of the street. I'm still about a block behind him as he passes Scoops & Scones and the Bee's Knees. But when he gets to Isabelle's Pet Shoppe, he goes up the stairs and enters. So Mom was right. I stand there trying to figure out what to do next. Follow him in?

A few minutes later, Isabelle comes out the front door and goes down the stairs. She turns and starts walking in the direction of her house. If she's going home this early, that must mean her nephew is there alone. That's perfect!

I go to the corner, cross the street, and lock up my bike. Inside the pet shop, Quincy is there. He's talking to some customer who's getting her dog shampooed.

"I can have him ready in an hour," Quincy says.

The woman, a lady I don't recognize, thanks him again. "He just got away from me at the beach, and he started rolling in that seaweed. Now, he smells awful. My husband says we can't drive with him in the car smelling like this, so I simply must get him bathed."

"Well, Mrs. Montoya, you know why dogs don't like to take baths, don't you?"

"No." She shakes her head, and her brow furrows.

"Because they don't want to go from a bark to a poodle!"

He grins at her, and they both laugh. Really? It wasn't that funny.

"Oh, you're hysterical, Quincy!"

"Well, thank you. Alright, let's see if we can take away some of the stress Banjo's little seaweed *soiree* caused."

Mrs. Montoya laughs again, and this time she puts her fingers under the dog's chin. "Banjo, you be good for Quincy! You don't know it, but he's doing you a huge favor."

When the lady leaves, Quincy hooks Banjo up to a leash near the pet-washing station. "Be good, boy." He turns to me, smiles, and says, "Sorry. I didn't see you when you came in. I'm Quincy. What kind of pet are you shopping for?"

Uh oh. "I don't have a pet right now, but I'd totally love to get a cat or a dog." Actually, a dog would be awesome! I step forward, hold out my hand, and introduce myself. "I'm Alex."

So he's the one Mom told me about. I can see why Veronica's crushing on him. He's super cute in a rugged surfer kind of way. He's wearing a tee shirt that says, 'Dyslexics of the World - Untie!'

I point at his shirt. "That's kinda funny."

"A friend gave it to me in school. He thought it was a good joke." He cranes his neck forward and looks at me. "So, you're looking for a dog? Follow me."

He walks over to the counter, where there are playing cards all laid out in seven piles. One card is face up on the top of each pile, and some of the piles have cards facing up that are alternating between red and black. "Are you playing solitaire?"

"Oh, yeah. It helps me pass the time." Again, he gives me another super cute grin. "My aunt doesn't mind."

"Cool. Awesome job," I say as he hands me a business card.

"My aunt hasn't sold dogs or cats anymore because it's a cruel practice. But she had these printed up for people who want to adopt. The front side has the phone number for the local rescue here in Seaside Cove. They only have one or two dogs at any given time, if that. On the other side is the San Ladron Animal Shelter. They have a lot more dogs, and you can adopt one there."

I get kind of a warm, happy feeling inside at the thought of adopting a dog from a shelter. "Awesome. I'll talk to my mom and dad. Hey, do you know a girl named Veronica?"

"Sure. We run into each other down at the harbor all the time. She's cool."

That's weird. He didn't say anything about her being his girlfriend. Do I dare ask if he likes her? Maybe not. If he's got Veronica in the friend zone and she doesn't know it, I don't want to be the one to break it to her. "We're friends." It sounds kinda lame, but maybe it will be enough to get him to tell me more.

"Nice." He says as he looks over at Banjo. "Anything else? I should get busy."

So much for getting him to open up. I take a step back. "Guess not. Thanks for your help. I'd better get home. My mom's gonna be wondering where I am."

He looks at me and smiles. "No problem."

"Cool." I hold up the card. "Thanks for this. I'll see if I can get my mom and dad to agree to adopt. If they do, I'll let you know."

He flashes me a thumbs-up, then looks down at the playing cards. He picks up a red card, hesitates, then places it below a black one. As I'm heading for the door, I hear him say, "Come on, Banjo. It's bath time!"

36

RICK

Tom Reynolds's assessment of Penny Feeney practically echoed around the room with its meaning. Penny would do anything for a thrill. "Are you sure? Would that include murder?"

Reynolds didn't hesitate in his response. His words were assured and deliberate. "Even though Penny is always outwardly calm and collected, inside, she's a ticking time bomb. She can get very angry, very fast. I've seen her go off in public once or twice. Let me tell you, it wasn't pretty."

Rick considered the implication as he made notes. Apparently, maintaining his subterfuge during his talk with her had been a good idea. "I see. Why do you think she told me you were still engaged?"

"To throw you off her trail. The woman's smart. She'd do anything to protect herself. That includes lying and manipulating people."

Rick frowned and looked out the window. It appeared that Penny Feeney could be far more dangerous and devious than he'd given her credit for. "Do you feel like she manipulated you?"

"Definitely. I didn't realize it at first, but slowly I began to see what she was doing. She was always trying to lure me into questionable situations. Being around her was like living on a razor's edge. At first, it was exciting, but it soon became way too stressful for me."

"Thanks. This has been very helpful. When's the last time you heard from her?"

"If you had asked me that question yesterday, I'd have said I haven't talked to her since our breakup. But yesterday, she left me three messages. She said if someone called, she wanted me to lie. She practically begged me to say we were still together. I figured she was pulling another one of her scams. That's why I was cutting you off in the beginning. I didn't realize she was in trouble with the cops."

"What exactly did she say in her message?"

"You mean like word for word?"

"As close as you can get."

"Well, let's see. It was something to the effect of, I might be in some trouble. I told this guy we were still engaged, so if anyone calls, just tell them we're still together." He paused, then added, "It was something like that. I didn't keep the messages because I had no intention of lying for her."

"Had she ever gotten violent with you, Mr. Reynolds?"

Rick could almost feel the man's anxiety as he waited through a silence that dragged on for longer than was comfortable. "Yeah. A couple of times. I've never hit a woman in my life, but I came close the last time."

"Do you mind telling me what happened?"

"We were at this bar shortly after we got engaged. Some guy made a pass at her because she was kind of encouraging him. You know, making eyes at him."

"While you were with her?"

"Yeah. It was like she wanted me to see her do it. Anyway, we got into an argument when I called her out on how she was acting. Things quickly escalated until she threw a punch at me. It didn't hurt, but it took me by surprise. I've never seen anyone with such anger in their eyes. I walked out on her. She started calling me names, but the next day, she apologized and told me how she'd been in this abusive relationship. She claimed that because of her ex, she'd completely lost it and reacted like he would. When she said she never wanted to go through something like that again, I felt bad about the way I'd just cut her off."

"So you took her back?"

"Like a fool, yeah, I did. The last time it happened, I realized she was never going to change. I knew then it was time for me to move on."

Rick thanked Tom for the information and asked him to call if he could think of anything else.

"Look, man, I don't want any trouble with the law, but I also don't want to be letting her back into my life."

Rick assured him he wouldn't be in trouble and thanked him again before ending the call. He sat back in his chair, turning over all the details of Penny's past in his mind. He had no idea what to do now. Was she dangerous? Or simply devious? Could she really have killed Gideon Styles? He dialed Adam's number.

Adam listened to Rick intently before responding. "That's a pretty damning story," he said. "I think we should pay this woman a visit and get the truth out of her. At the very least, I need to make it clear she has to stick around. She seems like our most promising suspect."

When they arrived at the Inn, Adam knocked on the door to Room 207, but there was no answer.

"Let me check with Ray," Adam said. "See if she's checked out."

"While you do that, I'll take a little walk," Rick said.

Adam frowned but followed Rick. At the bottom of the stairs, Adam looked at Rick again. "Anything I should know?"

Cocking his head in the direction of the doorway where he'd first spotted Penny on the walkway, Rick said, "I'll be over there, watching the door."

After throwing Rick a quick thumbs-up, Adam wove his way along the path through the gardens while Rick took up his position. Barely two minutes later, the door to Room 207 opened, and Penny Feeney came out with a duffle bag slung over her shoulder.

Rick sent Adam a quick text to let him know Penny was on the run, then went to the bottom of the stairs. When she saw him, she swore to herself and glared at him.

"You're not going anywhere, Ms. Feeney," Rick said.

With one hand on the railing, the other holding a white-knuckle grip on the bag strap, she hissed, "Who sent you? And how much do you want?"

Rick stepped forward, his gaze steady. "All I want is the truth."

Behind him, Rick heard Adam's voice. "And I'm the Seaside Cove Chief of Police, Ms. Feeney. Unless you have a very good explanation as to why you're leaving, I may be detaining you for questioning in the murder of Gideon Styles."

The hard lines on Penny's face cracked, and she seemed to sag against the railing. "Please," she said, her voice low and desperate. "I didn't do it."

Adam stepped forward. "We're taking you in for questioning."

Penny practically spat the words, "We? So you're a cop? You told me you were a reporter!"

"I used to be. Now, I consult with the local police on murder investigations. And you seem to be at the center of this one."

She slumped down until she was sitting on the stairs, letting the bag rest cockeyed next to her. "I can't believe he's gone."

Good act thought Rick, thankful that he'd spoken to Tom Reynolds and had some insight into what this woman was capable of. "Let's start at the beginning," he said. "Why did you come to Seaside Cove with Gideon?"

Penny looked up, her gaze solemn and sad. "I hadn't seen him in three months. We'd broken up for the umpteenth time, but he called and said he wanted to get back together and that this was a perfect place to have a romantic reunion."

"Why'd you lie and tell me you were still engaged?" Rick kept his voice level, but his resolve was firm. He was not letting this woman play any more games.

Her cheeks flushed red. "I don't know. Pride, maybe? I didn't want to admit that I just dropped everything to be with Gideon." She paused before continuing. "When we arrived in Seaside Cove, he seemed distant and distracted. He said he was working on something big."

Adam stepped forward. "Do you know what he was working on?"

Penny shook her head and sighed. "No. He wouldn't tell me. That's the truth." She looked back at them, her eyes filled with tears. "That's all I know. I swear it."

"She's lying, Adam," Rick said confidently.

"I agree. Ms. Feeney, please stand up. You're coming with me."

Her jaw tightened, and she rose from the stairs with a determined look in her eye. "Where are you taking me?"

"To answer more questions," Adam replied.

Adam took out his handcuffs and advanced towards her. She held up her hands in surrender and allowed him to fasten them securely around her wrists. She shuffled beside him as he led her away. As Rick watched the scene unfold, he felt sure this wasn't Penny's first time in cuffs.

When they got to the police station, Adam guided her to the interrogation room. One of these days, he thought, this town really needed to invest in better accommodations for the police. Especially if they had to keep dealing with criminals like Penny Feeney.

37

RICK

THE SEASIDE COVE POLICE DEPARTMENT'S 'interrogation' room was one of those spaces that, over time, had become the equivalent of a kitchen junk drawer. Because it had a coffeemaker and a small refrigerator, it was used as a break room. In addition, more and more boxes had accumulated in one corner, making it also serve as a storage room. A filing cabinet took up space next to the 'supply corner.' A table and four chairs filled the rest of the space. Consequently, while the room's physical dimensions had never changed, the feel of the room had grown tighter and smaller over time.

Penny sat on one side of the table while Rick and Adam sat side-by-side opposite her. Ancient fluorescent bulbs cast a cold, stark glow over everything. The window that looked out into the rest of the station provided the only source of natural light.

Rick remained silent while he watched Penny fidget in her chair, struggling against the handcuffs Adam had chosen to leave on more for effect than anything. They'd both agreed that she posed little physical threat, but they also felt it was necessary to send a clear message that this was not fun and games time. Penny shot quick, darting glances towards the door as if she were planning an escape route. But in the end, Rick was sure she understood the futility of any attempt to escape.

Adam sat next to Rick, his brow creased in concentration. "We searched your room," he began, his voice steady and calm. "We found three sets of credit cards and IDs that aren't yours. We haven't checked them out yet, but we'll confirm soon enough that they're either stolen or outright fakes. They're all for men, so they're obviously not yours. And we already know the Russell Caraball credit card was used by Gideon Styles at the Rusty Nail."

Penny's face paled at the mention of Gideon's name. She swallowed hard, her eyes filling with tears. "I didn't," she croaked, but Adam held up a hand.

"We know about your past, Ms. Feeney," he said. "Your relationship with Mr. Styles, your criminal activities. What did you do with the gun that killed Styles?"

"I don't own a gun. I hate them," she croaked.

Rick watched as her face crumpled. She was clearly getting the message. But whether her emotions were just an act, due to being caught, or even perhaps the death of Gideon, he couldn't tell.

Adam continued, laying out the evidence they'd found. As he spoke, Rick's mind raced. They had to be closing in on the truth, even though some things still didn't add up. What they needed was more time—and more evidence.

The ringing of Adam's phone broke the tense silence. When Adam excused himself to leave the room, Rick wanted to curse the phone call. Adam was the one who could apply the real pressure here. Besides, he had mixed feelings about Penny.

Despite her past, despite everything he knew about her, there was a certain vulnerability about her that tugged at Rick's heartstrings. Was that why she was so good at what she did? Because she had the ability to cloud someone's judgment? Maybe. Whatever his mind told him, Rick's feelings wouldn't go away for some reason. "How did you obtain those credit cards and the IDs, Penny?" he asked softly.

"Gideon gave them to me," she replied.

"Really…why?" Rick demanded.

"He wanted me to have them in case something happened." Penny hesitated before continuing, and when she did, her voice faltered. "He said that if he didn't come back, I should use them to get away."

Rick might have bought the act—Penny sounded incredibly sincere and worried. But there was a problem. She was still in town. She hadn't used the resources she had to make an escape. "You're lying to me again. Gideon used the card for Russell Caraball at his lunch with Tyler Winkle. Let's try this scenario, you came here to be with Gideon, but he wanted you to work instead. You got into an argument. You shot him, then stole what was in his wallet. You would have gone to his room and cleaned it out, too, but you decided it was too risky because you weren't sure how closely we'd check the room for DNA."

"No! That's not true. He gave me that card and the ID."

"When?"

"After the lunch."

"Why?"

"Why what?"

"Why would he give you a man's ID?"

Penny shrugged and started to gesture like she intended to flip her hand nonchalantly but winced instead. "Can I get these taken off?"

"No. I'll consider it after you tell me the truth about the credit cards."

"Fine. Gideon realized he'd made a mistake at the restaurant. He wanted to make sure they wouldn't be found, but didn't want to destroy them, either. He gave them to me for safekeeping."

"Why wouldn't he have just put them back in his room with the others? You're not thinking this through, Penny. You can't lie your way out of this."

"I'm not lying!"

"Then you have a problem. Being caught with Russell Caraball's ID and credit card puts you in contact with Styles after he left the Rusty Nail. That makes you one of the last people to see him alive. The DA will use that against you. I'm sure if you cooperate with us, things will be better for you."

"I'm trying to cooperate."

"Let me rephrase that then. If you tell us the truth, Adam would be willing to talk to the DA. If you don't, he'll recommend they consider the theft and possession of those cards a felony. You're facing serious jail time just for those two charges alone."

"But..."

"There's no but here. Right now, the murder charge is also on the table."

Penny bit her lower lip. Her eyes darted around the room as if she were again looking for a way out. But there was none. Her shoulders slumped in defeat as she seemed to realize she was trapped. "I didn't kill Gideon. I loved him."

Rick fired back, "Sure you did. But the stats say something different. One in ten murders is classified as intimate. That fits you and Gideon. So there's a one-in-ten chance you had a motive to kill him. Bad odds when you're talking about the rest of your life in jail. Now, do you want to stop lying to us, or would you rather have me tell Adam this is pointless? Surely you don't want to be facing charges for murder, identity theft, fraud—do I need to go on?"

Penny let out a deep breath. With her confidence visibly eroding, Rick was ready to gamble. Maybe she was ready to stop playing games with them.

The door opened, Adam entered, and asked what he'd missed. Rick decided it was time to take his shot. Could he move this interrogation forward? "Penny and I were just having a little chat, that's all. The good news is she's decided to level with us. Haven't you?" Rick looked across the table at her.

"Yes, I'm ready to tell the truth." She paused, then looked up at Adam and Rick. "I didn't kill Gideon, but I did take the credit cards from him before he died."

Rick wasn't about to let her off so easily. "Why? Was it because you argued?"

"No. I didn't do it because we argued. I needed to protect myself."

"From what?" Adam pulled a pen from his pocket and positioned it over a yellow-lined notepad.

"Because I think Tyler caught on to what we were doing."

"Which was?" Rick prompted.

Penny inhaled sharply. "Gideon was smart. He'd dug into the Secret Ingredient Bakery's history. He knew the value of the recipe. He had the whole family legacy down. How Robert Winkle Jr. inherited the business from his father. How he passed it on to his son. And how the son nearly bankrupted the business and committed suicide. He knew it all."

"He did all this research before he contacted Tyler Winkle?" Rick asked.

"Of course. It didn't matter whether Gideon was playing poker or turning a deal, he always knew his opponent. He knew all about how Tyler's sister was murdered. He loved that kind of stuff. Tyler and his niece never stood a chance. Gideon had all the facts about how devastated they were. It made it easy to manipulate them."

Rick's stomach cringed. If Tyler had discovered this, would he have wanted revenge? And then, Adam asked the question Rick feared was coming.

"You say you think Tyler Winkle had figured out what you were up to. Does that mean you think he murdered Mr. Styles?"

Penny shifted in her chair. “All I know is that Gideon was dead when I found him. I was on my way back to my room when I heard a shot. My first thought was that Winkle had figured it all out, and so I went running. When I got to the parking lot, Gideon was lying on the ground. There was a pool of blood, and he wasn’t moving.”

“So rather than calling the police to report the murder, you stole the credit cards?”

“Yes. I knew that if you found them, you’d start to ask questions. I didn’t know he’d used the Caraball card at lunch. He must have been pretty rattled. The easiest way to stay out of things was to get rid of the evidence, so I pulled out Gideon’s wallet and took the extra IDs and credit cards.”

For Rick, something still didn’t add up. While it was true that Tyler’s temporary amnesia could have been caused by the trauma of committing murder, he didn’t seem like the type of man to do it. Rick shifted in his chair and searched Penny’s face for a clue as he asked, “You said you thought Tyler Winkle figured it all out. What, exactly, are you talking about?”

“That Gideon never planned to pay for the recipe. We were originally going to do this a little while after Gideon had his first meeting with Tyler. Then Tyler upset everything by moving here because that little brat of a niece got herself in too much trouble.”

“So when they moved to Seaside Cove, you had to start all over again?” Rick asked.

Penny hesitated, then took a long breath. “Gideon always planned to steal the recipe. He was sure he had Tyler fooled, but I think Winkle was onto us. That’s why he killed Gideon and why I felt the need to protect myself. I’m afraid I’m next.”

38

ALEX

I'M UNLOCKING MY BIKE FROM a lamppost when a gust of salty air teases my hair. The scent is one of a kind. Mom calls it the tang of the sea. I can hear the calls of seagulls as they circle overhead, just watching and waiting for a tourist to drop almost any kind of food.

Hopping on my bike, I ride toward home and the marina. I can't help it if they're in the same direction. And if I run into Veronica on my way home, that's not my fault, either. Right? Besides, I've realized it's not Veronica I'm afraid of. It's her uncle.

At the roundabout, I see Veronica leaving the harbor. Her fiery-red curls are blowing in the wind, and she's got this walk. It's kind of like she owns the whole town. It's totally epic.

"Hey, Veronica! Wait up!"

She turns around, her cheeks flushed pink from the chill, and her emerald eyes sparkle with a hint of mischief. "Alex!" she calls out.

Her voice sounds fakey, like she's pretending to be thrilled to see me. Whatever. I don't really want to be her friend, anyway. "What's going on?"

"Nothing. I was hoping I'd bump into you, though. Have you had any time to look into Gideon's death? Any clues so far?" Her voice is a blend of concern and curiosity. She searches my face like she expects to find a hint of what I might have discovered.

My heart starts to thump in my chest. She never actually came out and said, "Hey, Alex, would you…?" but I don't want her calling me a slacker, either. Besides, I'm not working for her. I'm doing this to get information about her and her uncle. I take a deep breath and tell her I haven't had a chance to do anything and that I got detention in school.

Veronica just laughs. "Yeah, it's tough being a teenager." She takes my hand in hers and squeezes it. "But we'll figure it out, okay? We're going to get to the bottom of this together."

Wow. That's like a total turnaround from thirty seconds ago. But then I remember, that's how she is. Super flakey. And maybe, a little vulnerable. I wonder what she'll say if I tell her I just came from the pet shop. "Hey, have you met Quincy Knox? He's Isabelle Murdoch's nephew. He's super cool and cute, too. He's older than you, but that doesn't matter, right? He's working at Isabelle's shop now."

"You were there?" she snaps. All of a sudden, the whole friend thing is over.

"I was talking to him about getting a dog. Why are you so mad? Wait! He's not your boyfriend, is he?"

Her face flushes to about the shade of her hair. Then, the anger is gone, and she's giving me a little girl smile. "Yeah, he is."

"Whoa! Really? That's awesome."

"He's been to law school," she says proudly.

"You like him. A lot. Don't you?"

She's not answering, but the smile's getting bigger. Oh yeah, she's got it so bad. I wonder how she'll deal with the serious questions. The things Chief Cunningham's gonna want to know. "Have you heard anything about the missing recipe?"

"Nah." She shrugs. "It'll turn up. I'm sure of it."

Another turnaround. The last time we talked, she was super angry about it. Now, it's like no big deal. "You're not upset about it?"

Veronica shoots me a glare that could freeze a desert. "Of course I am! I'm just trying to deal with it better. The recipe is super important. It was stolen from me. And I'm going to find out who stole it. They're going to wish they hadn't by the time I get done with them!"

"So you don't think Gideon Styles stole it?"

She shakes her head, her wild curls blowing in a sudden gust of wind. I shiver, suddenly wishing I'd brought my jacket instead of running out so fast.

"No, it wasn't him. It was a woman. And she wasn't working alone."

"How do you know that?"

"I just know. Okay." She takes a deep breath and looks away. "I saw her. She's going to pay for what she did."

I don't know what to say. She's planning something, and all this talk of making people pay has got me worried she might try to do something super bad. "When did you see her?"

Veronica looks around like she's expecting someone to be listening in. Duh. We're all alone. But now she's looking worried. Her tough image is fading fast. Kind of like she's actually afraid of something.

"Veronica? Are you scared?"

She crosses her arms and gives me that epic eye roll and the determined look she can get on her face. "She was bent down over the body. I think she killed him. And then, when she looked up, she saw me. She has to be the one who trashed our house and killed that awful man. Because she's seen me, I'm afraid she'll come after me next. That's why I need you to find out who she is."

Whoa. If she wanted me to find this woman, why didn't she tell me this before? And if it's all true, Chief Cunningham should know about it. "You're sure she saw you?"

"Totally sure. She looked right at me."

"What was she doing bending over the body?"

Veronica shifts her weight, her eyes darting around again. She whispers, almost too low to hear. "Getting rid of the evidence."

Evidence of what? "Veronica, you're not making any sense. If you saw the killer, and she saw you, why wouldn't you go to the cops?"

"Because of my Uncle Tyler. It's why he lost his memory."

What's she getting at? My dad said it happened 'cause of some kind of stress. "What do you mean?"

She crosses her arms over her chest and puts one leg out in front of her. Her voice turns kind of edgy. "My uncle's been acting really strange lately. He's forgotten the entire thing where I fell into the planter. I thought at first he was faking it because he was working with Gideon, but now I don't think he is. It's like he's totally blanked on everything to do with that day."

"My dad said your uncle's memory loss is for real." But losing his memory because he's trying to protect Veronica? That makes no sense. She totally needs to talk to an adult about this. "You gotta tell Chief Cunningham. If you saw this woman, and she really was the killer, you have to tell him."

"I can't."

She shakes her head, and I can see fear in her eyes. She can't go to the cops? What is it she isn't telling me? "You're holding something back. What is it?"

"No. It would break him."

"Who are you talking about?"

"My uncle."

"What about him?"

"He doesn't know that I know."

"Does he have a secret or something?" I hold my breath while I wait for her to answer. This is it. The answer Chief Cunningham wants. And I'm only seconds away from finding out what's going on.

She turns away from me and looks out towards the ocean. Standing there with her hair blowing in the wind, she reminds me of those statues of women shipbuilders used to put on the front of ships. Mr. Gray told me all about them. He called them Neptune's wooden angels. He said they were supposed to bring the sailors good luck, but all I see when I look at Veronica is trouble.

"Veronica, I can't help you if you don't tell me the truth."

"It's about my mom's murder. My Uncle Tyler was supposed to work the day my mom was killed. He got drunk the night before and was too sick to work the next day. Me and my mom were supposed to go to the beach, but she had to cancel so she could keep the bakery open. My uncle went to a super dark place after that, and we never talked. He's supposed to be my guardian, but he doesn't know me at all. Things were getting better between us after we moved here, but he's been this total stranger ever since the recipe got stolen."

She stops, hugs herself again, and then her green eyes light up with a fire inside. "It all makes sense. My uncle needed money. He pretended to sell the recipe to Gideon Styles, but he didn't want to turn it over, so he staged the robbery. He took the recipe from the safe, then hired that woman to trash the house. When Gideon Styles found out he'd been scammed, he came after my uncle. Don't you see? They were working together, so they were both in on the murder. But she must have killed him because I saw her right near the body. She wants to get rid of me next to cover her tracks."

My breath catches in my throat. So that's it? That's why she won't go to the cops? Because of some bogus theory about her uncle trying to con a conman and two people committing murder? Nuh-uh. I'm not buying it. "The chief had your uncle checked out by a doctor. The memory loss is for real."

"Of course, it is! He's in way over his head, and the stress got to be too much. My uncle's behind this. But I can't have him sent to jail. My mom would never have wanted that."

Wow. She really believes her uncle was behind the whole break-in thing and the murder. But that raises a million questions. "Have you ever seen your uncle with this woman?"

"No, but she had to have had a key to get into the house."

"Nuh uh. She could've picked the lock."

"That's a real thing?"

How does she not know this? "For sure. Why would your uncle want to steal his own recipe? And why would he hire someone to trash his house? Veronica, I think you need to look at other options. Like maybe this woman wasn't working for your uncle. Maybe she was working for Gideon Styles, and they had a falling out."

Oh, snap! And that would mean if her uncle found out what Gideon was doing, he might have wanted to get revenge. For sure, a double-cross would totally be a motive for murder. And it might even force him to forget what he'd done.

39

RICK

A SENSE OF CALM. As Rick sat at the kitchen island, he realized that's what Marquetta's domain radiated. The granite countertops with their white marbling gleamed under the soft overhead lighting. The walls, a pale seafoam green, added to the aura. It was exactly what he needed after the day he'd had. Sitting here, he felt the day's stresses begin to melt away. And with Marquetta sitting to his right, her attention focused on the steaming bowl of soup before her, everything suddenly felt right.

"I thought this would be a good choice for dinner," Marquetta said. "I decided that if you had to work late, Alex and I could eat on time, and it would be easy to heat up later if you wanted something."

Rick kissed her and said, "Well, surprise. I'm on time."

Alex's blue eyes sparkled. Rick studied her, wondering how the conversation they were going to have would go. After the interrogation with Penny Feeney, he was more convinced than ever that getting Alex away from Veronica was the best course of action.

"So, kiddo, what did you do with the rest of your afternoon?"

Alex grinned. "I stopped by the pet shop," she announced. Her excitement practically bubbling over.

Rick exchanged a glance with Marquetta, who raised an eyebrow. This might not be good. Were they going to have 'the pet talk' again?

"And why did you do that?" Marquetta asked, her tone curious.

"I want a dog," Alex declared, her voice full of conviction.

"Really, Alex? We've talked about this before."

"But Daddy, it would be a rescue dog. We'd be saving a dog's life! " Alex's brows furrowed in determination. "I think it would be awesome."

Her empathy and enthusiasm were heartwarming, but he also knew they had to be practical. "A B&B is hardly a place for a pet. We've got guests, and some of them could have allergies."

"I know."

"And dogs are a big responsibility. With everything else going on, I don't think it's a good idea."

"Daddy, I can handle it!"

Rick rubbed at his temples. He could see the stubborn set of Alex's jaw, a trait she'd inherited from him. He admired her spirit, but he also knew how and when to choose his battles.

He looked at Marquetta, who was trying to hide a smile. "What's your opinion on this?"

To Rick's surprise, Marquetta's eyes twinkled with amusement. "I think we should let her try. It might be good for her."

Rick groaned, burying his face in his hands. "I can see I'm outnumbered here."

Alex cheered, throwing her arms up in victory. But then, her smile faltered. "But maybe it's not a good idea," she admitted, her shoulders slumping. "With the B&B and all."

Rick felt a surge of pride and relief. His little girl was growing up, learning to make mature decisions. But his momentary euphoria was quickly replaced by sadness. Growing up meant she'd be going to college. Getting married. Maybe leaving Seaside Cove. He forced a smile, reached across the table, and gave her hand a reassuring squeeze. "We'll figure it out, kiddo."

Just then, Rick's phone buzzed with a text from Adam. He quickly read the message and muttered, "Oh, no."

"What is it, Rick?" Marquetta asked, concern etching her features.

Rick looked up, meeting Marquetta's gaze. "It's about Penny Feeney. He had to let her go."

"Who's she?" Alex asked.

"She's one of our main suspects in the murder investigation."

Alex gasped. "That must be her!"

It was the last thing he wanted to do, and the first thing he knew he needed to do. "What have you heard, Alex?"

"Veronica was telling me about a woman she thinks is working with her Uncle Tyler." She rambled on with a story about double and triple crosses. The woman had a deal with Tyler. He had a deal with Styles. But Tyler wanted to double-cross Styles, who learned about it, and the only solution was to get rid of him.

The complexity was enough to make Rick's head spin, and as the story unfolded, Rick made mental notes, but he also noticed the look on Marquetta's face. She was hurt. He could easily see that, and so could Alex. By the time Alex finished, Rick had counted numerous clashes between Veronica's version and what Penny had told them. He also suspected Marquetta was very upset with Alex.

When he tried to ask, Marquetta set her jaw and picked up Baby Jack. She took a long breath, then gave Rick a weak smile. "I think I'll take the baby upstairs and feed him. You two finish your dinner."

"Mom! I didn't go looking for her. Well, I did, kinda, but the pet shop was totally safe because it's a business. All I wanted to do was make sure Quincy really was her boyfriend and see if he could tell me anything about Veronica or her uncle. But he told me they were just friends, so I decided I'd better not push. And then Veronica was leaving the marina just as I was riding by on my way home."

Alex stood and started toward her, but Marquetta held out her hand and shook her head. “Not now, Alex.” She turned and walked away.

Rick’s insides twisted as he watched Marquetta leave. This was the first time Alex had deliberately lied to Marquetta, and he knew the hurt she was feeling. He’d gotten used to it over the years. He’d had thirteen years to watch Alex’s determination grow stronger. But Marquetta, she’d barely had three, and never had Alex deliberately gone against her wishes.

“You hurt her, Alex,” Rick said solemnly.

“Daddy?” Alex stood there, tears streaming down her cheeks. “I didn’t mean to. I wasn’t actually gonna talk to Veronica, but then she just showed up.”

“Really, Alex? You know how I feel about coincidences.” After letting out a deep sigh, Rick said, “Sit down. We’ve talked so many times about there being consequences to your actions. This is an example of what happens when you aren’t completely honest. Not only can you put yourself in danger, but it hurts to know you don’t completely trust us. To be honest with you, your mom expected more from you.”

Alex swiped at her cheek to wipe away another tear. “What do I do? How do I fix this?”

“This isn’t something you can fix, Alex. Once you break someone’s trust, you can never really undo that.”

Rick’s gut twisted again as he watched Alex’s turmoil. He’d hoped this day would never come, but now that it was here, he could only encourage her to try and never make the same mistake again.

“Come here, kiddo.” He opened his arms and pulled Alex close to him. Her shoulders shook, and even though she was getting older and taller, she still felt frail and small to him. She was, after all, his baby girl. And she’d always be that no matter what she did.

He stroked her back and let her cry on his shoulder. When she'd cried herself out, she muttered, "Daddy?"

"What, kiddo?"

"I'm sorry."

"For what?"

"For all the times I've done the same thing to you. I'm gonna do better."

Famous last words, thought Rick. "I'm sure you will." He pushed Alex away and looked at her. "Part of this is my fault. I never should have agreed when Adam asked you to help out. Unfortunately, we're now in the middle of an investigation, and it appears you may have some critical information. I have to ask you a few questions. To begin with, in this theory of yours about who killed the victim, what makes you so sure Veronica's uncle didn't do what she thinks he did?"

"Veronica almost had me believing her uncle did it, but it doesn't make any sense. If he'd made a deal to sell the recipe but then pretended it was stolen, that man could have sued him to get his money back. Right? Besides, if Veronica's Uncle Tyler was so upset over his sister's death, why would he put Veronica in danger?"

"That's very adult thinking, kiddo."

Alex sat slowly in the seat next to Rick's. The redness in her eyes gradually seeped away as she talked. "Besides, Veronica never saw her uncle with that woman, and once Chief Cunningham took her into custody, she'd have ratted out Veronica's uncle if she wanted to save herself. But she didn't, so he can't be behind the murder."

"Okay, so what do you think happened?"

Alex's eyes widened, and she said slowly, "I think someone else is involved. Someone who wants to hurt Veronica." She paused before continuing, "Someone who was watching her closely enough that they knew when to swoop in and kill." Her voice rose in excitement as she spoke, her face lighting up with the possibilities. "Maybe someone who was even there when it happened. Someone who could have seen or heard something they could use to their advantage."

Rick considered her theory before asking, "What about Veronica? Is she in any real danger?"

Alex looked around her before replying, "I don't know, but I think you need to ask this woman questions about Veronica. That's the only way we'll figure this out."

She looked up at Rick with determination, and he knew what was coming next. Once again, it felt like someone had just stabbed him in the gut with a knife.

40

ALEX

My sneakers squeak against the polished wood as I creep into the master bedroom. Mom is sitting on the bed with a couple of pillows propped up behind her. Sometimes, she calls it her hushed haven—the place where she can nurse my baby brother without any interruptions. The room smells of the lavender soap she insists on using. A lamp on her nightstand casts long shadows across the room, making the familiar furniture look like hulking beasts waiting to pounce.

Mom's eyes are closed. Her lips are drawn in a tight line. She's humming softly, an old lullaby she says her mom used to sing to her. As I stand there quietly, my heart breaks for so many things—for not having spent more time with her since the baby was born, for not having her as my real mom so she'd have sung that song to me when I was a baby, and most of all, for having lied to her about meeting up with Veronica. My dad's right. I broke the trust we had. How can I ever make it up to her?

I shuffle closer, my heart pounding in my chest. I feel like I'm standing over a black hole, about to dive into a big, black, empty space.

"Mom," I whisper. My voice sounds strange and foreign in the quiet room.

She opens her eyes slowly, like it costs her something. Her gaze lands on me, and there's a flicker of surprise before she gives me a weak smile.

"Alex," she says, her voice still filled with hurt and sounding cold as a winter frost. "Did you help your dad with the dishes?"

"Uh-huh," I stammer, rubbing my hands on my jeans. "I wanted to say how sorry I am."

"Sorry? For what?"

"For seeing Veronica," I mumble, hanging my head. "I know you didn't want me to."

"You're missing the point, Alex."

"I am? But I thought you didn't like her."

There's a silence. The air feels so thick it makes it hard to breathe. It's like I'm choking or something. Then, Mom laughs. It's a soft, sad sound that doesn't quite reach her eyes.

"Sweetie, whether I like Veronica or not isn't the issue. The problem is that you lied to me so you could hang out with her. You helping her at the Rusty Nail was admirable. I'm proud of you for trying to help someone in distress. But sneaking around and lying to me? It's the one thing I thought you'd never do." She shakes her head. "This doesn't mean I love you any less."

"But now you'll always wonder if I'm gonna do it again."

"Yes. You can't just say you're sorry and expect it to make everything okay. Life doesn't work that way."

I swallow hard. "No, but it's a start, right?"

Mom gives me a hurt look, then shifts my brother to her other shoulder. "Alex, there's no magic wand you can wave to suddenly make everything the way it used to be."

I wince. Alex. She only uses my name when she's mad. Or upset. I guess she's both. "I know, Mom." My voice sounds strange in my throat, like I've swallowed sand or something. "But I have to try. I love you."

Suddenly, my brother gurgles, breaking the tension. We both look at him, and he beams at us, his tiny fists waving in the air.

"See?" I say, grinning despite everything. "Even Baby Jack agrees with me."

Mom chuckles, her eyes softening as she looks at me. "You're impossible, you know that?"

"I know." Suddenly, heat rises up my chest and into my face, and the room is getting even hotter and stuffier, and I can't hold back the tears.

She pulls me close and lets me cry on one shoulder while Baby Jack makes funny noises on the other. "Oh, Sweetie, from now on, if you disagree with me about something, tell me. I understand that we won't always agree. But let's not lie about it, okay?"

Between the sobs I'm choking out, I manage to say, "I never want to hurt you again."

"It's bound to happen, Sweetie. It's all a part of growing up." She chuckles and looks me in the eye. "For now, I just take solace in knowing that someday you'll face this same situation with your own daughter."

Oh, gawd. Really? That's like total karma payback.

There's still a long way to go, a million apologies to be made, and a thousand secrets to unravel. But for now, this is enough. For now, we're okay. As I sit beside Mom on the bed, her arm still rubbing my shoulder, I think that maybe, just maybe, things will get better. And maybe, just maybe, we'll find our way back to each other.

September 13

Hey Journal,

I snuck into Mom and Dad's room tonight while Mom was nursing Baby Jack. It was so quiet in there. Like you could hear a pin drop. I swear I felt like I was standing on the edge of a cliff, about to tumble down into nothingness.

I told Mom I was sorry. For seeing Veronica and for breaking our trust. And you know what she did? She laughed. Not a happy laugh, but a sad one. It was like she couldn't believe what I was saying.

Mom told me that my apology doesn't fix everything. That hurt, Journal. But she's right. I can't change what I did. I get it now. Life isn't a fairytale. You can't take your relationships for granted.

Things were kind of tense, but then the funniest thing happened. Baby Jack gurgled and smiled at us. It was like he was telling us everything would be okay. We had a good cry, Journal. A really good one. And then we made a deal. From now on, no more lies. If I disagree with Mom, I'll tell her. And she promised to do the same. It sounds kinda scary but also kind of freeing. What do you think, Journal? Could this be the beginning of something better than we had before?

Let's hope. Right? Here's to new beginnings, Journal. And to not messing up again.

xoxo,

Alex

41

RICK

LOOKING OUT THE WINDOWS ALONG the west wall of the kitchen, Rick soaked in the early morning light. He only had a minute or two to take this in before Marquetta would finish the breakfast she'd been preparing for Leo and Lily Carmichael.

Marquetta's movements seemed almost automatic as she alternately cooked and shot occasional glances at Rick. At one point, he said, "We're fully booked tonight. There's no way they can extend their stay again."

When she looked at him, Marquetta's gaze was focused. "This isn't about the Carmichaels, Rick. And you know it." She turned back to the stove without saying another word.

Having seen the worry lines etching his wife's forehead, Rick knew he'd have to wait until she was ready to talk. He let his gaze return to the outside world. This was his favorite time of day. He loved the morning light and how the sun cast long shadows across the patio to create a stark contrast between light and dark. Especially on mornings like this, when his thoughts were a jumble of theories and worries, it seemed to mirror his inner turmoil. It beckoned to him as if the light itself encouraged him to visit and clear his thoughts.

"Rick," Marquetta said suddenly, breaking the silence. "I'm worried about Alex."

Taking her hand in his, Rick looked into her eyes. "I knew that's what was bothering you. I'm worried, too. I have a feeling, though, that we might be thinking about different things. Why are you worried about her?"

"It's Veronica," Marquetta confessed, her eyes meeting his. "I've heard some things about Tyler. He's been getting angry with the locals, and I'm just…" She trailed off and turned back to the stove.

Rick felt a chill run down his spine. Ever since his conversation with Alex, Tyler had been on his mind. "What have you heard?"

"I didn't say anything last night because I knew it would make Alex more curious, but the man has a short fuse. At least, that's what several of the shopowners are saying. They've been talking, Rick. They're all wondering if he might be Gideon Styles's killer."

"After you left the dinner table, Alex and I had a conversation about Tyler and Veronica. Based on what you're telling me and what Alex said last night, Adam and I should be taking a closer look at him. At the both of them. Based on what the shopowners saying, does it sound like he's done anything violent?"

"Not so far, and I'm not saying he will." Marquetta winced, then lifted the skillet from the stove and deftly transferred the scramble for Leo Carmichael into a serving bowl. "I'll tell you the rest after you get this to the lovebirds."

Rick delivered the orders and, as he placed Leo's scramble in front of him, told Leo he was thinking of having the same thing.

Leo rubbed his palms together as he inspected the masterpiece on his plate. "Chorizo, potatoes, peppers, and onions. Man, I never get to eat like this. Babe, we might have to stay longer. A lot longer."

Lily rolled her eyes. "I'd feel bloated all day if I ate that. But this fruit plate is divine."

"I hope you both enjoy. Unfortunately, Leo, as much as I'd love to have you extend your stay, we're fully booked. And I can guarantee you won't get food like this at the Seaside Cove Inn. Ray only has a grab-and-go pastry bar."

"Bummer. Then I'm going to enjoy my last breakfast."

After refilling coffee mugs and checking on the other guests, Rick returned to the kitchen for the next order. At eight-thirty, the breakfast service closed for the day. Rick was looking forward to the scramble Leo had ordered earlier when he pushed through the butler door and found Marquetta and Lydia talking.

"Don't worry," Lydia said. "I'll get started on the cleaning. You just relax and have breakfast with Rick."

"Thanks, Lydia. The Jensens have already checked out of the Starboard Room. Why don't you begin there? By the time you're done with that, I should be able to lend a hand."

"No worries. I'm happy to take the load off of you. You focus on the baby this morning. It's a light day." Lydia let out a hearty laugh. "Besides, you two saved me. Thank goodness I don't have to put up with Ray Villari and his perpetual foul moods. I'll be forever grateful that you hired me."

After Lydia left the room, Marquetta sat on her stool at the island. "She's been a lifesaver, Rick. I don't know how I'd have gotten through this pregnancy without her."

Rick chuckled. "She's part of the family now. We couldn't get rid of her if we tried." He poured a mug of coffee for each of them and sat next to Marquetta. Now, what's this you were saying about Tyler?"

After going back through the story and hearing more specifics about the rumors circulating about Tyler Winkle, Rick felt that Tyler's possible guilt was all too real. "The truth of it is that I'm getting worried about Tyler Winkle. It's hard to believe, but do you think he could be the killer?"

"I don't know," Marquetta admitted, her tone filled with uncertainty. "But if he is, and Alex is involved with Veronica, that could be a problem."

The thought left a sour taste in Rick's mouth. "Alex shouldn't be getting near Veronica—or Tyler. Adam's agreed to tell her she's off the case, but the big problem is Alex doesn't know how to let go." The words tasted like ash on his tongue. The idea that his daughter could again be involved with a potential killer terrified him. Especially because he hadn't put his foot down when Adam first came up with the idea.

For several seconds, Marquetta's eyes held a faraway look as if they were seeing but not perceiving. Then, the lines around the corners of her eyes crinkled, and she narrowed her gaze, focusing on Rick. "And what if Veronica did see something? What if she saw this woman kneeling over the body? That could put her and anyone near her in danger."

Rick felt his heart skip a beat. "If it's true, she'd be scared for her life."

"And if it's not?"

The fear in Marquetta's gray eyes materialized as if it were standing right next to her. The coffee pot gurgled loudly, breaking the tension. They both jumped, and Rick knocked over his mug, sending coffee across the table. He started to curse under his breath but stopped when Marquetta laughed and handed him a towel.

"Smooth, Mr. Atwood. Real smooth."

He grinned sheepishly while he mopped up the mess. "At least I didn't spill it on me."

"That's my hubby. Always looking for the silver lining."

As much as he wanted to agree, Rick's mind was still racing, trying to devise a plan to protect his daughter while he tried to figure out who had murdered Styles. The truth was, no matter who had done it, he didn't want Alex caught in the middle of the investigation.

Rick's phone rang as he wiped up the last of the spilled coffee. Seeing it was Adam, he answered quickly, determined to put all of these issues to rest. His family was having enough turmoil, and it needed to stop.

"I've got some news," Adam said, his voice low and urgent.

"What is it?" Rick's heart started to race again. They really needed a break.

"It's about Tyler Winkle and his possible involvement in his sister's death."

"What? Are you saying you think he had something to do with it?"

"Covering all the bases. Right after the break-in, I placed a call to the detective who was in charge of the investigation. She mentioned that they received a tip about Tyler's whereabouts when his sister was murdered. It turns out he had no alibi. He claimed he'd gotten drunk the night before and called his sister to work for him."

"He told us that, Adam."

"I know. But what he didn't mention was that he also called his sister multiple times throughout the day of her murder. The phone records alone didn't prove anything because Winkle claimed he felt terrible about her having to work for him and was just checking to make sure she didn't need help. But if he felt so terrible, why didn't he go in and let her have her day off? It's almost like he was keeping track of her."

"But why? Why would he want to kill his own sister?"

"The detective believes there was some kind of sibling rivalry involved. Maxine was the one who saved the business. Tyler was basically just a hired hand. And, according to my contact, he wasn't doing that great of a job. In fact, Maxine was grooming Veronica to take over the business."

"So at least part of what Veronica's been telling us is true," Rick said.

"Exactly."

The idea seemed preposterous, and yet, not. Rick had seen firsthand the lengths people would go for money and power. Survival was no different. And now, with these rumors circulating about Tyler having a short fuse and his possible involvement with Penny Feeney—was it possible the man had played them all?

"It's just a theory at this point, but it's worth looking into," Adam said. "Let's face it. He had the perfect opportunity when she was making the bank deposit. She was alone, and it was the perfect time to take over the business. He had both motive and opportunity."

"What about a gun? Did they find any evidence linking him to the crime scene?"

"No. If he owned a gun, he'd purchased it on the black market. Then again, the murder weapon was never found."

"So the investigation just, if you'll pardon the expression, died."

"Basically. But there was one other thing the detective on the case didn't like." Adam paused; the background silence was filled with the sounds of shuffling papers.

"Come on. Don't keep me in suspense," Rick said.

"Okay. The night before Maxine was killed, not only did Tyler get drunk, but he also got into a fight at a bar. The detective says it was a pretty nasty brawl, but the guy he got into it with was in the service and was shipping out. Nobody wanted to bring charges, so that never came to light until later."

Rick let out a low whistle. "Adam, Marquetta's been telling me what some of the shopkeepers are saying about Tyler. That he's got a short fuse. Have you heard anything about this?"

"Yes. And that's another reason I'm thinking we need to have another conversation with Mr. Winkle. See if he can shed any light on this. Can you come by, and we'll go pay him a visit?"

"Give me an hour."

Rick turned to Marquetta and shared Adam's theories about Tyler. When he finished, he said, "I keep going back to our conversation with Veronica and how she has this strained relationship with her uncle. I'm concerned that Tyler's temper might make him prone to commit violent acts. Maybe that's why he's forgotten the day of the murder."

"Maybe," Marquetta said. "But have you or Adam considered the possibility that Tyler is being manipulated?"

"By?"

"Veronica. Think about it, Rick. That girl is very, very good at manipulating people. You've seen it yourself."

Rick swallowed hard, held Marquetta's gaze, and said, "Yes. I have."

42

ALEX

Today feels like it's been the longest day of my life. I can't believe how bad I feel about my mom. I worked so hard to get her and my dad together, and then I totally blew it just because I took our relationship for granted. I'm never gonna make that mistake again. Sasha and Robbie wanted to have lunch with me, but I told them I had things to do. I don't want to have to talk about it, and I know Sasha will figure out something's wrong.

Right now, it just feels like the whole entire world's mad at me. Even the sun. It feels like it's blazing hot, and it never gets hot in Seaside Cove. Over here by the D Building, I can hide away from everyone. The corridor is shady, so I can hide from the sun, but I keep thinking about how much I need to fix my mistakes. If only.

Then, I stop and gasp. Veronica is hunched over with her back against the wall. Her fiery red hair is spilling over her shoulders like a waterfall. Sitting there all by herself, she looks like a lost kitten. Her eyes are all red when she turns to face me.

"Hey," she says.

"Hey," I say back. Talk about awkward. What do I do now?

She gets up, her wild curls bouncing with the movement. "I'm thinking about running away." Her voice is shaky, and it sounds almost…broken. She keeps watching me like she's waiting to see my reaction.

I blink at her, my heart pounding in my chest. "Uh…what?"

"I said, I'm running away."

"That's not what I meant, Veronica. I mean, why?" Oh, man, why did I do that? Why am I getting involved? I should turn and walk away. No, run. But she looks so lost.

Her cheeks get super bright red, almost as red as her hair. "I got a text from my boyfriend. He wants to talk with me," she says, her voice sounding super excited. "You can't tell anyone."

I stand there, not knowing what to say. I should comfort her. Right? Make her realize running will only make things worse. But then there's my mom. And my promise. Oh, this totally sucks. I'm gonna hate myself if I don't try to stop her. "You can't run away."

She looks at me, desperation in her eyes. "Why not? I can't deal with my uncle anymore. I don't want to live with all of his rules." She shrugs and picks at a chipped nail. "My uncle's being a jerk, school is boring, and my boyfriend is the only good thing in my life right now."

Silence hangs heavy between us, broken only by the distant yelling and laughter of kids playing on the playground. That's it. Kids on the playground. If one of them went missing, everyone would be looking for them. "You're only seventeen. The cops will get involved. You could get your boyfriend in trouble. You don't want to do that to him. Right?"

Her eyes start to glisten with tears. I can see how broken she is. I didn't see it before, but now I do. She wants to escape from her problems, but she needs to understand you've gotta face them, not avoid them. The thought just stops me cold. That's exactly how I ruined things with Mom. I lied instead of telling her the truth.

I take a deep breath and gently place my hand on her shoulder. "I get it. Things are tough right now, but running away won't work. Let's talk to someone. Someone who can help."

"Who? Not your dad. He works for the cops. All he'll do is tell my uncle."

"What about my mom? She's cool. Right?"

My heart skips a beat as I wait for Veronica to say something. A few seconds later, she does. "Okay. Yeah, I liked your mom."

I'm super relieved. Mom will know what to do. I pull out my phone, dial her number, and wait while it rings. "Come on, come on." But she doesn't answer, and the call goes to voicemail. I mumble, "She must be resting."

"I'm outta here," Veronica says, then starts toward the school exit.

I grab her shoulder. "Wait! Do you know Miss Redmond?"

Veronica stops and turns to look at me, confusion evident on her face. "Miss Redmond? Yeah, I talked to her when I started here. Why?"

I smile, feeling a glimmer of hope. "She's the school counselor. She can help us figure out what to do."

Veronica hesitates before she lifts her chin in the direction of Miss Redmond's classroom. "You go get her. I'll wait here. I'm not going into any office. They might lock me in and make me wait for my uncle."

She cuts off my protest with a nasty look that tells me to do what she wants or else. Her jaw is set, and there's total determination shining in her eyes.

I take off toward Miss Redmond's classroom, hoping to get there and back before Veronica decides to run. Miss Redmond is standing at the blackboard writing. She gives me a polite smile. Oh, man, I've totally blown that relationship, too. My life sucks right now. No. It's my relationships, and that's because I haven't taken my own advice.

"Miss Redmond?"

"Yes, Alex?" She puts down the chalk and the eraser she was holding and looks directly at me.

"I wanted to apologize for acting the way I have lately."

I should tell her about Veronica right away, but instead, I keep trying to apologize and start going on about how I was playing matchmaker for her and Barrington Rhymes. When I'm done, she puts her hand over her mouth to hide a smile.

"Alex, I know Barrington quite well. I'm the liaison between his company and the school."

"Huh? What's that?"

"His company is trying to get us to pilot a program to help small schools provide better educations to their students. We've had several meetings since he's been here. Actually, I'm not quite sure why he's hung around so long."

"He's cute, right?" Oh, crap. Why did I say that?

Miss Redmond blushes and can't quite hide her smile. "Yes, he is. But I do not want you interfering in my life anymore. Do you understand?"

I nod. Got it. Her personal life is off limits. "Totally. But that's not why I'm here. My friend Veronica needs someone to talk to."

She looks at me closer, and then her blue eyes widen behind her glasses. "Veronica Campbell?"

"Yes, ma'am."

"Where is she?"

"On the other side of the D Building. I'll show you."

Miss Redmond shakes her head. "No. Absolutely not. This conversation needs to be strictly between her and me." She strides out the door with a purpose I've never seen in her before. Or maybe it's just that I never noticed it.

Standing at the door, I watch Miss Redmond walk toward the D Building. Sasha comes and stands next to me, crossing her arms over her chest to mimic the way I'm standing. "Hey, what's up?" she asks.

I wince, then look at her. Her brown eyes look worried. Sasha's had so many problems at home because of her mom being sick. And I haven't been there for her lately. "I'm sorry I've been such a lousy friend."

She shrugs. "Hey, we're like still learning life. Right?" She laughs quietly and smiles at me. "Besides, you've only been a lousy friend for a week or so, and you were a good one for a lot longer than that."

I reach out and hug her. We hold onto each other tight. "I'm gonna do better, Sash. I promise."

She gives me a final squeeze, then says, "For sure."

I pull in a quick breath when I see Miss Redmond coming back from the D Building alone. When she gets closer, she shakes her head. "She was gone, Alex. I'm calling Chief Cunningham."

"Who's gone?" Sasha asks.

"Veronica," I say. "Wait. At lunch, you were sitting where you could see Building D. You didn't see her, did you?"

"Oh, yeah. She was looking at her phone. I think she was texting somebody."

"Her boyfriend," I say.

"What boyfriend?" Miss Redmond asks.

"His name's Quincy, and he works at Isabelle's Pet Shoppe. He's her nephew."

"Sure, I remember him. The last I heard, he went off to attend law school."

"Yes, ma'am."

Miss Redmond frowns. Now, she's looking super worried.

Veronica doesn't want me to say anything, but I've gotta do the right thing. I've gotta face this no matter how mad it makes her. "I think she's going to run away."

"I have to call the police before anything happens to her." Miss Redmond excuses herself and goes into the classroom.

I feel my stomach drop at the thought of something terrible happening to Veronica. She's been through so much already, and I can't help but feel responsible for part of it because if I had told an adult instead of trying to handle things on my own, she'd probably still be here in school. Safe.

My phone rings. It's my mom. Oh, no. What am I gonna tell her? Sorry, I messed up again?

43

RICK

RICK WAS SITTING ACROSS FROM Adam Cunningham when Adam's phone rang with a call about Veronica Campbell. Adam immediately put the call on speaker. Within seconds, Rick realized that no matter how he felt about Veronica personally, he hated the idea of something happening to her.

"I don't know where she could have gone, Chief. I've heard she got a message from her boyfriend. One of my students says the boy in question is Isabelle Murdoch's nephew, Quincy Knox." Miss Redmond's voice practically dripped with concern.

"Let me guess, Alex told you that." Rick hadn't intended to say the words aloud and winced at his knee-jerk reaction.

There was a momentary pause before Miss Redmond responded. "Yes, how did you know?"

"Just an educated guess, Miss Redmond. You know Alex, she always finds a way to be in the middle of things."

Adam looked across his desk at Rick. "Don't tell me you already have a lead on this case."

"Not exactly," Rick said. "But based on Veronica's past behavior, I think it would be worthwhile to check with Isabelle's nephew."

Adam had a grim look on his face. "Legally, Veronica Campbell is still a minor. I hope this young man realizes he could be facing serious charges if he has a relationship with her."

It wasn't just the legal implications that bothered Rick. He also found himself oddly worried about the emotional price Veronica might pay. "Let me run down to the pet shop and see if Quincy is working. If he's not, I'm sure Isabelle will know where he is."

"Chief, I wish I could help, but I'm already late for a class," Miss Redmond said.

"You did the right thing by calling me, Francesca. Do me a favor, though. If Veronica shows up, call me right away."

"Will do."

Rick was already out of his chair by the time the conversation ended. "I'll let you know what I find out. You're still following up on Penny Feeney?"

"Yes," Adam said. "I have a lead on another possible 'business partner' of hers. I should be getting a call any minute."

Upon exiting the front door, Rick strode down Main Street toward isabelle's Pet Shoppe. He walked, his thoughts racing around the subject of Veronica's influence on Alex's behavior. Marquetta had told him just this morning about her conversation with Alex last night. It shocked him that Alex had already done exactly the opposite of what she'd said she'd do.

He approached the front door of Isabelle's Pet Shop, still unable to put his finger on why he was so concerned about Veronica. Maybe, deep down, he knew Veronica needed someone to stand up for her and protect her. From who, though? Her uncle? Or herself? He remembered the troubled girl who'd sat in front of him just a few days ago. Maybe Veronica really was nothing more than a troubled kid.

The brightly painted storefronts of the quaint seaside town made it look like a scene from a postcard. And yet, here they were, once again investigating a murder. In addition, he was trying to protect a teenage girl from making a choice that could ruin multiple lives. He took a deep breath, steeling himself for the conversation ahead.

Inside the shop, Quincy Knox was busy playing a game of solitaire. He didn't seem to notice that Rick had entered and continued humming to himself. Lean with sandy blond hair, Rick could see how a girl like Veronica would be infatuated with him. Quincy's movements were precise, his focus absolute. Rick watched him for several seconds before clearing his throat.

"Sorry to bother you," Rick began, his voice steady. "I don't think we've met. I'm Rick Atwood. I run the Seaside Cove Bed & Breakfast."

Quincy ran his fingers through his long hair and gave Rick a tentative smile. After introducing himself, he stopped, tapped his finger on his chin, and snapped his fingers. "You're Alex's dad. Did she talk to you about a dog? Do you have any questions?"

Rick took a deep breath and decided to cut right to the chase. He had a feeling Quincy would appreciate it. "I actually came to talk to you about Veronica Campbell."

The young man's smile faded, and his expression turned guarded. "What about her?"

Quincy ran his fingers through his hair again, and Rick hoped the young man didn't view his directness as unnecessarily harsh. "Do you mind if I cut straight to the chase?"

"Please do. I'm getting kind of concerned that I'm in some sort of trouble. Has she accused me of something?"

"Have you been seeing her?"

"Well, yeah. I see her around. She's a nice kid."

Struck by the phrasing, Rick suddenly began spinning all sorts of theories. What if Alex had misread what Veronica had told her? What if Veronica misunderstood this young man's intentions? Or what if he was just lying? Something was off, and he needed to push further.

"Odd that you should call her a kid. She's seventeen."

"I know." Suddenly, Quincy's entire expression turned to one of surprise. "Oh, I get it. You think we're dating or something? Really? No way, man. She's total jailbait. I want nothing to do with that kind of trouble."

"But you've been seeing her around town."

Quincy shrugged, "Sure. She's been following me around like a puppy. She keeps showing up down at the harbor. I like it down there, and I guess she figured that out."

"Is there anything more than just seeing each other? Maybe a relationship?"

The young man's guarded expression turned into an amused smile. "I'm way too old for her. Or anybody else who considers the word totally a complete sentence."

Rick held back a smile at that. "Have you been texting her?"

"Yeah, I have. I guess I never should have given her my number. Now, I get stuff from her all the time."

"And today?"

"She was having a tough day, so I sent her a message to cheer her up. It was just a little something to brighten her day." He raised his hands with his palms up. "In their darkest hour, kind words become a tower. Hope blooms, a flower." Quincy held Rick's gaze, and his voice became softer, more apologetic. "You know, when somebody's down, you've gotta help pull them up. Right?"

"I don't question the sentiment, Quincy. Your involvement with a young girl does concern me, though."

There was a hint of regret in Quincy's eyes as he talked. "I get your point. Look, I'm sorry. I didn't mean to lead her on or anything."

Rick studied Quincy's face. He looked sincere. He sounded sincere. Maybe he was, but Rick needed to be sure. "And you're not interested in her? Romantically?"

Quincy laughed, a short, bitter sound. "Do I look like a guy who'd go after a teenager? No. Veronica is a friend, nothing more."

Just then, a parrot perched nearby squawked loudly, mimicking Quincy's last words. "Friend, nothing more! Friend, nothing more!"

Rick considered pressing Quincy further, but the only outcome he could foresee was little gain for a lot of pain. He chuckled as he gestured at the bird. "Well, I guess that settles it. You've got a witness."

Quincy grinned at the parrot. "Yeah, a real reliable one."

Rick left the pet shop feeling slightly relieved but also more worried. If Quincy didn't have a romantic interest in Veronica, then why was he spending time with her? Was this strictly a one-sided relationship? He started toward the police station, but when he got to the corner, he spun on his heel and hurried back to the pet store. Quincy had returned to his game of solitaire and was again engrossed. However, he did look up and smile.

"Forget something, Rick?"

"Just one question. What time do you usually go to the harbor?"

"When I get off work. My aunt keeps kind of a crazy schedule, so I work around that. I get down there most afternoons, though. Why?"

"Just curious," Rick said. He excused himself, rushed out the door, and called Adam as he walked toward the harbor. The call went to voicemail, so Rick left a message and told Adam where he was going.

At the roundabout, he scanned the docks. A few boats were moored, but it was relatively quiet. Two customers stood at the outdoor service window of the Ugly Worm Bait and Tackle shop. And, out on the edge of the dock, a lone figure sat. Even from this distance, he recognized the fiery red hair.

"I found you," Rick said as he followed the roundabout. He crossed the asphalt parking lot with its faded white lines for parking spaces and a profusion of potholes. As he passed Gray's Sailing

Charters, he spotted Joe Gray and waved. Joe returned the gesture, looked out over the marina, and stroked his chin as he sat on one of his deck chairs.

When Rick was close enough for Veronica to sense the vibrations from his footsteps on the wooden planks, she turned. Her bright smile faded immediately, and her shoulders slumped. "Oh," she said. "It's you."

Sadness filled her eyes, and Rick felt a twinge of guilt. He was probably the last person she wanted to see, but he hoped she would at least hear him out. And maybe this time, she'd tell him the truth.

44

RICK

THE SALTY BREEZE TUGGED PLAYFULLY at Veronica's fiery red curls. She sat, studiously ignoring Rick, while he waited. She'd been expecting Quincy Knox. He was just sure of it. The light in her eyes. Her smile. The way it had all evaporated in the instant she'd seen him. Regret filled his veins in anticipation of what he was about to do. With what he needed to do. He had to tell her about his conversation with Quincy. But he couldn't. Not yet. Otherwise, he would destroy any chance of furthering the investigation into Styles's death.

"Veronica, you told me when we first met that Gideon Styles wanted your secret recipe. Do you still feel the same way?"

Veronica twisted to face him, her green eyes flaring with determination. "Yes, I do. He wanted it, and Uncle Tyler was going to sell it to him."

"The odd thing is, the recipe hasn't turned up yet. Do you know if your Uncle Tyler has been contacted by anyone about it?"

"My uncle's not talking to me. He says he doesn't remember anything. He's lying."

"We had him checked out by a physician who said the condition is real. What makes you so certain that the doctor's wrong?"

Veronica's expression softened, her determination giving way to sadness. "Because I've known him all my life. Uncle Tyler was good to me before Mom died. He was never forgetful. He always had a sharp memory, especially when it came to what people liked and didn't like. A customer could come into the store, and he'd remember their name and their order until they came back." The sadness parted, giving way to a reminiscent smile. "He remembered birthdays and holidays, and he always made me feel special."

"And now?"

"It doesn't matter anymore. I don't need the recipe. And I don't need him."

"Why's that?"

"Because I remembered it!" Her green eyes flared in defiance. "I can't believe I forgot it for so long, but I finally remembered it. And now, I don't need anyone, including my Uncle Tyler, anymore."

"You do realize that you're still underage, and you can't just take off on your own. Don't you?"

"I'll sue for emancipation. I have someone who can help me."

It wasn't exactly a bombshell. He'd been expecting something like that. He'd also bet anything Quincy was the someone. So much for not needing anyone. Her confidence also made him wonder which one of the two was taking advantage of the other. "Do you have an attorney?" Rick asked nonchalantly.

Veronica set her jaw and stared out at the ocean. "I don't have to answer your questions. You're not a cop."

Rick paused for a minute, letting her outburst dissipate on the wind. When he saw a slight softening in her jawline, he said quietly, "You have a lot of anger inside. Don't you?"

"Someone killed my mother! And they never found the person who did it!" Her eyes flared with emotion. "At least I can do something about that now."

Rick's heart ached for her. He'd seen firsthand how the pain of losing a loved one could eat away at those left behind. "I understand your need for closure, but don't let it consume you, Veronica. Sometimes, things are just out of our control."

Veronica ignored Rick, her eyes now fixed on some unseen point near the horizon. Considering the weight of her burden, Rick felt it was only a matter of time before she exploded with emotion again. And all that would do is to delay the inevitable.

"I know you're feeling angry. I also know you blame your Uncle Tyler for much of what's happened. Running away isn't going to solve your problems. My guess is you'd need help with that. And that could put whoever helps you in jeopardy. You should be aware that there could be severe consequences for the person who helps you."

Veronica whipped around to face him. "What are you talking about?"

"I'm going to be blunt, Veronica. You think Quincy Knox is going to help you solve all your problems. Don't you?"

Veronica's jaw dropped, but then she shook her head and laughed. She reached out and playfully slapped Rick's arm. "Don't be silly. Quincy? He works for his aunt in a pet shop. He can barely take care of himself, let alone help me find justice for my mother."

Rick raised an eyebrow. "Then why have you been spending so much time with him?"

Veronica's smile faded, and she looked away. "I don't know. I guess it's just nice to have someone around who knows what it feels like to lose a parent. But you're right. He can't solve my problems for me."

Nodding as though he understood, Rick began ticking through the possibilities. From the first meeting at the B&B, he'd sensed that there was something not right with Veronica Campbell. Now, he was sure of it. On top of solving Styles's murder, now he had to stop this girl from ruining a young man's life.

Rick reached out and placed a hand on Veronica's shoulder. For now, he had to let her think she was still in control. "Good. I'm glad we understand each other. Look, I've got to get back to solving a murder case. Adam's following up on some information about Penny Feeney."

The look of shock on Veronica's face was unmistakable. Somehow, Veronica knew Penny. How could that be? And how well did they know each other? Was she the one Veronica thought would help her? Not Quincy?

"You look surprised," Rick said.

"I didn't know you already had a suspect. That's all. So you don't think my Uncle Tyler had anything to do with the killing? You think it was this woman? What was her name? Penny Feeney?"

Rick drew on Adam's standard line, an impassive look and a polite, "Sorry, but I can't talk about an ongoing investigation." He stood, gave Veronica a parting smile, and said, "I'll see you around."

Without waiting for her to reply, Rick turned and walked away. He had so many thoughts rushing through his head that he barely noticed Joe Gray still sitting on the deck of his houseboat, taking in the scene. Rick dismissed Joe from his thoughts and reached for his phone. He had so many ideas to share and talk through with Adam. He dialed Adam's number as he headed for the roundabout.

"I don't think Veronica Campbell's as much of a victim as we thought she was," Rick said when Adam answered.

There was a short pause on the other end of the line before Adam responded. "What do you mean?"

Rick recapped his conversation with Veronica. When he finished, he said, "To top it off, she seemed shocked when I mentioned Penny Feeney's name. I think they know each other."

"Look, buddy, there's no way Veronica's our killer. She was never alone during the time of the murder."

"I understand that. But you remember how she had a complete meltdown when she thought she'd lost the recipe, right? Well, now, she's claiming that she remembered it and doesn't need the stolen copy. There are too many inconsistencies, Adam."

"Okay, buddy, but I think we need more than some accusations to crack Ms. Feeney."

"I agree. That's why I'm going back to Isabelle's Pet Shoppe. Quincy should be off work now, and I want to see what Isabelle can tell me about him."

Rick ended the call as he climbed the stairs to the shop's front door. This time, when he entered, he got an entirely different greeting. As he'd learned the very first time they met, Isabelle Murdoch was not one to ignore her customers.

45

ALEX

THE CLASSROOM IS A SEA of empty desks, except for mine. I'm sitting in the back, feeling like a lone island. A totally lone island. I'm gonna be in big trouble when Mom gets here, all because I told Miss Redmond about Veronica wanting to run away. After that, she called my dad, who told her to call my mom, and then Miss Redmond made me sit here while she grades papers. The only sounds in the room are the hum of the overhead lights and the scratch-scratch-scratch of Miss Redmond's pen on paper.

The door swings open, and my mom spots me sitting in the back row. She gives me what I call her Mom Look. I'm so dead. I only get that stare when I'm in huge trouble. She's got Baby Jack on her hip. She's all confidence and color, her brown hair tied back with a bright red scrunchie. Yup. I'm in so deep.

"Hey, Frankie," Mom says casually as she approaches Miss Redmond's desk.

Frankie? My mom knows Miss Redmond? My brain explodes 'cause I had no idea they were friends.

Miss Redmond looks up. Her face opens up with a bright smile. "Marquetta. It's been too long." She stands, smooths her dress, and approaches my mom. She holds out a finger for Baby Jack, and her voice goes up a little. "Is this the little guy? Isn't he adorable?"

"Frankie, meet Baby Jack. The man who keeps me awake at night."

My mom and Miss Redmond giggle as something I never thought I never saw coming happens. Miss Redmond goes all gaga over Baby Jack. While my teacher coos and tells my little brother what a strong grip he has, I sit in the back feeling kinda jealous. Baby Jack's getting all the good attention. Wait'll it's my turn. I bet Miss Redmond isn't gonna be all goo-goo, gaga then.

Finally, it happens. Miss Redmond seems to realize this isn't just a social call. She clears her throat and says, "Marquetta, thanks for coming in. I talked to Rick, and he suggested I call you so we could talk about Alex's involvement with Veronica Campbell."

Oh, man, there it is. My life is over. I'm gonna be grounded until I get married, maybe even longer.

"He called me, too," Mom says. "He's concerned about Veronica's involvement with Isabelle Murdoch's nephew, Quincy. Rick went to the shop and spoke to Isabelle. Apparently, Isabelle is worried, too. She's noticed a change in her nephew's behavior recently."

"Quincy always cracked under pressure. Do you remember how it took him months to get over that disaster during the science fair?"

Mom shakes her head and winces. "I felt so bad for him. Poor guy."

I'm super curious, so I ask, "What happened?" Whatever. I can't get in any more trouble than I'm already in. Right?

Miss Redmond motions for me to join them, and I feel a lump in my stomach. Maybe I was wrong. I walk slowly, kinda feeling like the longer I take, the better this might get.

"Do you know what specific gravity is, Alex?" Miss Redmond asks.

Oh, man. Now we're having a science test? This is so not fair. "Isn't that like what makes a person able to float in the ocean?"

"Basically, yes. It's a way to compare the density of one substance to another. Seawater has a higher specific gravity than tap water. Quincy was two years behind us. He was always trying to keep up, and so he set up an experiment to demonstrate specific gravity. The problem was that he kept calling it pacific gravity. Mrs. Dickinson, who didn't realize Quincy was dyslexic, didn't pull him aside and explain his mistake quietly but made an example of him in front of all the other kids and their parents."

"Oh, man. And kids can be so mean."

"Exactly. It took months for the commotion to settle down."

"So Quincy's dyslexic?" I ask. "You mean he like switches letters around? Is that why he plays cards?"

Miss Redmond shrugs. "It could be. Maybe he thinks it helps him. There are quite a few tools for dyslexics these days. And some card games can help them."

My mom shifts Baby Jack on her hip. It looks like she's getting kinda tired, and I'm about to ask if she wants me to hold him when Miss Redmond reaches out. "Here, let me. He's so adorable."

Baby Jack seems to love the whole trading-off thing. He smiles and coos like crazy.

"He likes you," I say.

Miss Redmond beams at me. "I like him, too."

"Frankie, what's your impression of Veronica Campbell?" Mom asks.

"I don't know very much about her. She's new at school. I see her sometimes with other girls, but that's about it. I talked to her when she first transferred here, but she was very quiet."

"She's super mad about her mom." I tell them how she blames her Uncle Tyler for her mother's death and add, "She's totally down on her uncle. One time, she even said she thinks he had something to do with her mom's murder."

Miss Redmond's face darkens. I can't help but notice how she hugs Baby Jack a little tighter like he's gonna ward off the bad stuff we're talking about.

"None of that came out when we talked. I wish I'd have spent more time with her. Tried to get her to open up."

"It wouldn't have worked," I say. "She can totally shut down when she wants to."

Mom nods. "Alex is right. I wanted to talk to you in person because of something Rick told me after he talked to Isabelle. He's convinced Veronica is manipulating Quincy. He thinks she's using him to escape from her uncle."

"And if she is that good at manipulating others, I might never have suspected it," Miss Redmond says, her voice super heavy with concern.

Mom looks directly at me. "What do you think, Alex?"

What? She's asking my opinion? Maybe this isn't gonna be so bad after all. "He said she was cool, But he didn't act like he was crushing on her or anything. It was just like the opposite. Like she was the one who was all into him. Mom, I was only trying to find out how he felt about her. I went to the pet shop to ask him about Veronica."

Miss Redmond makes a face, then says, "Quincy never was a very good liar."

"You're right. I guess we'll find out. Rick and Adam are going to call him in. I'm sure he'll tell the truth if he's still the same innocent boy he was in school." All of a sudden, Mom's eyes get wide. "Uh oh. Frankie, you'd better give him back to me. I think somebody needs a change."

Miss Redmond blows out a small breath as she hands Baby Jack back to Mom. Then, she giggles, "What did you give him for lunch, Marquetta?"

Mom laughs. “Believe me. It doesn’t matter much what he eats. Can I take Alex home?”

“Sure. She’s done nothing wrong. Quite the opposite. Marquetta, you should be proud of her. She came to me when she discovered that Veronica was thinking of running away.”

“But…” I blurt. “But you made me sit at my desk.”

Miss Redmond gives me kind of a mock stern face. “That’s true. But do you remember what we talked about, Alex? Personal space.”

“Oh. I get it. I won’t interfere again.” I’m disappointed because Miss Redmond really is pretty cool. And the fact that she likes Barrington Rhymes makes it super hard not to get involved.

“Good girl.”

Mom cradles Baby Jack on her hip. “Hey, Frankie, you should come to dinner. It’d be fun to catch up.”

“It sounds delightful, but I don’t want to impose.”

“Oh, don’t be silly. We have a house filled with people all the time. It would be nice to have someone I’ve known for more than twenty-four hours to talk to. How about tonight? Lydia helped me get dinner on before I left to come down here. It’s nothing fancy, just roasted chicken with roasted vegetables. Believe me, there’s plenty. Especially if Rick works late with Adam.”

Miss Redmond smiles, and her cheeks get kinda pink. “It would be nice to have someone to talk to for dinner.”

“It’s settled, then. Stop by at about five. We’ll eat at five-thirty.”

“Should I bring something?”

“Your appetite. And if you want, a bottle of wine. But that’s not a requirement.”

“Okay. I’ll see you then.”

On the drive home, Mom says, “As soon as we get home, I’ll change Baby Jack. You, young lady, your job is to find Mr. Rhymes and invite him to dinner.”

"What? But I just got in trouble for interfering in Miss Redmond's love life."

"You're not interfering. You're simply inviting Mr. Tall, Dark, and Mysterious to our dinner table. I'm the one who's meddling."

"Uh, okay. I can invite him."

"Good. And, by the way, Sweetie, I hope you were taking notes. That's how matchmaking is done."

I can't keep the grin off my face for the rest of the drive home. If there's one thing I've learned today, it's that my mom is way cooler than I ever could have guessed.

46

RICK

RICK PUSHED OPEN THE DOOR of the Seaside Cove police station, saw Deputy Kama sitting at her desk, and said hello. "Nice to see you back, Amy. Feeling better?"

"I felt fine yesterday, but you know how the doctors are. I'm glad to be back at work. The chief's waiting for you. Go on back."

Adam was at his desk, hunched over a yellow notepad filled with what looked like a chicken's scratchings. He'd taped photos of their suspects and the victim on the wall behind the desk. It wasn't something they'd done in the past, but Rick supposed a few visuals couldn't hurt their process. Adam's hair was sticking up in tufts as if he'd been running his fingers through it or maybe trying to tear it out. Definitely, visuals couldn't hurt.

Adam looked up and motioned for Rick to join him. "What's up?"

"I just finished talking with Isabelle Murdoch."

Adam's green eyes, though weary, were suddenly attentive. "What did you learn?"

Rick sat on the edge of the desk and gave his friend a knowing look. "We've got a murder board now?"

Looking over his shoulder, Adam snickered. "First class, right? Amazing what you can do with some tape, a few photos, and a wall. Why are you so upbeat?"

"We might have a new way of looking at things. From what Isabelle told me, it sounds like we had the roles backwards. I don't think Quincy Knox was trying to take advantage of anyone. I think he might be more of a puppet than a mastermind."

Adam rubbed his tired eyes, which were now bloodshot and weary. "You're talking about the girl? Veronica Campbell?"

"Yes. It appears she's more mature than we gave her credit for."

"Meaning?" Adam grabbed the notepad and flipped to a clean page.

Rick sat, eager to share what might be an opportunity to change the lack of progress they'd seen so far. Even though they'd only worked the case for a few days, he wanted to move on and put this entire affair behind them. He looked up at the wall and said, "You're kind of light on photos. All you have are Styles, Penny Feeney, and Tyler Winkle."

"I'm working on a budget here, okay? Besides, Feeney and Winkle are our only suspects. So what did you find out at Isabelle's?"

"Quincy was working when I got there. He denied having any interest in Veronica, but I couldn't stop wondering why he was spending time with her if he was telling me the truth."

"Logical question. I assume you asked him about it. What did he say?"

"That she was too young for him and that she was just a friend." When Adam made a face, Rick continued, "I didn't believe it either. So, when he told me he liked to go to the marina when he got off work, I decided to see if she was there."

Adam made a note. "We should check with Joe Gray and Jennifer Martin. Maybe one of them has seen her."

"Already done. I struck out with Jennifer, but Joe had seen her and Quincy together."

"Guy's better than a security camera," Adam snickered.

“You’re right. Not only had he seen Veronica, but he knew about her past, including her troubles with the police before they moved here. He also said that when she was with Quincy, she was, and I quote, ‘all googoo-eyed’ over him.”

“It certainly sounds like she wants something more than just friendship from that relationship. But how does that help us?”

“On its own, it doesn’t. But when I talked to Isabelle, she said she’s concerned about Quincy’s relationship with Veronica. She’s noticed how he’s paying less attention to his duties at the store and seems more distracted lately.”

“Isn’t that the pot calling the kettle black? Isabelle’s not exactly one hundred percent in the cognition department.”

“Yes, but Isabelle has a medical condition that’s causing it. Quincy, on the other hand, has no real excuse other than being distracted by someone or something. If he is truly being manipulated by Veronica, it could explain the sudden change in his behavior. Maybe he’s denying his interest in her because that’s what she wants him to do.”

“So you’re seeing Veronica as some sort of puppetmaster? Seems like a stretch.” Adam scribbled some notes on the notepad. “Do you think I should add her to the list as a possible suspect?”

“I don’t know. Not yet. But if Quincy is interested in her romantically, it could mean he’s doing her bidding.” Rick slumped down a little in his chair and rested his chin on his knuckles. “We know how much Veronica seems to have hated Gideon Styles. So I wondered if maybe she’d convinced Quincy to kill him.”

“Great. Ripped from the headlines. Another boyfriend commits murder to impress his girlfriend. Maybe I should take a photo of him and add him to the wall.”

“You mean the murder board,” Rick smirked.

"I don't think three or four photos classify as much of anything. Let's just stick to calling it what it is—a wall."

"Whatever you say. You're the Chief of Police. Anyway, I had the same idea about Quincy when I talked to Veronica at the harbor. I figured before I got too carried away, I'd find out if he had an alibi. Turns out he does. According to Isabelle, he was working at the time of the murder."

"Doing what?"

"Picking up supplies in San Ladron."

"So he was an hour away. Makes it hard for him to be our killer." Adam groaned.

"Right. And neither is Veronica because she was with me at the time someone shot Styles."

Adam shook his head, planted his elbows on his desk, and huffed. "So what exactly was your point in all this? You came here to tell me that two people we didn't consider suspects aren't?"

"Not at all. I still think Veronica is involved. I just think we had the wrong accomplice."

"Feeney," Adam said. "The one person with the most to gain from Styles's death."

"Exactly. And if she's the killer, that means she's been lying to us this whole time." Rick rubbed his temples. "The big question is, how do you get an accomplished liar to suddenly tell the truth?"

"By boxing her in with evidence. It's our job to follow every lead, no matter how unlikely it may seem," Adam parroted back the message Rick had drummed into him since their first case.

"Are you mocking me?" Rick snickered.

"Not at all. Well, maybe a little."

Rick let out a frustrated huff. "I hear you. And you're right, but it does feel like we're going in circles sometimes."

As the two men continued to discuss their findings, Rick felt like a dog chasing its tail. When Adam's gaze went past him, he turned to see what had caught Adam's attention. Isabelle Murdoch was talking to Deputy Kama. Isabelle had a piece of paper in her hand and was shaking it as she talked.

Deputy Kama stood and escorted Isabelle back to Adam's desk. "Sorry to interrupt, Chief, but Mrs. Murdoch has something she wants you to see."

"That's right," Isabelle said adamantly.

Rick's eyes widened at how fired up Isabelle seemed. She was five-foot-two and heavyset, and Rick typically thought of her as the friendly grandmother type, but right now, she reminded him of a bulldog on guard as she practically shoved the paper into his face.

"Is everything okay, Isabelle?" Rick asked.

"After our conversation, I couldn't let it go. You need to see this. It's a receipt for the supplies Quincy picked up in San Ladron. This proves what I told you is true."

"Isabelle, I didn't doubt you."

"It didn't sound that way to me." She jabbed a pudgy finger at the paper. "That's Quincy's alibi. It proves he was in San Ladron at the time of your murder." She shook her head defiantly. "I thought it might be important for your investigation."

Rick and Adam quickly scanned the document. "Thanks for bringing this in, Isabelle," Rick said. "I apologize for upsetting you. But you really didn't have to do that. Honestly, I believed what you told me."

"Oh." Isabelle's expression softened, then she said, "Well, I didn't want you having any doubts about Quincy. He might be naive, but he's a good boy. It's that girl who is the bad influence. She's trouble, I tell you."

"Thank you, Isabelle," Adam said gratefully. This helps narrow down our suspect list. You can be assured that we're looking into all possibilities here." Adam gestured behind him at the wall. And, as you can see, Quincy's not even on our murder board."

Isabelle squinted at the wall for a minute, then said, "That's a murder board? Chief, the mayor should give you a bigger budget." Suddenly, she stopped and looked closer at the wall. "Who's that man in the middle? Is that your victim?"

"Yes. Gideon Styles."

"He looks familiar," Isabelle said as she tapped her chin with her finger. "Hmmm...I'll think of it. Well, I have to go."

Isabelle said a polite goodbye and left. When she was gone, Rick felt a sense of relief. "I think this clinches it, Adam. Quincy and Veronica both have solid alibis. That only leaves us with one suspect."

"I disagree," Adam said. "I think maybe we have two. I haven't ruled out Tyler Winkle."

"I suppose you're right. I guess I just don't want it to be him. The guy's been through so much." Rick paused and pointed at Adam's yellow notepad. "You were making notes when I walked in. Anything you care to share?"

"Like you, I think there's something here that doesn't make sense. We're sure Feeney stole the recipe, but when you think about it, she stopped talking after she told us she conspired with Gideon to steal it. She never actually said she had it."

Rick now understood where Adam was going with this. "So maybe she wasn't the one who actually stole it? Is that where you think Tyler comes in?"

"What if he removed the recipe from the safe?"

"Why wouldn't he have told us when we were there about the break-in?"

"It could be he wanted everyone to think it had been stolen. And now that he's forgotten what he did, it really is lost."

Rick considered Adam's theory. It was no worse than the others they had. And maybe better. Other pieces fit with the scenario. "So Penny broke in to steal the recipe, realized it was gone, and trashed the house. Then, when she reported back to Styles, he blew up, they argued, and she killed him."

"She confesses to the break-in and the theft of the recipe because the penalty's a lot less than it is for murder."

It was clear that there were still many unanswered questions surrounding the theft of the recipe and the murder of Gideon Styles. Rick and Adam continued to brainstorm, trying to piece together all the information they had gathered. At one point, Adam stopped, made a note, and tapped his pen on the pad of paper.

"I wish we'd have found Feeney right after the shooting. At least then we could have tested for gunshot residue."

Rick rubbed his neck as he spoke absently. "That would have been nice. It would have made things pretty simple. It's not necessarily too late now."

Adam frowned as he looked at Rick. "Typically, the window's only four to six hours. There have been cases where there's been residue present up to five days after someone's discharged a firearm, but that's the rare exception. I'm sure you already know that, though."

"True. But if it's present, we know she's our killer."

"And if it's not, it doesn't prove a thing."

Rick gave Adam a crooked smile. "Maybe she doesn't know that."

Adam's green eyes reflected a mix of amusement and seriousness. "You're right. I'll bet she doesn't. I'll have Kama conduct the test."

47

RICK

STANDING OUTSIDE THE INTERROGATION ROOM watching Deputy Kama swab Penny Feeney's hands, Rick whispered under his breath, "She's never going to fall for this."

Adam whispered back, "What was that?"

"Sorry. I didn't realize I said that out loud. This is such a long shot. Maybe one in a million chances that it will work."

Adam's expression turned serious. "I know, but it's the only shot we have without any solid evidence against her."

"What if she's not our killer?" Rick asked.

"Then who is? She's the only one who makes sense. She had a motive—"

"We think."

"What? Are you on her side now?"

"No," Rick said and grimaced. "I'm just getting worried that we've missed something."

"We've looked into everyone else involved, and they all have alibis or no motive."

"I don't know, Adam. I still think we're missing something."

Rick looked over his shoulder at the photos on the wall. He spoke faster as he realized that, indeed, they had missed an entirely different motive. "What if this murder had nothing to do with the stolen recipe? What if the burglary is unrelated to the murder?"

Adam gazed at the photos as Rick continued, his mind racing with the new possibility.

"We've been so focused on these guys as suspects that we haven't even considered any other possibilities."

Adam's expression was thoughtful. "Could be. You're suggesting we try looking at it through a different lens. You could be right. Maybe we've been focused on the wrong motive."

"Exactly. Let's get back in there and finish this interrogation. We're not ruling out Penny just yet, but we'll also start exploring other leads," Rick said with determination.

They entered the interrogation room. So far, they'd been lucky because Penny hadn't asked for an attorney. Both Rick and Adam were reluctant to push her too hard. If they did, she might decide to take the easy out, which was an option neither wanted to consider. As they sat, Rick watched Penny's face. She was a tough one to crack, that's for sure. But he sensed something in her eyes, some deep-down reluctance to tell the truth. Almost as if she were holding back to protect someone else.

"Look, Penny," Rick began, his tone serious yet empathetic. "We know you were close with Gideon. We won't have the results of the gunshot residue test until later today or tomorrow. The Chief and I don't really think you killed Gideon, which leaves us with the question of who did. How many enemies did he have? Would they hate him enough to commit murder?"

Instead of avoiding his eye contact, Penny suddenly turned a laser-focused gaze on Rick. "That baker, for one," she shot back. "There were plenty of others, but most wouldn't know how to find him."

Adam placed his hand on the yellow notepad and slid it across the table. "Let's be more specific, Ms. Feeney. How many others? Why don't you help your case and write down some names?"

The intensity in her voice that had been there before suddenly softened. She hesitantly took the pen and scribbled down a few names before sliding the notepad back across the table.

"I don't know if any of them could have done it, but they all had grudges against Gideon for one reason or another." She focused on the boxes stacked in the supply corner of the room for a few seconds, then shook her head. "I never thought anyone could hate him that much."

The list consisted of four names, none of them familiar. Rick scanned the names again. They were common. It was the kind of list that could take them at least a week to weed through. On a hunch, Rick pushed the list back at Penny. "That's not enough. We need to know how to contact these people. And what their connection is to Gideon."

The crowsfeet around Penny's eyes crinkled. She cocked her head to the right and twirled a lock of near-black hair around her finger. She inched closer to Rick and smiled. "What's in it for me?"

"A chance to walk out the door free," Rick replied cooly.

To his side, Rick could tell that Adam wasn't comfortable with the answer, but Rick had a feeling he now understood Penny Feeney. He'd dealt with people like her before. The players. The manipulators. The confident liars. He fully expected her to spin a tale and let her words flow freely. Each sentence might be punctuated with a laugh, a knowing look, or a coy shrug. She'd weave in small anecdotes to ensure her listeners would be captivated by her story. She'd be so convincing that even if they knew she was lying, they'd want to believe her.

She held Rick's gaze, her blue eyes locked onto his. He recognized the move. It was intended to make him feel seen, heard, and understood. What he hoped she didn't realize was that he'd seen this game play out many times and knew how to deal with it.

"Hang on a second, Rick, I have an offer for Ms. Feeney," Adam said.

"Okay," Rick said tentatively. He supposed that if he could go off script, Adam could do the same. "What did you have in mind?"

"Ms. Feeney, I'm pretty sure this list of names is nothing more than a wild goose chase. So, before we let you start telling us a fairy tale about all these people and how your ex-boyfriend wronged them, here's my offer. You stop playing games with us and tell us the truth about what happened on the day of Gideon Styles's murder. In exchange, I don't start digging into your past. You see, this is a small town PD, and we don't have much to do other than hand out parking tickets to tourists. So if you don't want me digging into your past and finding crimes other law enforcement agencies will want to question you about, I'd suggest you start being straight with us."

Oh, man, was Adam laying it on thick, but Penny didn't seem to know whether he was telling the truth or lying. Why not add a little more fuel to the fire? "The Chief is right, Penny. As you can see, I've got plenty of time to sneak away from the B&B to help out here. I've got a lot of contacts from my old newspaper days. For instance, there's your ex's claim that you stole a painting from him. We could contact the Pokerville PD and have them reopen the investigation."

"That's right," Adam said confidently. "By the time we're done, we'll know every detail of every crime you were ever involved in."

Penny's smug facade faltered, her eyes darting between Rick and Adam. Rick admired Adam's bluster. It might have been just what they needed. And bringing up Tom Reynolds showed that they had done some digging into her past. She had to be wondering how deep they'd be willing to dig. Either she could take the deal to avoid having them dredge up something incriminating in her past, or she could continue playing games and risk getting caught in even more lies.

"Sounds like a good offer to me," Rick said, trying to keep his tone neutral. He didn't want Penny to think he was on her side just yet.

Penny's eyes narrowed, and she chewed at her bottom lip before finally speaking. "Fine. You want to know what happened that day. I'll tell you if you give me immunity from the murder charge."

"I thought you said you didn't kill Styles. Why would you need immunity?" Adam's voice grew in intensity.

"I didn't kill him!" She buried her face in her hands and shook her head. "Gideon always thought he was so smart. I told you before. From the beginning, he never planned on paying for the recipe. He had me go to the house because that idiot baker told him he was keeping the recipe under lock and key in his bedroom. How stupid do you have to be to tell a guy like Gideon right where the safe is?"

Rick ignored the question and responded with one of his own. "You keep saying you were in the house to steal the recipe, but what about all the damage? That place looked like it had been hit by a hurricane."

"It wasn't me," Penny said. "When I got there, the place was already ransacked."

Adam responded by resting his elbows on the tabletop and focusing intently on Penny. "You're saying someone else broke in before you?"

Penny's eyes flitted around the room, and when they settled back on Adam, they were large and pleading. "I swear, I didn't do it! I just wanted the recipe. That's all."

"Okay, let's say we believe you," Adam said, folding his arms across his chest. "If it wasn't you, who broke in and vandalized the place?"

Penny's eyes darted around the room. "I don't know. I really don't. That was the other thing about Gideon. He kept things compartmentalized."

Rick leaned forward, his curiosity piqued. “You know this because he’s done it before?”

“Yes. He’d hire one person to do one thing and someone else to handle another. He figured if either one was ever caught, they couldn’t implicate anyone but themselves.”

“Unless they told the authorities who hired them.”

Penny smirked. “It would never happen. Gideon made sure everyone was loyal to him. He had dirt on everyone.”

Rick had learned a long time ago that if you dug deep enough, you could always find something in a person’s past. Sometimes you just needed an excavator. If what Penny was saying was true, it meant Gideon was one of those people who knew how to do the digging. “So you’re saying someone trashed the house before you got there, and you have no idea who it was. Sorry, Adam, but I don’t think that’s enough. She’s admitted to being in the house. I think you should charge her with breaking and entering, theft, and vandalism. Even without the murder, she could be facing a long prison stretch.”

Penny bit her lip again. “Okay, okay. What if I tell you where you can find the recipe? Let’s call it a sign of goodwill.”

“That would be a good start,” Adam said. “Where is it?”

“I gave it back.”

“Really?” Rick scoffed. “Who’d you give it to?”

“Before I answer that, let me show you something else.”

Rick hid a smile at Penny’s resourcefulness. The woman was prepared for all contingencies. What other tricks did she have up her sleeves? He said, “Okay, we’ll play along. What is it you’d like to share with us?”

She leaned back in her chair and crossed her arms over her chest. Suddenly, her tone shifted, becoming assertive and confident. “I’m not the one who trashed the house,” she said firmly. “And I have proof to back it up.”

"Really?" Adam locked his gaze onto Penny's. "What kind of proof?"

"Bring my stuff in here, and I'll show you something."

Adam stood, went to the door, and asked Deputy Kama to bring in Penny's belongings. When the deputy returned, she laid a plastic bag containing a set of keys, a pocket knife, some pepper spray, and a scrap of paper on the table.

"That paper? It was on the floor in the living room when I got there."

Deputy Kama pulled the paper from the bag and handed it to Adam. He read it, then passed it to Rick. While Rick read the short note, Adam asked, "And the significance of this little diddy is what?"

Chaos born of me,
In regret, I seek your peace,
Forgive my storm's roar, please.

As Rick considered the words, he realized that they had indeed been looking at this case all wrong. He thought about Penny's words—*Gideon had dirt on everyone*. If he was right, the person who'd ransacked the house hadn't wanted to do it but had been forced to be there by Styles. Rick said, "It's a confession, Adam. And maybe a plea for help. And it might be just the break we need."

48

ALEX

IT DOESN'T TAKE ME LONG to find Mr. Rhymes. He's in the living room, sitting on one of the couches, looking like he's misplaced his favorite book or something equally tragic. His deep blue eyes are clouded over with confusion, and he's tapping a B&B pen on a notepad he's got perched on his lap.

"Hey there, Mr. Rhymes. You look like you just lost a game of tic-tac-toe to a five-year-old. What's up?" I plop down on the couch next to him.

He rests the pad on his lap and playfully tosses the pen at me. "Take your pen back. It doesn't work."

I pick it up and start to take it apart, but he gently takes the pen from my hand. I stammer, "How about if I get you another pen? I'm sure it'll work." I can't believe it. We just got this supply in. And my dad was so sure the guests would love them.

"It won't write the words I need," he snickers. Then, he shakes his head. "Don't worry. There's nothing wrong with the pen. I have a bad case of writer's block."

"What's that? Sounds serious."

"It is," he says with a dramatic sigh. "Today, I've lost my focus. I think my muse has taken an unexpected vacation. I've been trying to coax her back, but she seems quite determined to enjoy her break."

Huh? What's a muse? Or, maybe, who? Could it be Miss Redmond? "Is your muse like a real person?" I ask, trying not to sound too excited.

He looks at the flames and then begins to ramble. "No, a muse is your inspiration. Your fire, if you will. There's a harmony to life. Synchrony that speaks of unity. It's like those flames. See how the oranges, reds, and yellows mingle together to create a radiant exhibition of colors that warm not only the room but the hearts of those watching?"

Wow. "Mr. Rhymes? Are you feeling okay? You sound like you're on a roll. In fact, you don't sound very blocked to me. I think maybe you're just writing about the wrong thing. Or person."

He stops and gets one of those stupid grins on his face that I used to see on my mom's and dad's faces when they first met. It was how I knew they belonged together.

"You could be right, Alex. Maybe I should think about writing something different."

"Hey, I never asked. How did your dinner with Miss Redmond go?"

His face lights up." Wonderful. Frankie is an amazing woman." He stops, shakes his head, and says, "No. That's inappropriate. You're a bad influence on me, Alex. I should be focusing on my work. My boss is starting to grumble about how long I've been here. I'll be leaving Seaside Cove soon. I've run out of excuses for staying here."

Oh, no. He can't leave. Not yet. Time to go for it before he convinces himself he should eat alone. "My mom asked me to invite you to dinner. Tonight."

He makes a face. "Oh, I don't know. Do you normally do that? Invite guests, I mean."

Duh. No. "Only for special occasions."

He looks at me kinda funny. His blue eyes are clouding over again. "What's the special occasion?"

"My favorite teacher's coming to dinner."

Shaking his head, he still looks confused. "Who's your favorite teacher?"

"Miss Redmond," I say with a smile.

"Oh!" It takes a few seconds before the confusion gives way to excitement like the fog gives way to the sun on a warm morning.

Oh yeah, Operation Epic Recovery is totally gonna rock his world.

49

RICK

AFTER REVEALING THE NOTE SHE'D found in Tyler's home, Penny had made more demands for immunity. While Adam wrangled that situation, Rick went to Tyler's house. The drive would have been quick, but just as Rick was making the final turn onto Tyler's street, a movement at the opening of a narrow alley caught his attention. He parked, then backtracked on foot and watched a man walking his dog.

The alley was now cast in long shadows that danced with the leaves rustling gently in the evening breeze. The warm hues lent an air of tranquility to the otherwise mundane scene. The man Rick had seen earlier moved at a leisurely pace. There was a relaxed rhythm to his steps, a contentment in his demeanor as he watched his small companion explore the world around them.

The dog, a pint-sized bundle of energy, meandered from one interesting scent to another, his nose to the ground and his tail wagging enthusiastically at the variety of enticements. The leash connecting man and dog seemed to serve not as a restraint but as a lifeline, a symbol of their shared journey. The man allowed the dog to lead. He seemed patient and understanding as he let his hand follow the pull of the tether between them.

When Rick stepped into the alley, the crunch of his shoe on dirt caught the dog's attention. The tranquility exploded into chaos as the dog snapped and barked furiously at the intruder. The man halfheartedly tugged on the leash and encouraged the dog to settle down. After what felt like an eternity, he reached down and scooped up the dog.

"I guess you scared him."

Surprised at the man's matter-of-fact tone, Rick said, "That makes two of us. My name's Rick, by the way."

The man smiled and said, "I'm John. Sorry about that; he usually doesn't react so strongly to strangers."

Rick chuckled and replied, "No worries. I guess I just have one of those faces."

The dog squirmed, but John clutched his small companion to his chest and clucked at him. When he looked at Rick, he asked, "So what brings you down this alley? It's not exactly a usual spot for a stroll."

"I'm actually doing some work with the Seaside Cove Police. Were you aware that there was a recent break-in at one of these homes?"

The man's jaw dropped. "No. Really? In the forty years I've lived here, this has always been such a quiet neighborhood." He looked down at his dog and grimaced. "We kind of keep to ourselves these days. All our friends are gone."

Rick scanned the alley beyond where the man stood. "Does this alley connect to all of the homes on the block?"

The dog squirmed again, and this time John made a face. "Alright, alright. Just don't bark at the man. Okay?" He lowered the dog to the ground. This time, the dog growled, but he seemed to have accepted Rick as more of an intrusion than a threat. John was also apparently satisfied that the situation was under control because he looked up and continued, "The new people don't use it at all. Originally, we all put our garbage cans out here, but now, with those new mechanical-arm trucks they use, we have to haul the cans out to the street."

Gazing past John and the dog, Rick studied the back of the third house on the block—Tyler's house. "So if someone came through this alley during the middle of the day, they probably wouldn't be noticed?"

John gestured at the homes along the alley. "I doubt it. Most of these people work and don't get home until suppertime." John suddenly stopped and eyed Rick. "Who did you say you were?"

Rick reintroduced himself and explained his role as a police consultant. With John and his dog apparently satisfied that he wasn't a danger, Rick asked a few more questions, more out of an attempt to be polite and friendly than to gain information. He then excused himself and circled around the block to Tyler's house. Standing in front of the old Craftsman, the conversation with John ran through Rick's thoughts. He turned and looked across the street at the home of the only person on the block who had seen anything of any value. Mrs. Maynard had described a woman leaving the house, but she hadn't seen anyone else. Maybe that was because she couldn't have.

As he ascended the steps to the wide front porch, Rick decided he was starting to believe Penny Feeney's version of the day. There must have been two people who'd broken into the home. He knocked on the door, now anxious to get a look at the back entrance.

Tyler Winkle opened the front door and peered at Rick from behind the screen. "Ah, Rick. Getting kind of late in the day, isn't it?"

"Unfortunately, the days for both me and Adam have gotten much longer lately."

"Sure. I guess so. What can I do for you?"

"I have some questions about the day of the break-in. Have you got a few minutes?"

"I suppose. I don't really remember anything, though." Tyler pushed open the screen door and gestured for Rick to enter.

The room was even neater than it had been on his last visit, a far cry from the chaotic mess it had been on the day of the break-in. Furniture had been arranged thoughtfully, and knickknacks were now on the shelves instead of scattered about the floor.

Tyler gestured for Rick to take a seat, but Rick declined. "This will only take a few minutes. Was the house empty most of the day you met with Gideon Styles?"

"I would have been here until I left for lunch, so that would have been about eleven-thirty. Veronica had school, so she left early. That's the last thing I remember from the day. Why?"

"We now believe there might have been two break-ins that day. One was committed by Penny Feeney. She's the thief who stole your secret recipe."

Tyler's eyes widened. "Do you mean you have it?"

"Have what?" Veronica asked as she entered the room. She was in the process of texting someone, but when she looked up from her phone and saw Rick, her face hardened. "What are you doing here?"

"I just wanted to ask a few questions about the day of the break-in."

Veronica made a humphing noise and rolled her eyes. "Whatever." She turned to her uncle. "I have some shopping to do. I'll be back in a couple hours."

"No, Veronica. We've talked about this."

Rather than shooting back with the fire Rick expected, Veronica resorted to a childlike pout. Her voice went up an octave as she wheedled, "Uncle Tyler. I need some personal items. Girl stuff."

Tyler suddenly flushed and stammered a quick, "Oh. Okay."

"Before you go," Rick said. "As I was telling your uncle, we're now operating on the theory that there were two break-ins." He told her about Penny and the note, then went on to suggest how a second intruder might have come in through the back door.

"Uncle Tyler? You didn't get that lock fixed?"

"No. I forgot."

Veronica gave him one of her signature eye rolls and muttered another, "Whatever."

"What's wrong with the lock?" Rick asked.

"It froze up on us the first week we moved in. I jimmied it open so we could go in and out, but when I told the landlord, he said that since I'd damaged the lock, it was my responsibility to fix it."

Rick pointed toward the back of the house. "Can I see it?"

"I guess." Tyler started toward the kitchen, and Veronica looked like she was going to make a break for the front door.

Stepping in front of the girl to block her exit, Rick looked her in the eye. "Veronica, I need you to wait a few minutes. I have several questions for you, too."

After a dramatic huff, she grimaced. "If I have to."

"Thank you," Rick said. "Now, let's all have a look at that door. I may have a solution for you."

Tyler led the way. Rick gestured for Veronica to follow her uncle, and then he brought up the rear. It took only a moment to diagnose the problem. The old hardware had indeed frozen up, and the solution was probably quite simple—remove all of the hardware, clean the components, loosen the set screw, then put it all back together if there were no broken parts.

"I have a handyman that has fixed several of these for us around the B&B. He'd be happy to take a look at it. He and his wife have three boys, so I'll bet he'd be willing to fix this for you for, say, a dozen muffins?"

Tyler gaped at Rick, then said, "That's all? I thought it would cost me a fortune to have someone come in."

"I'll have him call you tomorrow," Rick said, avoiding the obvious answer. Yes, indeed, it should cost more than a dozen muffins. But he saw these people as needing a little kindness right now, so he'd make the arrangements. "We think whoever did this damage wanted to hurt you. It's possible we have a lead on the person who ransacked your house. They left behind a poem, and I'd like you both to take a look at it."

Veronica's hand went to her throat, and she swallowed hard. "A poem? What kind of poem?"

"It's called a haiku," Rick said as he reached for the paper. At the buzzing of his phone, Rick checked the screen. It was a message from Adam.

Feeney says she gave the recipe to the girl.

Rick pocketed his phone. If Penny had returned the recipe to Veronica, then why hadn't she said something? There was only one reason he could think of—she was planning on making her escape. He smiled, pulled the paper from his pocket, and said, "Here it is." He handed the paper to Tyler, forcing Veronica to read over her uncle's shoulder. He watched her face closely, now suspicious of every move she made.

50

ALEX

MOM'S IN THE KITCHEN LOOKING kind of flustered. She's retying the scrunchie in her hair, shaking her head, and muttering to herself. She keeps repeating Lydia's name and asking what she's done.

"What's wrong, Mom?"

"Oh, good, you're back. Is Mr. Rhymes coming to dinner?"

"For sure."

"Excellent." She grabs a piece of paper and a pen and plops down onto her stool at the kitchen island. It looks like she's writing out a grocery list. "I need you to go to the store, Alex."

Uh oh. This is serious. She called me Alex. "What happened?"

"Lydia used the last of the potatoes for dinner and didn't tell me. That's so unlike her," she says as she writes out a list with two more items—onions and bell peppers. She stops, looks at the clock, then me. "Maybe I should do this myself. A bag of potatoes will be pretty heavy on your bike."

"It's no problem." I don't dare tell her I gave Sasha a ride on my bike the other day—she'd freak out.

She fusses a little bit but finally gives in. I grab my backpack so I can put the onions and peppers in there and balance the load better, then take off. On my way, I slow down when I get to Marina Park so I can look out over the harbor.

I hold my hand up over my eyes because the sun is now hanging out over the ocean. It's such a pretty sight with the light glinting off the smaller waves like diamonds sparkling on a sea of blue-black.

There's no sign of Veronica or her boyfriend. That's okay because if they were here, I'd probably only get in trouble. I get back on my bike and head for the market. After I lock up my bike, I look down the street. Isabelle's Pet Shoppe is there. I'd kind of like to see if Quincy is working. But just as I'm trying to make a decision, my phone pings with my mom's message tone.

I pull the phone from my back pocket and read her message.

No dawdling.

I realize I'm grinning from ear to ear as I read it again. She totally knows me. I text back that I'm heading into the market right now. I grab a cart and head for the produce section. The market's getting a little busy. It's mostly people I recognize. A few are tourists. You can always tell because they look totally lost. When I get to the veggie section, I see Mrs. Murdoch and Lydia. Lydia's standing in front of the section with the bell peppers, and Mrs. Murdoch is in front of the onions.

I wave to Mrs. Murdoch, then go say hi to Lydia.

She looks up, smiles, and gives me a funny look. "Alex? What are you doing here?"

"Mom wanted me to get potatoes, onions, and peppers for breakfast tomorrow."

"Why would she do that? I left her a note telling her I'd used the last of them and would pick them up this afternoon."

"That's weird. Mom didn't say anything about a note. Maybe she missed it."

Lydia laughs. "Or maybe she just wanted to make sure you got some exercise."

I laugh along with her, grab a few onions, and plop them into my backpack. "I'm gonna get what's on my list. It's no big deal if we have extras, we'll use them up in a day or two. Where'd you leave the note?"

"Right on the counter. I got a call from Traci about her wedding." Lydia stops, closes her eyes, and shakes her head. She reaches into her pocket and pulls out a piece of Seaside Cove stationary. "Oh no, I wanted to make a note about Traci's wedding, so I put the note to Marquetta in my pocket. I forgot to put it back on the counter. I'm so sorry, Alex."

Mrs. Murdoch, who seems to be debating between a red and a yellow onion, laughs. "Oh, Lydia, if you only knew how many times I've put notes in my pocket and forgotten about them. I usually find them when they fall apart in the laundry."

We all laugh, and then I tell Mrs. Murdoch about the red onion being better for her than the yellow. Her cheek quirks up like she's tasting something nasty. "That's what my doctor told me, too. You know what? I'm not going to worry about it. I never have liked red onions. They're way too strong for my taste."

She puts the red one back and the yellow one in her cart.

"How's your nephew doing?" Lydia asks.

I totally know why Lydia's asking the question. She loves to gossip. But then, so does Mrs. Murdoch. For the next couple of minutes, she goes on about how unfair the police are being to her nephew, all because he's interested in a girl. Then she starts telling us what a terrible influence the girl is.

Even though she doesn't mention a name, it's obvious she's talking about Veronica. I feel like I should defend my friend, but that's kinda hard to do with the way she treats people. "I don't think it's because she wants to be bad. She's been messed up ever since her mom was killed."

Lydia looks around and lowers her voice. "I heard she's been in trouble with the law on several occasions. Alex, do you know anything about that?"

Oh man, I should not have let myself get dragged into this. Now, what do I do? "I'm not sure," I say, even though Veronica's told me all about it. "I think she got kind of lost for a while."

"I heard that's why her uncle moved them here," Mrs. Murdoch says.

"And then, someone broke into their house! What brought that on?" Lydia clucks her tongue a few times.

"What about the murder?" Mrs. Murdoch gasps. "I heard the man who died was doing business with her uncle. They were at lunch right before it happened!"

This is so not fair. They're gonna trash Veronica and her Uncle Tyler just because they're new to town and have had some hard times. "My dad's working with Chief Cunningham to find the killer. They have some leads they're following."

Lydia narrows her eyes. "And your dad believes that girl could really be innocent?"

I can sense the judgment in Lydia's tone, but I stay calm. "He believes everyone is innocent until proven otherwise. And Veronica has a solid alibi for the time of the murder."

Mrs. Murdoch shakes her head disapprovingly. "Well, I hope they catch the killer soon. We don't need any more trouble in this town."

"I think we should all keep an open mind," I say firmly. "There's a lot we don't know yet."

"Really?" Mrs. Murdoch says.

Lydia's face lights up. She wraps her arm around my shoulders and smiles at me. "Alex? You've been holding out on me. Do tell."

51

RICK

ANGER HARDENED TYLER WINKLE'S FACE as he read the haiku. He clenched his jaw and grumbled, "This is ridiculous. Who would do such a thing?"

"I have an idea, but don't yet have proof," Rick replied.

Tyler passed the paper to Veronica. Her fingers trembled as she read it again and again. She absolutely knew far more than she was revealing. How did he get her to talk, though? Her eyes flicked up to Rick's, then down again to the words on the page. "I don't understand," she said, her voice trembling. "Where did you get this?"

"It was left on the floor in the living room by the person who ransacked the house."

The last hints of color in Veronica's cheeks drained. She croaked, "Who gave it to you?"

Rick's tight-lipped frown seemed to further shake Veronica's confidence. No question, she knew. He wanted to kick himself for having taken so long to see what should have been obvious. The haikus were the key. Their killer had left them a valuable clue to his or her psychological makeup. High intellect. Attention craving. Rick would bet money they took pride in their work and wanted to leave a unique mark. This was someone with a complex, creative mind. Someone who liked to play mind games. Or would send the police on a wild goose chase while they sat back and watched in amusement.

"I didn't get it from anyone, Veronica," Rick lied. "I found it on my own."

"No! You got it from her." She practically spat the last word.

"Who, Veronica? Penny Feeney?"

"Yes." Veronica smirked and crossed her arms over her chest. "And she gave the recipe back to me."

"What?" Tyler's voice boomed. "Why did she do that?"

"It belongs to me! Not you," Veronica snapped.

"I'm your guardian. You should turn it over to me," Tyler demanded.

"Shut up, Tyler," Rick said. "You two can argue over who the recipe belongs to later. Who should have it is not the issue here. You made a deal with Penny Feeney to have her return it to you. Didn't you, Veronica? Why didn't you say anything sooner?" Rick had plenty of other questions, including the big one of how had she even known Penny Feeney?

"I didn't think it was important," Veronica said defensively.

"I doubt that. You knew exactly how important it was, and you knew we were still trying to find out who'd stolen it. How did you find Penny Feeney?"

"She contacted me."

"How?" Rick demanded. "Young lady, you have been lying all through this case. You've manipulated everyone to your own advantage, and now, unless you come up with some answers, you could be in a lot more trouble."

"Stop this!" Tyler demanded. "Can't you see she's hurting?"

"No, Tyler. Interfering in a police investigation is far more serious than shoplifting. Veronica, you have thirty seconds to answer me. After that, I call Chief Cunningham, and he'll ask Penny Fenney directly. She's in custody right now and is desperate to save her own skin, so I'm sure she'll tell us all about how you contacted her."

"No! I didn't. I ran into her at the harbor. That's the truth."

"When was this?" Rick demanded.

"Yesterday afternoon."

"What time?"

She hung her head. "About three."

Tyler watched his niece, his face a mask of disbelief. Tears welled in his eyes. He croaked, "What have I done to you, my poor girl?"

Rick ignored the man's reaction, letting him wallow in self-pity. How ironic it was that Rick had been waiting for Penny to return to her room right about then. And when she'd gotten back at closer to four, she'd already disposed of the recipe. "Why did she give it back to you?"

"She said she felt bad about stealing it. She admitted that Gideon hired her, and said that with him being dead, she didn't have a way to get rid of it, so she wanted to try and do some good with it."

"How did she know who you were?"

"No clue. I didn't ask her. She just walked up to me, told me she had it, and asked if it was mine. I said yes."

Rick looked at Veronica, conflicted as he almost always seemed to be when dealing with her. There were so many things wrong with her story. For starters, he doubted that Penny would give up anything so easily unless there was something in it for her. "You know, if you had just told us this from the beginning, there wouldn't have been all this trouble."

"I'm sorry," Veronica said, tears forming in her eyes.

She was good, thought Rick. Very good. But maybe he could throw her off her game. "Why were you at the harbor?"

"I like it down there."

Rick waited barely a heartbeat before he delivered the line he hoped would shake her confidence. "I imagine you do. Especially because that's where you're having your secret rendevous with Quincy Knox."

Veronica's jaw dropped, then she glared at Rick. "I don't know what you're talking about."

"Don't lie to me, Veronica. I know all about your infatuation with Quincy."

"Alex told you about him, didn't she? I knew I shouldn't have trusted her!"

"Actually, it wasn't Alex. There are plenty of eyes in this town. When you have a meeting in a public place, you're bound to be seen by someone. Now, answer my question. Were you there to meet Quincy Knox?"

"I thought he might be there, but he wasn't."

Finally, he was getting some answers. Maybe even the truth. The puzzle was starting to take form. "Was Penny there to meet Quincy?"

Veronica screwed up her face. "Ewww. Why would he want anything to do with her?"

Again, the emphasis proved her dislike of Penny Feeney. A dislike so intense she couldn't even appreciate Penny returning something she wanted. It was the kind of reaction he'd expect from a young girl in love. Maybe, deep down, Veronica felt threatened by Penny. He was certain there would be no arguing the point, and that Veronica would probably lie to protect her vanity, so he decided to let it go and focus on proving Quincy had been the third player in Gideon's little game.

"What about that haiku?" Rick pointed at the paper in her hands on which the words he'd almost memorized were written.

Chaos born of me,
In regret, I seek your peace,
Forgive my storm's roar, please.

* * *

Veronica's gaze dropped back to the paper, and she read through it again. "You think this is about me?"

"I do. In fact, it's possible you wrote it. The first line refers to your anguish since the day your mother died. It pains you to say that you'd like to find peace. And finally, you want forgiveness. You should know that I'll be having Adam check to see if you were at school on the day of the break-in."

Veronica's jaw dropped, and she planted a hand on her chest. "I didn't write this!"

Tyler exploded, too. "How dare you!"

Rick had to admit, it was an excellent demonstration of indignation by both of them. "All I'm doing is trying to find the truth. Because one of these haikus was left here and another was left on the murder victim, I suspect whoever ransacked your house also killed Gideon Styles."

While Veronica stammered weak protests about how ridiculous it was that she might have damaged the house where she lived, Tyler's anger eroded into shock and fear.

"Veronica?" Tyler stammered. "Please, tell me."

Her voice cracked—a tear brimmed on her lower eyelid. "I didn't. Uncle Tyler, I swear, I didn't do it."

Tyler's jaw tightened, and he looked at Rick. "You should leave."

Rick straightened up and looked back at him. "It would be better if I didn't because if I do, Adam will be coming back here. You don't want that." Turning to Veronica, Rick felt a desire to believe her. But there were so many signs. Still, he had to keep an open mind. "Veronica, if you didn't do it, then you have to tell me what happened here."

She took a deep breath and wiped away her tears. "I don't know. I really don't."

"I think you're still holding back," Rick pressed. "You've seen something like this haiku before. Haven't you?"

Tyler placed a comforting hand on Veronica's shoulder. "We'll figure this out together," he assured her. "But please, be honest with the man."

The girl looked on the verge of breaking, but Rick wasn't sure if that would result in another lie. There was one way to get the unvarnished truth—her phone. Who had she been texting when she walked into the room? She'd been smiling, so it had to have been a friend—probably a boyfriend.

"Let me see your phone, Veronica."

"What? No! That's private."

"I'm investigating a murder and the break-in that occurred in your home. This isn't a game. Someone killed Gideon Styles. And I believe that's the same person he hired to vandalize your home. Do you really want that person going free?"

Veronica took a deep breath, and when she spoke, her voice cracked. "He wouldn't do that to me!" Her voice quivered as she whispered, "He wouldn't."

"Who's 'he', Veronica? Quincy?" Rick waited and tried to coax her again when she didn't answer. "Please, let me see the phone."

As the first tear tracked down Veronica's cheek, her fiery red hair seemed to be the only remnant of her equally fiery spirit. She pulled her phone from her back pocket, unlocked it, and handed it to Rick.

An odd combination of relief and regret washed over Rick as he read the last text message.

Your fiery spirit,
Like the waves crashing ashore,
Captivates my heart more.

* * *

And as he scrolled through the messages that had come before, the feeling grew. This message proved Veronica was not the author of the haiku left in the house. But she had been in touch with the killer all along. Tears were now streaming down her cheeks. She had her arms crossed before her and clutched herself like she was cold.

"What is it?" Tyler asked.

Rick didn't answer at first, but instead looked at Veronica. "You understand what this means?"

Rather than answering, she snatched the phone from Rick's hand and ran for the back door.

52

ALEX

OH, MAN. THIS IS LIKE super stressful. I'm standing between two adults who want me to gossip. I don't know what to do, but I also hate the idea of betraying my mom's trust. Not again. I promised her I wouldn't gossip anymore. And I can still see the hurt in her eyes from when I lied to her. No, I can't do it. I'm already pushing back because of Veronica. No matter how much I might want to say something, I can't break my mom's trust again.

I pull away from Lydia and grip the handle of the grocery cart so tight it almost hurts. "Nuh-uh. I've already said more than I should."

Mrs. Murdoch gives me a stern look. "Alex, this is important for our safety and the safety of our town. We've had a murder here. People are scared. Everyone wants to know when the killer will be brought to justice."

Lydia is looking at me with a light in her eyes. She winks at me and shakes her head at Mrs. Murdoch. "No, Isabelle, Alex is right. We have no business getting involved in this. We're just trying to gossip." She gives my shoulder a squeeze. "Mija, you're doing the right thing. Don't get involved in this old-lady gossip mill."

"Who are you calling old," Mrs. Murdoch demands.

"It's not me, I'm like thirteen," I say.

Lydia snickers, then says, "Good point."

Mrs. Murdoch breaks into a smile and laughs. "Okay, you're right. I'm the oldest one in this group. I suppose I should know better. Besides, I need to get back to the store. Quincy wanted a little time off this afternoon, and I promised him a nice dinner because he's been doing such a wonderful job."

"Quincy was super helpful when I was in the store. He told me all about how to adopt a rescue dog. He was cool about it. By the way, I wish I could work for you, Mrs. Murdoch. I never get to play cards when I'm working."

"What?" Mrs. Murdoch frowns. "Cards?"

"He was playing solitaire when I was in the shop."

"Oh, yes. That's to help with his dyslexia. The doctors told his mother when he was very young that certain types of card games would be good for him. I suppose that's why he always carries a deck of cards around. He also likes writing his little poems. They don't make sense to me, though."

"What kind of poems?" I ask.

Mrs. Murdoch screws up her face. "Oh, whatever did he call them? Hey-something? Hi-something?"

"Haikus?"

"That's it!"

"We've got a guest at the B&B who loves those. He's been teaching me about them."

"Really? I should introduce Quincy to him. Maybe he could give Quincy some advice. Oh, Alex! I have something you need to tell your dad. I remembered where I saw that man who was murdered. He was coming into the shop as I was leaving. He was very abrupt. Not a very nice man at all."

"Wait. Gideon Styles went into your pet shop? When?"

"I think it was Tuesday."

"That's the day he was killed, Mrs. Murdoch."

Her eyes get wide. “Really? I didn’t realize that. What a coincidence.”

No way. That’s one of my dad’s big rules. There are no coincidences. Oh, crap. If Quincy wrote the haikus like the one left at the murder scene, then maybe Veronica’s in trouble. I have to text her. Now.

“I gotta go!” I back my cart away, then head toward the front of the store. Halfway there, I decide this is taking too long and stop. I pull out my phone and text Veronica.

Stay away from Quincy!!!

53

RICK

Tyler Winkle stood in the middle of the alleyway behind his house bellowing his niece's name, "Veronica!"

Rubbing the back of his neck while scanning the area, Rick felt like an idiot. Rather than running after the girl, he'd honestly expected her to come back and had waited about thirty seconds before following her. With that kind of head start in this maze of streets and alleys, she could have gone anywhere. Rick's shoulders slumped as he took a last look up and down the alley. "She's gone. She just vanished."

Tyler called out for his niece again, but there was still no answer.

"I'll call and report that she's missing. We can start a search. Don't worry. This is Seaside Cove. She can't get very far," Rick assured Tyler.

Unfortunately, he knew there was one way she could prove him very wrong. If she connected with someone who had a car, someone like Quincy Knox, all bets were off. He dialed Adam's number and paced as the phone rang.

"Adam, it's Rick. Veronica has disappeared. I'm concerned she might try to find Quincy Knox. I have a feeling he's our killer."

There was a long huff on the other end of the phone. "The mayor's little budget stranglehold is killing me. Okay, I can free up Deputy Kama. I've still got Ms. Feeney to deal with."

"We really have to work on the mayor. Without an actual jail cell or another deputy, you're really limited. Okay, have Amy cruise the neighborhood around Tyler Winkle's house. I'll do the same."

Rick disconnected the call. He also checked the message that had come in from Alex while he was talking to Adam. When he finished, he muttered, "Oh, great." He immediately redialed Adam's number.

"Now what?" Adam asked.

"Just got a message from Alex. Apparently, Isabelle Murdoch saw Gideon Styles going into the pet shop while she was on her way out on the day of the murder."

Adam groaned. "So we have a connection we didn't have before."

"That's not all. Quincy is a card player. Alex saw him playing solitaire, but Isabelle says he always carries a deck of cards with him. Adam, it's not a big stretch to think that Quincy might have a gambling addiction. Maybe he owed Styles money."

"Which could have given him motive. You've also got me wondering if his alibi is as airtight as Isabelle claims. Hang on a second while I check something." While Rick waited on hold, he began walking toward Tyler, who was talking to a young woman with an Irish Setter. He stopped when Adam came back on the line. "Just as I thought. The document Isabelle gave us shows the scheduled pickup date, which was the afternoon of Styles's murder. But there's nothing saying what date it was when Quincy actually picked it up. I'll call and see if they have a record."

"So he could have been here after all," Rick said, his voice feeling heavy and sad for Isabelle.

"Right. He could have picked up the order the following morning, and Isabelle would never have known."

"We still don't know who owned the gun that killed Styles, so I think we need to be on the lookout for Quincy."

"As soon as I can free up Kama, I'll have her stop by the pet shop to see if he's there. I can have her bring him in for questioning. Let's save some time. Can you check Isabelle's house? It's only a few blocks from where you are. Could be where our missing girl is, too."

"I'll let you know what I find out." Rick walked toward Tyler and the young woman with the Setter. A bit apprehensive after the last encounter with a dog, Rick approached cautiously. But, when the Setter saw Rick, she began to bounce around as if she were ready to play fetch, catch, or lick the new guy's face.

The girl shook her head as she tried to focus on Tyler. "No, I haven't seen her." The corners of her mouth turned down slightly, and she gave Rick an apologetic look. "Sorry, she likes people. She always wants to play. Come on, Brandy, let's let the men finish their search." She gave the leash a gentle tug. Brandy gave Rick one last longing look, then followed her owner.

"Tyler, I'll drive around the neighborhood. I'll also check the home of Isabelle Murdoch. It's possible Veronica will be there. Why don't you stay home? If she shows up, call me immediately."

After a short debate, Tyler agreed to sit tight while Rick began his search. Rick started with a drive around the block. When that turned up nothing, he expanded his route to the next set of streets. It didn't take long to realize his method wasn't working. He'd just covered the same street twice and felt like he was driving aimlessly as if a clue might appear by magic. He needed help. And the person who knew Veronica best was Alex. He dialed her number as he made the next turn.

"Hey, kiddo. Thanks for letting me know about Quincy. I think we're very close to solving this case."

There was an uncharacteristic pause, then Alex said, "What if I was wrong?"

"How so, kiddo?"

"I didn't think of it before, but there's somebody else who likes to write haikus. It's Mr. Rhymes."

"Hang on." Rick pulled the car over and sat silent as he tried to think of what to do next. "Where are you?"

"I'm on my way home from the market."

"Go inside and stay there. Wait. Have you called your mom yet?"

"I was just gonna do that."

Rick stared out the windshield, his mind racing. There were two options, and he couldn't do both. He had to choose between finding Veronica, tracking down Quincy, and now, checking out Barrington Rhymes.

"Daddy?"

"Sorry, kiddo. I was just thinking." Which choice was the right one? He had too many options and could only pick one. His mind made up, Rick said, "Alex, I want you to go home. When you get there, I want you and your mom to go to a safe place where you can be alone. Then, call me. If I don't hear from you in fifteen minutes, I'm going to assume you're both in trouble, and I'll call Adam. Understand?"

"Got it. What are you doing?"

"Looking for Veronica and Quincy. She ran out of the house, and I think she's trying to find him because she believes he can help her run away."

"Daddy, she really likes Quincy."

"I know, kiddo. But I'm not so sure he feels the same. Now, go home. Do as I asked. Okay?"

"I'm on it."

Rick took a deep breath as he disconnected the call. He quickly dialed Adam's number and filled him in on the situation as he drove to Isabelle Murdoch's house. By the time he arrived, they'd agreed that finding Quincy was their top priority—unless Alex didn't call soon.

Standing on the sidewalk, Rick inspected the house for signs of life. He saw nothing. The drapes in the upstairs bedrooms and the dormer were all closed. The windows were dark, and the French doors leading to the small front porch were closed.

He walked quickly to the front door, knocked on the gleaming, lacquered wood, and waited. When there was no response, he passed between the two white columns framing the front entrance and went around the side of the house. The grass, though lush and green, needed to be mowed, and Rick noted that there were no footprints matting down the grass anywhere. He walked all the way around the house, went back to the front door, and knocked again. His frustration rose as he scrutinized every window and door for any sign of movement or activity.

Rick checked the time. Alex would be calling him in a few minutes if all was well at home. He started the engine and called Adam as he drove away from the curb. "There's nobody at Isabelle's house. Have you heard from Amy?"

"Nothing so far. It looks like Veronica has learned to avoid being seen in Seaside Cove. Do you want me to have Kama stop by the B&B?"

Rick made a left turn onto Whale Avenue, which would lead him directly to the downtown. "No. I should be hearing from Alex in two or three minutes. Has Amy gotten to Isabelle's Pet Shoppe yet?"

"No. Can you go?"

"Sure. I'll check to see if Quincy's there, but if I don't hear from Alex by the time I get there, I'm going home instead." Rick disconnected the call and hit the gas, realizing that with Adam and Amy both tied up, there was nobody to give him a speeding ticket.

As he pulled into the alley behind Isabelle's Pet Shoppe, Rick's phone rang. He checked, saw that it was Alex, and said a silent thank you. He tapped the screen to answer. "Hey, kiddo. All's well there?"

"Hey, Rick."

"Marquetta? Why are you calling on Alex's phone?"

"Because you really didn't give her much time. She's out locking up her bike. She dragged me into the kitchen, handed me her phone, and told me to call you while she went back out to put it away. Everything's under control."

"Good. And Barrington Rhymes is acting normally?"

"Actually, he's not here. I haven't seen him in the last half hour or so."

Rick balled his fist and pounded it on an imaginary tabletop. Rhymes had been missing for about the same amount of time as Veronica. "Marquetta, did Alex say anything about Mr. Rhymes?"

"No. She was in a huge hurry when she got here. What about him?"

"He's an expert on haikus. It's something that our killer used to leave clues."

"You think Mr. Rhymes is a killer? I can't believe it. You're way off base on this."

"I hope so. Text me when he shows up. I'd really like to cross him off our suspect list. And tell Alex to stay put. I don't want to have to be worrying about her getting involved."

Marquetta chuckled. "Don't worry. I'll lock her in her room if I have to. And Lydia's on her way with the groceries we need for morning, so I can have her help me."

"Given Alex's propensity for finding trouble, it might just take the two of you."

54

ALEX

AFTER LOCKING UP MY BIKE in the shed, I see Lydia's car pull up in front of the B&B. She's got the groceries from the market, and I know she wants to get home to her family, so I go out to see if she wants help. "Hey, Lydia," I say when I get to the front yard. "Let me help you with those."

"Oh, Alex, thank goodness. This bag broke because that new bagboy overloaded it. I told him not to pack it so heavy, but he did it anyway. I've got one of my cloth bags in the trunk. Would you put what's left in the paper bag and the loose groceries in my cloth bag and bring it in for me? I'm in kind of a hurry."

"No problem." Especially because the minute I walk through the front door, Mom is probably gonna put me under lock and key.

So while Lydia takes the potatoes and another sack into the house, I start collecting the loose veggies. The onions are on opposite sides of the trunk. How'd that happen, anyway? There are three loose peppers, so I grab those and stuff them into Lydia's cloth bag.

While I'm transferring the stuff from the ripped bag into Lydia's cloth bag, I hear someone whisper my name. "Alex!"

I pull away from the trunk, shocked to see Veronica standing in the shadows. "Hey, what are you doing here? Everybody's looking for you."

"I know," she says, her voice urgent. "I need your help."

"What? Why me?" I don't mean to sound whiny, but that's how it comes out.

I guess Veronica didn't notice. She just goes on like I didn't say a thing. "They're looking for me because of those stupid haikus. Now the cops think Quincy killed Gideon Styles."

Duh. Not just the cops. Me, too. Unless it's Mr. Rhymes, but he's too nice. It couldn't possibly be him. "Veronica, all the pieces fit."

"He didn't do it. I know him. He wouldn't kill anyone. You have to help me prove it."

"Why do I have to help you? If he didn't do it, he should just turn himself in, and Chief Cunningham will eventually get to the truth."

"Quincy can't turn himself in because of that woman. She's twisted everything around. Now she's trying to hide what she did by blaming him. The cops have already made up their minds. They're convinced he's guilty."

My heart is pounding as I look at her. Do I believe her? She's lied to me before. No. I should go back inside, call my dad, and tell him what's happening out here. He'll want to know where Quincy is. But by the time he gets here, Veronica and Quincy could disappear together. And what if she's right? What if the cops are chasing the wrong guy while the real killer goes free?

"Come with me. I'll prove it to you."

I shoot a look over at the front of the B&B. I should get in there. I don't have my phone. Mom won't know where I am. Both her and my dad will be worried. I can still see Mom's face. Hear her voice. So many things. So many emotions. She was proud when I helped Veronica. And hurt when I lied to her. But she'll be scared to death if I don't get back inside right now.

Veronica grabs my arm. I try to resist, but her strength catches me off guard. I realize she's bigger than me. Stronger. And as she practically drags me away from the house, I squeeze my eyes shut tight to block out the memory that comes flooding back. That horrible, horrible man. He grabbed me the same way. My insides are telling me to fall down into a little ball on the sidewalk and wait for my dad to save me. But my legs are numb. They don't cooperate.

Veronica shouts at me, "Come on! You're wasting time. You're the only one who can help me prove this. I need your help. You're my only friend. The only one who can help me!"

Me? The only one? Really? The memories are still coming at me like I'm walking through a nightmare. I guess I asked where we're going because Veronica says we're going to the marina. With one last pull, I jerk free of Veronica and the nightmare. Mom's right. Being around Veronica is toxic. "No! You have to stay away from Quincy!"

"I can't. He texted me and said he needs my help."

"No. He's the killer, Veronica. It's the only thing that makes sense. And if I let you go to him, you might wind up dead, too."

"I'm going to him, Alex. With you or without you. If something happens to him or me because you wouldn't help, you'll have to live with that the rest of your life." She turns and stomps away, her fiery curls bouncing angrily with each step.

Oh my God. Now what? Veronica's right about one thing. If I let her go alone and she winds up dead, I'll have to live with that for the rest of my life. Would Mom agree? Would she hate me for turning my back on Veronica now? Mom's words echo in my head—*I'm proud of you for helping someone in distress.*

I hate myself for what I'm about to do, but I want to make Mom proud again.

"Veronica! Wait! I'm coming with you."

55

RICK

THE TINKLING OF A TINY, silver bell over the entrance of Isabelle's Pet Shoppe announced Rick's arrival. The store smelled of pet food. A welcoming display of vibrant toys greeted him just inside the entrance. The display was new, and Rick wondered if it might be one of Quincy's suggestions. It was smart marketing. He wondered what would happen if someone like John came in. Would he find something perfect for his little furry companion?

Isabelle's famed cockatoo, Wallace, screeched loudly from a perch near the front window, then mimicked something resembling, "Full house!"

Rick found Isabelle at the back of the store in an area designated for grooming pets. He walked up to her with determination in his steps.

"Isabelle, we need to talk." Rick said firmly.

Isabelle turned to face him, a puzzled expression on her face. "What's going on? Is everything alright?"

Rick explained what he'd discovered about Veronica and Quincy. "Do you know where your nephew is?"

A look of horror crossed Isabelle's face. Her hand went to her heart as she said, "No, I don't. I wish I did." She reached below the counter and pulled out a small notepad. She thumbed through the pages, which were filled with artistic doodles and cursive writing, and stopped on the last page. “That girl is ruining his life. And if she’s running away, Quincy might be planning on going with her. Read this!”

Isabelle shoved the notepad toward Rick. It was another haiku. Or, rather, the iterations to create one. It had taken the author several attempts. Words had been crossed out and replaced until the author had been satisfied with the final version.

Meet me where sun sets,
Hand in hand, we’ll chase our dreams,
Under starlit pathways.

“Quincy wrote this?” Rick said.

“Yes, this is his notebook. He’s so artistic and he made all those wonderful drawings.”

Isabelle started in about how talented her nephew was and how much help he’d been around the shop. She described how he’d been helping her with product displays, grooming the pets, and more. The only thing he had trouble with was numbers. As she prattled on, Rick recalled his conversation with Barrington Rhymes about the haiku they’d found at the murder scene. He began counting syllables. There were five in the first line, seven in the second, and six in the last. It was the same pattern of breaking the rules. Rhymes wasn’t their killer. He professed himself to be a purist. A stickler for the rules of a traditional haiku. He would never have written any of those haikus.

Flipping back a few pages, he found another haiku. Then another. All followed a similar pattern of breaking rules. Rick swallowed hard, then looked at Isabelle with sadness in his eyes. “I need to take this, Isabelle.”

“Oh, I don’t know, Rick. That’s Quincy’s personal property. I feel like I’m betraying his trust.”

"I know, but this is important. It could help us find him and Veronica before he makes a terrible mistake." He left off the other half of the notebook's importance—it was evidence in the murder investigation.

Isabelle hesitated, then her shoulders slumped in resignation. "Alright, if you think it will help get that girl out of our lives. Bring it back to me when you're done with it. Please?"

Rick promised he would, then turned to leave. As he passed by the Cockatoo, he said, "Goodbye, Wallace."

"Royal flush! Royal flush!"

Turning back to Isabelle, Rick asked with a smile, "Isabelle, when did you teach him that?"

Isabelle gave Rick a blank look. "I didn't. I guess Quincy did. Wallace is very intelligent, you know. He learns new words easily. Of course, he doesn't understand them, but I guess Quincy was having fun teaching him."

Poker hands? Why would Quincy choose poker terminology? Why did he carry a deck of cards around? He might if he was fascinated with the game. Or addicted. Rick scanned the colorful display of pet toys and then looked back at the grooming station. "Why did your nephew leave law school, Isabelle?"

"He said he found the law boring. He wanted to do something where he could connect with people."

Doing retail? In a pet store? "So he didn't graduate?"

Isabelle shook her head sadly. "No. He said it was so competitive for those scholarships, and he was so tired of it that he just wanted a change. Why all these questions, Rick?"

"Indulge me for one more moment, okay? Does Quincy play poker?"

Isabelle seemed to think for a minute, then said, "I don't think so. Why in the world would you ask that?"

Seeing the worry on her face, Rick knew he had to come up with something. But revealing his worst fears was not what he wanted to do. "I just want to make sure we find him and bring him back safely. That's all."

Putting her hand over her heart, Isabelle clucked, "Thank goodness. For a minute, I thought you were trying to blame him for something."

"I want the same thing you do, Isabelle. To make sure he's safe." Rick gave Isabelle a parting smile, then hurried out the front door. As he went down the front steps, he thought about the haiku. *Meet me where sun sets*. That could only be one place—the marina. He was also sure Quincy had texted the haiku to Veronica. If he was right, it was where he'd find her, too.

On his way back to his car, Rick was about to call Marquetta when his phone bleeped with Adam's ringtone. "What's up?"

"I wanted to see how things are going. Any luck with Isabelle?" Adam asked.

"Maybe. Hey, Penny Feeney and Leslie Mendez both said something about Styles being big on gambling. Can you ask her if she's ever heard of Quincy Knox?"

"Sure. Hang on. I'll put you on speaker."

A few seconds later, Rick heard Adam ask Penny if she knew Quincy. Before she could answer, Rick said, "Penny, Veronica Campbell is only seventeen. She's with Quincy Knox. You know where this is headed, right? If you've ever heard that name before, you need to tell me. Right now."

Penny muttered, "Oh, my God. Seventeen?"

"Well, Ms. Feeney?" Adam demanded. "You could be an accessory to kidnapping, perhaps another murder, if you know Knox and don't tell us."

A few seconds later, Penny cleared her throat. She croaked, "Gideon was always good at pulling people into his web. He never told me how he got his hooks into Quincy, but while he was at law school, Quincy became a regular at Gideon's poker games. Quincy's problem was that he was brilliant, but he was easily manipulated. He could never read people. So he lost. A lot. Quincy lost his college savings, plus he owed Gideon over five grand when he disappeared. Gideon was furious. He'd never had anyone skip out on a debt before. Gideon was never a patient man, either. He was always in a hurry to get things done. So, the fact that there was this naive kid who owed him a bunch of money and just fell off the face of the earth drove him nuts."

"Do you think Quincy murdered Gideon?" Rick asked.

"Yes. There's no way I can prove it, but he was there."

"Where, exactly, is 'there'? Ms. Feeney?"

"Where…Gideon…died. I didn't know Quincy was in Seaside Cove until I saw him watching me. I was bending down over Gideon's body. That's when I was trying to get the credit cards I told you about. I didn't want you to suspect Gideon had multiple identities. Quincy came up to me and accused me of killing Gideon. He said he'd say he saw me do it if I told anyone he was there."

So much suddenly made sense. Styles had stolen Quincy's college fund. Quincy had dropped out and disappeared but was found purely by luck when Styles walked into Isabelle's shop. Styles had probably threatened Quincy, who'd done his bidding, then killed him when he realized Styles would never stop squeezing him for payment. Then Quincy blackmailed Penny into silence when she found the body. The kid was smart. He'd learned plenty from Styles, including how to manipulate others. That raised the question of who was in charge of the relationship with Veronica. Quincy? Or Veronica? Maybe they both thought they were.

"Adam, can you bring Penny down to the marina? I think that's where we'll find Quincy and Veronica."

"Will do," Adam said. "See you there."

Rick called Marquetta, but when she answered, he could hear the fear in her voice. "Alex is missing," she said.

A river of conflicting worries ran through Rick's mind. He felt numb inside. How could this happen? "I thought you said she was just putting her bike in the shed."

"That's where she was when we talked. But she never came back into the house. Lydia brought over tomorrow's breakfast groceries and asked Alex to bring in one bag. That was the last we've seen of her. We've looked all over. The groceries were still in Lydia's trunk. I've checked her room, and Lydia's been around the house searching for her. Alex's bike is in the shed. She's just gone, Rick."

Rick's breathing quickened as he tried to come up with a logical reason why Alex would disappear. His palms felt sweaty, and he gripped the phone tighter. There were two possible answers, neither of them good. Alex had willingly gone to the center of the storm, or someone had forced her to go there. "Where's Rhymes? Did he come back?"

"No. I haven't seen him. Rick…if something's happened to her…"

"I know," Rick said, trying to sound comforting. The river was back in his head, rushing louder than before. Suddenly, saving Veronica from Quincy Knox, or even finding Quincy, was far less important than finding Alex. Then again, if she was at the center of things, she was with them.

There was no sense in going home. Alex wasn't there. "Do you still have her phone?" Rick asked.

"Yes. She left it with me when she was putting away her bike."

Without a phone, he couldn't track her whereabouts, either. Maybe that didn't matter. If he knew his daughter, she was probably with

Veronica and Quincy. In which case, he knew exactly where to find her. He hoped. "I think I know where she's at. Call me if she shows up, okay?"

"I will, but Rick? I'm scared. I should never have let her go outside alone."

Rick shook his head adamantly. "No. You couldn't have foreseen this happening. Besides, we both know that Alex always finds trouble. Just stay calm and let me know if she shows up."

"I love you, Rick."

"And I love you, too. I'll call you once I know she's safe."

Rick hung up and immediately dialed Adam's cell. He quickly rattled off his theory.

"So you think she's with Knox and the girl?"

"Exactly. And I think we'll find them all at the marina."

"You could be right," Adam huffed. "My deputy sure hasn't had any luck finding either of them. She's covered most of Seaside Cove, too. I'll have her meet us there."

56

ALEX

ALL I CAN THINK OF as I chase after Veronica is that I have to stop her from making the biggest mistake of her life. Quincy could be dangerous, and she's walking right into his trap. I catch up to her at the marina entrance. My heart pounds in my chest because Quincy is at the end of the docks looking out at the ocean. If he turns this way…

I grab Veronica's hand and force her to stop. "Listen to me. I hated Seaside Cove when we moved here. I had to leave all my friends. Everything I knew."

"That's not the only reason I'm leaving. Uncle Tyler is ruining my life."

I squeeze her hand and look her in the eye. "Is he? Really? Or is he trying to turn it around? That's why my dad moved us here. He could've just sold the B&B, and we could've stayed in New York. But he saw something I didn't."

"What?" Veronica shoots back.

"Hope. A chance to start a better life. Are you sure that's not what your uncle wants for you? A better life?"

Veronica's eyes soften, and I know I've struck a nerve. For a split second, I see a little girl who misses her mother and feels alone and scared.

"I don't know," she whispers.

"But shouldn't you know—I mean, like, be totally sure, before you run away?" I look past Veronica at Quincy. He's coming this way. We've got less than a couple minutes before he's here and can stop us from leaving.

She looks like she's torn, but finally, she says, "I guess."

"You can't guess, Veronica. You have to know, be totally, one hundred percent positive. Think about everything your uncle's done for you. He sold the business. He uprooted his life, too. Just so he could take care of you. He might've made some bad decisions, but he's trying. He loves you."

Veronica looks down at her feet, her hand still tightly gripping mine. I can see the conflict in her eyes, the doubt and confusion. I squeeze her hand again, willing her to understand.

"Please, Veronica. Don't run away. Talk to your uncle. Give him a chance. And if things still don't work out, then we can figure something else out together."

Veronica looks at me, tears shimmering in her eyes. "But what about Quincy? What should I tell him?"

I totally wish my mom was here. She'd know what to say. But maybe if I listen to her, because she says we're in each other's hearts, I'll find the words. "Tell him the truth. That you don't love him. That it's not fair to him or to you to continue pretending. That you need time and space to figure out your own life without anyone else telling you what to do."

Veronica still looks like she can't make up her mind, but she also seems a little relieved—like maybe she's finally getting it.

"And if he really loves you," I continue, "he'll understand and give you the space you need." Wow, I can't even believe I just said that. Mom's right. We're totally in each other's hearts. "You gotta know, Veronica. You've gotta be strong, and you've got like thirty seconds to decide. It's not fair, but Quincy's coming this way."

She bites her lower lip, then turns to watch Quincy. "You're right. I'm not in love with him."

Relief washes over me, but then it's too late because Quincy's saying hi and taking her hands and wrapping his arms around her. While he's holding her, he smirks at me over her shoulder, like he totally knows what I was doing and that he's gonna win anyway.

"Veronica, be strong," I say.

Quincy's smirk gets bigger. "Beat it, kid." A second later, he pushes Veronica back a little and says, "Babe, we have to go. Now."

In the pit of my stomach, it feels like I'm about to throw up because what if she goes with him? What if she decides to stay in this fake relationship and never figures out who she really is or what she wants? But then Veronica looks back at me, her eyes determined and clear. "I'm sorry, Quincy. I can't do this anymore."

She pulls away from him and walks over to where I'm standing, taking my hand in hers. "I need some time to figure things out on my own."

Quincy's blue eyes turn cold. His jaw tightens. "You can't change your mind. It's too late."

He reaches out to grab her hand, but instead of letting him turn this into a tug-of-war with Veronica in the middle, I yell, "No!" Then, we run.

It's too late when I realize we're running out onto the docks, not toward town. But I keep running anyway, pulling Veronica along with me. We both know Quincy's fast and strong, but I need time to think.

When I turn around, I see him coming towards us. He's not running. Instead, his walk looks determined. Like he knows we can't get away from him. Our eyes connect, and he reaches behind him. The sun glints off the gun as he lets it hang at his side. I get a sick feeling in my stomach that I'm gonna die, and he's still gonna get away.

Veronica grabs my arm with a grip that's driven by fear. "What should we do?" she asks.

We stop at the end of the dock. There's water on three sides of us. And in front of us is Quincy, looking super cocky and confident. "I dunno."

But when I see my dad's car and a Seaside Cove Police car pull into the lot, I think maybe this is gonna be okay. Assuming Quincy doesn't kill somebody trying to escape. I wanna kick Veronica when a second cop car pulls into the lot, and she points it out to me.

Quincy looks to see what Veronica is pointing at, and suddenly, he's not taking his time anymore. My dad and Chief Cunningham are running onto the dock, but they're still like a hundred feet away. Quincy's so close I can see the stubble on his chin.

"Enough. I've had it with you two." He takes two big steps forward and grabs Veronica by the arm. "Like to play games, little girl? Well, we're about to play the hostage game. You're my ticket out of here."

"You're hurting me!" Veronica squeals.

My dad and the chief are blocking Quincy's escape, but he's got Veronica. And a gun. We're out of time.

Quincy slips behind Veronica and points the gun at her head. He grinds out the words, "If you put up a fight, you'll be dead. Now, shut up and let's go." He yells at my dad and Chief Cunningham, "Move aside. We're leaving."

"You killed Gideon Styles, didn't you?" I demand.

"He was a no-good liar and a cheat. He stole my future from me—my self-respect. Yeah, I killed him. I did the world a favor." Quincy pushes Veronica one step forward.

My dad and the chief stop where they're at. Quincy looks rattled, but even with help so close, they might as well not even be here.

"Put down the gun, Sheriff," Quincy yells.

That's it! What Mom said about him. He was easy to manipulate. Would it work? "It's Chief!" I yell at him. I hope it doesn't sound like I'm scared because I'm totally freaked out, but when Quincy screws up his face and looks confused, I know Mom was right.

He looks over his shoulder at me. "What?"

"She's right," Chief Cunningham says. "I'm not a sheriff, I'm appointed by the mayor of this town. You went to law school, Quincy. You should know the difference between a sheriff and a chief of police."

Quincy looks like he's trying to come up with an answer, but then he gives up and shakes his head. "I don't care about stupid titles." He waves them away with the gun. "Move over. We're walking out of here."

I look down at his feet. He's right on the edge of the dock. His body's twisted so he can watch me, my dad, and the Chief. But if he falls, he might take Veronica with him. There's gotta be a way. "Take me, too," I say. "Two hostages are better than one. Right?"

My dad yells, "Alex, no!"

"It's okay, Daddy. I don't think Quincy wants to hurt anybody."

Quincy loosens his grip on Veronica, and the gun starts to waver. "No. I don't."

"Styles was blackmailing you. Wasn't he?" my dad asks.

"He tricked me. Made me think I could win at poker. But he was just a thief. And then when he showed up at the pet store, I had to do something." Quincy's voice trails off and kind of cracks. "I'm sorry, Veronica. I hated the idea of trashing your house, but he wanted me to make it look like a burglary. He said he'd tell my aunt about my gambling if I didn't do what he wanted."

He was being blackmailed? Well, that like never ends. He went to law school, and he doesn't know blackmailers never stop? Really? But then I think about what Miss Redmond said about him cracking under pressure. I take a step toward him. My heart is pounding so hard I think I might throw up. "After you did the job, he wanted you to do something else, didn't he?"

He looks at me, like he can't believe I figured out what happened. Then he does exactly what I want. He inches backward. He's starting to sound desperate, like this isn't going the way he planned. "That's right. He wanted me to kidnap her if his other plan fell through. Back up. Don't come any closer."

He starts to point the gun at me, but my dad and the chief step forward. That forces him to pivot and aim at them.

He's so close to the edge. All it will take is one tiny step. I inch forward. He sees me move and swings back to me. His foot goes off the edge. I reach out, grab Veronica's hand, and pull hard. She starts to fall, but when she tries to catch her balance, her foot catches Quincy's. There's a huge splash and then a lot of thrashing around.

Chief Cunningham, my dad, and Deputy Kama swarm us. My dad grabs me in his arms and pulls me to his chest. He keeps asking me if I'm okay, but I don't answer. I'm too caught up in Veronica's drama.

She's sitting on the dock picking at one finger. She looks up at me with the old fire in her eyes and shakes her fist at me. "Really? You couldn't have thought of something else? I've got a splinter and you made me break a nail!"

57

ALEX

September 28

Hey Journal,

It's been a couple weeks since Chief Cunningham arrested Quincy Knox for murder. After Quincy fell off the dock, things happened pretty fast. Veronica's Uncle Tyler showed up to take her home. My dad held onto me the entire time that the chief and Deputy Kama were fishing him out of the water and then putting him in handcuffs.

Later that night, the chief got a diver to go down and find Quincy's gun. It turns out the gun belonged to Gideon Styles and was the one that was used in the murder. We found out when the chief showed up for breakfast with my dad yesterday. Life is kinda getting back to normal around here, except that Baby Jack seems to be out of his singing phase. Mom says we'll just have to wait and see what happens next.

I was stoked because Veronica finally realized her uncle was doing things to make her life better. They actually started baking together last week. She texted me to tell me that her Uncle Tyler pulled a box out of storage that contained all the stuff Veronica's mom used when she started making chocolate. Kind of as an apology, Veronica brought over a small box of chocolate treats. When we tried them, my mom said Veronica is a genius chocolatier. It made me realize that she might have been just as connected to her mom as I am to mine.

While she was here, Veronica started talking about maybe opening a new shop right here in Seaside Cove. It would be awesome to have a chocolate shop here in town. But, I don't know. I think she's still trying to find her way in the world. Maybe it's chocolate, maybe it's acting. She is a total drama queen. And that's one reason I'm not sure I wanna be friends with her. The good thing about Veronica is that she made me realize I like Sasha and Robbie more. They like me for what I am, not for what I can do for them.

Whoa. That sounds kinda deep, Journal. Maybe too deep for a thirteen-year-old. I think I'll just go back to being a kid.

Bye for now,

xoxo,

Alex

PS Mr. Rhymes and Miss Redmond have been hanging out together a lot since the dinner my mom arranged. We all laughed a lot that night when we found out the reason Mr. Rhymes had disappeared. He spent almost an hour at the wine store trying to decide on the perfect bottle of wine for dinner! It was pretty epic because they both showed up with the exact same kind of wine!

www.ingramcontent.com/pod-product-compliance
Lightning Source LLC
LaVergne TN
LVHW100514110826
845146LV00002B/638
* 9 7 9 8 9 9 0 0 4 5 7 0 5 *